Praise for *The Heartbreakers*

"*The Heartbreakers* is both equally heartwarming and swoon worthy… I fell in love with Oliver Perry so fast. This book is feels-inducing and every girl's dream—with a side of Heartbreak."

—Anna Todd, *New York Times*
bestselling author of the After series

"When I wasn't reading this book, it was all I wanted to be doing. Adorably romantic and fun! I loved it."

—Kasie West, author of
The Distance Between Us

"Novak creates a titillating tension between her leads… Fans of boy bands will be on this like tattoos on Harry Styles's chest."

—*Kirkus Reviews*

"A fun summer romance that doesn't shy away from the deeper issues of family, illness, and self-discovery."

—*School Library Journal*

Praise for *My Life With the Walter Boys*

2015 Yalsa Teens' Top Ten Nominee

"This title will appeal strongly to boy-obsessed readers who will find the romance, particularly the chemistry between Cole and Jackie, to be quite engrossing and the teen voices credible."

—*VOYA*

"A fun, quirky read that will keep a smile playing at the corner of your lips."

—*TheGuardian.com*

"A very addicting book. The writing is strong and the characters kept me invested and turning the pages."

—*Teenreads.com*

THE HEARTBREAKERS

ALI NOVAK

sourcebooks
fire

To Wattpad, both my readers and the people behind the scenes, whose unwavering love and support made my dreams come true.

Published by Sourcebooks Fire, an imprint of Sourcebooks, Inc.
P.O. Box 4410, Naperville, Illinois 60567-4410
(630) 961-3900
Fax: (630) 961-2168
www.sourcebooks.com

Library of Congress Cataloging-in-Publication data is on file with the publisher.

Printed and bound in the United States of America.
VP 10 9 8 7 6 5 4 3 2 1

CHAPTER 1

Cara was clutching the latest edition of *People* as if it were the Holy Bible.

"If I didn't have you to bring me magazines," she said, "I'd go stir crazy locked up in this place."

"I had to fight off some soccer mom for the last copy," I told her. And I was serious. Fresh reading material was a hot commodity among inpatients and their families at the hospital.

Cara didn't hear me. She was already tearing through the magazine, eager to consume her daily dose of celebrity gossip. Beside her, Drew was camped out in the room's only armchair, staring down at his phone. From the scowl on his face, I knew he was either reading about last night's baseball game or discovering that the spotty Wi-Fi was being particularly fussy.

Unlike a typical day at the hospital, today I actually had something to keep me occupied during visiting hours. After pulling a chair up to Cara's bed, I started scrolling through the pictures I had taken with my new Canon. My parents had bought me the camera as an early birthday gift, and I had tested it out at the Minneapolis Sculpture Garden this morning.

"God, could he be any more perfect?"

I looked over, and Cara had the magazine open to an interview with one of the guys from the Heartbreakers, her favorite band. The headline read "Bad Boy Still Breaking Hearts." Underneath it was an abstract with a quote: "I'm not looking for a girlfriend. Being single is too much fun." When I glanced back up, there was a look on Cara's face—eyes avid, mouth partially open—that made me wonder if she was about to lick the page. I waited a moment to see if she would, but all she did was heave a sigh, the kind that implied she wanted me to give her a reason to gush over her favorite celebrity.

"Owen something?" I asked to be polite, but my attention was already focused back on my camera.

"Oliver Perry," she said, correcting my mistake. I didn't need to look at Cara to know she was rolling her eyes at me even though I had made my dislike of the band clear on multiple occasions, like every time she blasted their music through the house. I didn't care enough about the Heartbreakers to learn their names; they were just another boy band whose popularity would sputter out as fast as it had shot up. "I swear you're like a forty-year-old stuck in a teenager's body or something."

"Why?" I asked. "Because I don't know the name of some boy-band member?"

She crossed her arms and glared. Apparently I had crossed the line. "They're not a boy band. They're punk."

There were two reasons I didn't like the Heartbreakers. First and foremost, I thought their music sucked, which should be explanation enough, but I had another reason: the Heartbreakers tried so hard to be something they weren't, parading around as rockers when really, they were just a boy band. Sure, they played instruments, but no amount of vintage band tees and ripped jeans could mask the watered-down lyrics and catchy beats of songs that were undoubtedly pop. The fact that their fans had to constantly remind the world that the Heartbreakers were a "real" band only proved otherwise.

I pressed my lips together to keep myself from laughing. "Just because they site the Misfits and the Ramones as their inspiration doesn't make them punk."

Cara tilted her head to the side, eyebrows scrunched together. "The who?"

"See?" I reached over and grabbed the magazine. "You don't know what real punk is. And this," I said, gesturing down at the page, "is not it."

"Just because I don't listen to all your underground weird stuff doesn't make you more musically cultured than me," she responded.

"Cara," I said, pinching the bridge of my nose. "That's not what I meant at all."

"Whatever, Stella." Cara slid the magazine back into her lap. She looked away from me, shoulders slumping. "Honestly, I don't care if you don't like them. I'm just in a bad mood because I wanted to go to their concert."

The Heartbreakers had performed in Minneapolis this past month, and even though Cara had desperately wanted to go, she had decided not to purchase any tickets. It had been a tough decision, especially since she had been saving up for months, but in my opinion, it was the right one. Because, when it came down to it, it didn't matter how much she wanted to go. Her body was giving her all the signs that she couldn't—nausea, vomiting, and fatigue just to name a few—and she knew it. One important lesson that Cara's cancer taught us was that there's a time to be hopeful and a time to be realistic.

Two weeks had passed since Cara started her first round of chemotherapy. The treatment worked in cycles—three weeks where countless drugs were pumped into her body, followed by a rest period before the whole process started over again. Then, after the regular chemotherapy killed off all the bad stuff in her body, Cara would be zapped with a single round of high-dose chemo just to make sure the bad stuff stayed dead.

I was never really good at science, but Cara's trips to the hospital taught me a lot. Ordinarily, chemo doses are restricted to small amounts due to the threatening side effects. A higher dose might kill the cancer, but it also destroys bone marrow, which I've learned is kind of essential to life. But sometimes, regular chemo isn't enough.

That's how it was for Cara. After two recurrences, her doctors thought it was time for a more serious treatment, so once she received the high-dose chemo she would need to have an autologous stem cell transplant. An autologous transplant was where Cara's own stem cells were removed from her bone marrow prior to her treatment. The cells were frozen and kept safe during her chemo, and they would be given back by a blood infusion. Without it, she wouldn't be able to recover.

A small sigh escaped me, and I was careful with my words. "I'm sure there'll be more concerts in the future," I said and offered her a weak smile. "I'll even go to one with you if you want."

At this, Cara giggled. "Drew's more likely to join a cheerleading squad." At the sound of his name, our brother looked up and raised an eyebrow at Cara before returning to his phone.

"It was just a suggestion," I added, but I was glad she found it amusing.

"You, at a Heartbreakers concert?" she said, more to herself than to me. "Yeah, right."

At this, we both went silent. A thick kind of quiet settled around us; I could feel its weight bearing down on my chest, and I knew we were both thinking of stuff that was unhappy. Long days at the hospital tended to do that, and after a while, bad thoughts came more easily than the good ones.

A knock on the door pulled me back into my surroundings, and Jillian, Cara's favorite nurse, stepped inside. When I saw her, I glanced up at the clock and was surprised to see how fast the day had disappeared.

"Stella, Drew," she said, greeting the both of us. "How are you both?"

"Same as usual," Drew said as he stood up and stretched. "You?"

"I'm doing well, thanks. Just here to check up on Cara." To her she said, "You need anything, dear?" but Cara shook her head.

"Are you kicking us out?" I asked. Visiting hours would be over soon and that meant it was time for Cara's nightly meds, which included penicillin and a long list of other stuff I couldn't pronounce.

"No," Jillian said. "You still have time, but I figured you'd want to run down to the cafeteria before it closes."

The thought of food made my stomach rumble. I'd gone straight to the hospital from the sculpture garden, so I hadn't eaten anything since breakfast. "That's probably a good idea." I wrapped my camera strap around my neck and stood up. "See you tomorrow, punk."

I wanted to lean over and give her a kiss, but I couldn't.

Cara had non-Hodgkin's lymphoma. It was a type of cancer that originates in lymphocytes—white blood cells—which are part of the body's immune system. Normally, people with non-Hodgkin's were treated as outpatients. They would come to the hospital on a daily basis to receive treatment before going home, and during her first two bouts of cancer, Cara was an outpatient too. Every day my mom would drive her to the hospital and her drugs were administered through an IV. It normally took about an hour, and sometimes Drew and I would tag along and do homework in the waiting room.

But Cara recently had complications with her appendix and it had to be removed. Since her white blood cell count was so low, her doctors were concerned she was at risk of infection, and she had to stay at the hospital for a few weeks. When we visited, we were required to wear masks over our mouths, and we couldn't touch Cara because there was a chance we could get her sick.

I knew being away from home was hard for her, and it was frustrating that I couldn't even comfort her with a hug.

"You know where to find me," she said and rolled her eyes.

"Get some rest for me, okay?" Drew said in parting. Then he turned to me. "Ready? I'm hungry."

"Yup," I responded. "Me too." We said one last quick good-bye, and then we were out the door, heading in the direction of the cafeteria.

"Think they'll have those caramel pudding cups today?" Drew asked as we made our way down the familiar hospital halls.

"Man, I love those things," I said, "but I doubt it. Haven't seen any in a while."

"Lame."

"Yeah," I said, thinking about our day. "Pretty lame is right."

☆♭♫

Every day, Drew and I would mention one positive thing that had happened during the time we spent with Cara. The thing about hospitals is that they're breeding grounds for fear. If you don't constantly remind yourself about the good, the bad will seep in and take over. Because when one of your family members gets cancer, you all get cancer. It might not be the same kind, but it will still eat at you until there's nothing left inside.

The tradition started when Cara was diagnosed the first time, back when we were freshmen in high school. It hadn't really hit me that my sister was sick, that I could actually lose her, until she had a diagnostic treatment and stayed in the hospital while her doctors identified the location, extent, and stage of her cancer. Our mom brought Drew and me in to see her, and all around us were children in various stages of decline, some further along than others.

That was the first time I felt the fear. It buried its nails in my chest, lifted me clear off the ground, and said, "See those kids?

Those kids are actually dying." And that made me wonder—if my sister was here, did that make her one of those kids too?

"What's your positive?" I asked Drew when we reached his old Honda Civic on the far side of the hospital parking lot. He was fiddling with his keys, and even though I knew my door was still locked, I yanked on the handle.

"The caramel pudding cup," he said. The locks popped up with a click when he found the right key. "That shit was delicious."

"A pudding cup?" I repeated as we both climbed into the car. "That's your positive?"

"It's that or the fact that the Wi-Fi was in an obliging mood today."

I was battling with my seat belt, trying to untangle it and pull it forward, but Drew was being so odd that I let it fly back into place. "Are you being serious?" I asked as I stared at him. "Because I honestly can't tell right now."

"What does that mean?" he said. "Pudding cups are serious business."

I blinked slowly and deliberately. Up until today, our positives had always been meaningful, something to keep us going. If pudding became the only redeeming part of our day, then we were in trouble.

Drew started laughing, and I smacked him on the shoulder. "Not funny," I grumbled.

"I was only teasing, Stella. Lighten up."

"Sorry," I said, reaching for my seat belt a second time. "I only narrowly avoided making Cara cry today."

"You know why she's upset, right?" Drew asked me then. "She thinks she's never going to go to one of their concerts."

"Why does she have to be all negative like that?"

I didn't expect Cara to be sunshine and roses all the time. In fact, she deserved the right to be angry with God or the universe or whoever had dealt her the shittiest hand of all. But I hated when she spoke in definites—*I'm never getting out of here, I'm never going to college, I'm never going to see the Heartbreakers perform*—like her death was already a done deal. It made me feel like I had no control over my life, like it really was all left up to fate.

"No, not like that," Drew said. "Apparently there's a rumor going around that the Heartbreakers are breaking up. Some kind of rift between the members."

"Oh! Well, no surprise there," I said, but I silently hoped that the rumors weren't true. Shocker considering I wasn't much of a fan, but I wanted to prove Cara and her definites wrong. She would see the Heartbreakers perform because she was going to get better.

Placing his hand on my headrest, Drew craned his neck to see if there was anyone behind us before whipping out of the parking spot at full speed. Visiting hours were officially over, and some of the hospital staff had already left for the night, so the lot was relatively empty. When we reached the exit, Drew swung the car into the left-turn lane and flicked on his blinker. We both just sat there for a second, neither of us talking, as we waited for a gap in traffic.

I remembered that Drew had yet to answer my question, and I was the first to break the silence. "So what is it then?" I asked.

"What's what?"

"Your positive."

"Oh, right," he said, his head twisting back and forth as he checked to make sure there were no more oncoming cars. There weren't, so he slammed his foot on the pedal and shot out onto the road. "I came up with an idea for Cara's birthday present."

"Really?" I asked. I turned my full attention to Drew. "What is it? Tell me."

Not only was next Friday the Fourth of July, but it was also Cara's eighteenth birthday. It was mine and Drew's as well; we were triplets. Every year, we had a competition to see who could get each other the best present, and Cara normally out-gifted us. This year, Drew and I decided to team up and beat her, but so far, we had yet to come up with anything worthy of winning.

"Okay, you know how you've been going on and on about that photographer's art gallery?" Drew asked, glancing at me. "The one that's opening in Chicago?"

"You mean Bianca Bridge?" I edged forward in my seat. I had no clue what Cara's birthday gift had to do with my all-time favorite photographer, but wherever Drew was going with this, I had a feeling it would be good.

Bianca was my inspiration and everything I wanted to be in life. As one of the most famous photojournalists of the modern world, she was known for eye-opening street photography that featured people from all walks of life. I had painted a quote from her on my bedroom wall, and all my best pictures were tacked up around it: "The world moves fast, changing everything around us with each new day. Photography is a gift that can keep us in a moment forever, blissfully eternal."

Whenever someone asked me why I enjoyed photography so

much, I would recite Bianca's quote as if it were my own personal mantra. I was enthralled with the idea that, with one click of a button, I could somehow beat time.

"Yeah, her," Drew said as he sped up to make a yellow light. "It just so happens that her gallery is only a few blocks away."

"A few blocks away from what?" Drew was purposely dragging out his explanation to build suspense, which was nothing short of annoying. "Come on!" I was bouncing up and down in my seat. "Tell me!"

"No patience whatsoever." He shook his head, but there was a glimpse of a smile on his face. "It's a few blocks from a radio station where the Heartbreakers will be doing an autograph signing this weekend."

"Are you for real?"

Drew lifted his chin, and a smirk flashed across his face. "Well, Cara was really disappointed about not being able to go to the concert, and that got me thinking. There has to be something else Heartbreakers-related that would make her happy. So I googled a list of their public events. We could drive down and get one of their CDs signed or something."

"And?"

"And visit your art thing."

"Yes!" I exclaimed and pumped my fist in the air. "Cara won't stand a chance of beating us this year."

"I know," he said and brushed off his shoulder. "No need to thank me."

I rolled my eyes but smiled inwardly. Something inside my chest was shifting.

When Cara's cancer came back again, I knew it was different than the first two times. The knot in my gut told me that if this treatment didn't work, Cara would never get better. It was a heavy feeling to carry around, almost as if a hundred weights had been tied to my heart.

Even now, I knew there was nothing I could do that would make Cara's cancer disappear. But for the first time since the recurrence, I felt like those weights were slowly being cut loose. It was silly, because what would an autographed CD do? But if it could lift Cara's spirits, then maybe she stood a chance.

"Do you think Mom and Dad will let us go?" I wondered, chewing on the inside of my cheek. If they didn't, my surge of hope would dissolve and bring me lower than before.

Drew shrugged. "We'll be together," he said, "so I don't see why not."

"Okay, good," I said, nodding at his answer. "Are we really doing this? Road trip to Chicago?"

"Yeah," Drew said. "Road trip to Chicago."

CHAPTER 2

I pressed my forehead against the passenger-side window and let my eyes drift over the buildings slipping past me. Drew and I had been driving all night, and thankfully we arrived in Chicago well before the morning rush hour. It was still dark, but a faint purple light on the horizon hinted at the coming sun. Even though it was too early to check in, we were making our way through downtown to find our hotel. Drew wanted a place to park the car and leave our luggage.

I stayed awake during the drive to keep my brother company, and now I was too tired to focus much on anything. If I didn't get caffeine soon, I would never make it through the day. Just as my eyelids began to flutter closed, a green sign caught my attention. I shot straight up in my seat.

"Drew, stop! It's a Starbucks!"

He jumped, accidentally jerking the wheel to the left, and the car swerved a foot into the next lane. There wasn't much traffic to crowd the five o'clock streets, but I could see the alarm on his face.

"Jesus, Stella, you could have gotten us killed," he said and let out a shaky breath when he successfully pulled our car back into the right lane. "That scared the crap out of me."

"Sorry," I said as he found a parking spot on the side of the street. "Coffee's on me. What do you want?"

"Just a regular cup of joe. None of that creamer crap."

I wrinkled my nose. "That's disgusting," I told him as I unbuckled my seat belt.

"That's how you're supposed to drink it," he told me as he settled back into his seat to wait.

Grinning to myself, I climbed out of the car and headed toward the shop. When I stepped inside, a bell rang above me and the smell of freshly brewed coffee greeted me. There was one employee behind the counter, a middle-aged woman with frizzy hair, and she was taking the order of the only other customer in the shop.

As I waited for my turn, I studied the boy in front of me. He was tall and lean and must have been around my age, but I couldn't get a good look at his face. Light-brown, wavy hair poked out from underneath a beanie, and he was wearing a fitted white T-shirt, designer jeans, and a pair of gray Vans: simple but stylish. I couldn't help but look him up and down a second time. Normally I was into guys with big muscles and facial hair, but something about this boy was interesting. His whole look screamed artsy, and I liked it.

"That will be two ninety-five." I watched as the boy retrieved a wallet from his pocket, pulled out a five, and handed it over. After giving back his change, the woman said, "I'll be right back. Gotta grab the soy milk out of the other fridge."

"That's chill," he answered and tucked his money away.

The barista disappeared through an employees-only door, leaving me alone with the boy. As he waited for her to return, he beat his hands against the counter, re-creating the rhythm to a song. I cleared my throat to let him know he wasn't alone, and he turned, finally noticing I was standing behind him.

He offered me a smile. It was one of those full-face smiles accompanied by an adorable set of dimples, and all I could do was stare like an idiot. Something about him struck me, almost as if I knew him from somewhere, which was ridiculous since we had never met. I touched my camera out of habit, and his smile faltered. Neither of us moved for a moment, but then the boy forced another grin onto his face and waited, like he expected me to say something.

Unable to stand his gaze any longer, I glanced up at the huge chalkboard menu hanging above us. Even though I already knew what I was ordering, I deliberately studied each item. They really should have another employee working. He was still watching me, and I tried my best to ignore him.

"So," he said, finally ending the silence. "That's a nice camera. I take it you're into photography?"

I jumped at the sound of his voice. The boy was leaning back against the counter, his arms crossed casually over his chest. "Um, thanks," I responded. "It's an early birthday gift. And yeah, I'm into it."

"What kind?"

"Portraits are my favorite," I told him, as I fiddled with my lens cap, popping it off and on. "But I'll take a picture of just about anything."

"Why portraits?"

"Have you ever heard of Bianca Bridge?" I could feel a smile growing on my face, and I didn't wait for the boy to answer. "She's, like, the best photographer ever, and she does these amazing shots of people from all over the world. I'm actually in Chicago to visit her photo gallery."

"Hmm," he said, tilting his head to the side. "Never heard of her." Pushing away from the counter, he took a step toward me. The dog tag around his neck caught a beam of light from above, and it shimmered back and forth. "Mind if I have a look?" he asked and pointed at my camera.

My fingers tightened around it, and I hesitated. "Umm," I responded, not knowing what to say. The Starbucks employee trotted back into the room clutching a carton of soy milk, and when I glanced back at the boy, he lifted an eyebrow at me as if to say, "Well?" Slowly, I nodded my head. In any other instance I would have said no, but something about the boy was confident and charming. Plus, I wanted to see that smile again. I lifted the strap from around my neck, and he moved in to take the camera. As he did, his arm brushed against mine, making my skin prickle.

"Like this?" he asked and snapped a close-up of me. I found it hard not to grin. He was holding the camera all wrong and clearly had no idea what he was doing.

"No," I said, reaching over to help. "You probably have to adjust the focus. Here, I'll show you." I put my hand on top of his and demonstrated how to move the lens. The boy looked up at me for a moment, my hand still over his. This close to him, I could see the thick lashes that surrounded his dark-blue eyes, and my stomach flipped in circles.

He moved the camera up to his face. "Smile," he said, but I

looked away and let my hair cascade in front of my face. "What? The photographer doesn't like having her picture taken?" he asked as he snapped another one.

"Not really," I answered and took back my camera. Dropping the strap back around my neck, I held it in my hands and let out a huge breath. "I much prefer looking through the lens," I told him. I focused it on his face for a moment before swinging around to my right and capturing the barista at work. I held the camera up so he could look at the image on the screen. "It's best when they don't know you're looking at them. That way you get the real stuff. Real is when it's the most beautiful."

"What if they know you're looking?" He was closer now, and even though he had spoken in a barely there voice, I heard every word.

Taking a deep breath, I counted to three in my head to work up some courage. Then I stepped back and focused the lens on him. He leaned in with an unwavering gaze, but with the camera between the boy and myself, he was less intimidating. I only saw a subject. My finger hit the button three times before I pulled away to study the portraits. They were easily the best pictures I'd taken in a long time.

Finally, I answered him. "Those can be beautiful too."

His lips quirked up in a smile, but before he could respond, the barista finished his order. "All right, one caffe latte with soy," the woman said, handing the boy his drink. "Sugar's around the corner if you need it."

"Thank you," he told the woman, but he never glanced in her direction. He kept his eyes on me as he reached over and grabbed his drink. Finally, after three long seconds, he turned and made his way over to the sweeteners and stir sticks.

"Sorry about the wait," the woman continued. "What can I get for you?" I gazed at her with parted lips. I had completely forgotten why I was even standing in Starbucks. "Hon?" she prompted me.

"Right," I said, tucking a loose strand of hair behind my ear. "Um, can I have a grande of your regular brew and a tall hazelnut macchiato?"

"Anything else for you today?"

"No thank you."

She pressed a few buttons on the register. "Okay, that will be eight ninety-eight."

I pulled my wallet out of my purse and searched for a ten. "I know I have some cash in here somewhere…" I muttered to myself. I didn't want to have to run back out to the car—that would be totally embarrassing—but all I could find was my plastic, and I was only allowed to use that in emergencies.

"I got it." The boy slapped a twenty down on the counter and winked. My fingers fumbled as I looked between him and the money, and my credit card slipped out of my hand.

"Crap." I rushed to pick it up, but he was already there, bending down and plucking it off the floor. He turned it over in his hand as he straightened back up, his eyes glancing down at my name.

"Here you go," he said, holding it out for me to take.

"Um, thanks."

"It was nice to meet you, Stella Samuel." A half grin yanked on the corner of his mouth as he said my name. "Have fun at the gallery today." Then he turned and exited the coffee shop. I stood in place and watched the door swing closed behind him.

"Here you go, darling. One grande coffee and a tall hazelnut macchiato." The barista pushed the drinks across the counter to me. "Your friend left his change behind. Do you want it?"

"Keep it," I told her, not bothering to look back. I grabbed the cups and rushed out the door to ask the boy his name, but when I reached the sidewalk, there was nobody in sight.

"What took you so long?" Drew complained when I finally slid back into my seat.

"Oh, you know. Soy milk, camera," I rattled off. My mind was on that boy.

Drew choked on a sip of coffee. "You spilled soy milk on your new camera?"

"Huh?" I focused my attention back on him and then realized what he was asking. "Oh, no. Never mind, it was nothing."

My brother watched me for a moment before shaking his head. "Drink that caffeine up. I think you need it."

☆ ♭ ♫

"That was awesome!" I exclaimed as Drew and I stepped out of Bianca's gallery.

Unlike this morning, I felt energy streaming through my body, enough for me to skip the five blocks to the radio station where the signing was taking place.

"Maybe not the word I would use," Drew responded.

"Oh, come on," I said, bumping my shoulder into his. "Don't you feel inspired?"

"Not overly," he replied. "We just spent all morning looking at a bunch of pictures on a wall."

This conversation was familiar. I'd had similar experiences with every member of my family in the past, times when I'd shown them new Bianca pieces that I was obsessing over. Nobody ever appreciated the photos, and I'd learn to shrug off their lack of interest. Mom liked to blame her sister, my aunt Dawn, for what she referred to as my "artistic arrogance," which was when I got all snobby about a certain photograph and tried explain the vision behind it.

My aunt Dawn was one of those posh, East Coast ladies who drank martinis like water and only bought art if the price tag had enough zeros. One time, when I was twelve, she took me to an art auction in New York. We spent three hours meandering through rows of artwork, and Dawn taught me which paintings were quality and which were not, a skill no twelve-year-old should be caught without. Of course, her definition of quality was vastly different than mine. Dawn's choice of favorites hinged on who the artist was, not the subject, while I preferred the black-and-white photographs tucked away in the back of the gallery. There were different people in each image, which made me wonder who they were and what they were thinking.

"But they were pictures that mean something," I said, turning to look at Drew. I knew he wouldn't understand, but that didn't stop me from hoping he would. I wasn't snobby about art the way Dawn was or the way my mom thought I was; I was just passionate about photography. And my mom could only blame that on one thing—my not-so-typical high-school experience.

When Cara first got sick, our mom made an effort to try to keep my and Drew's lives as normal as possible. But Cara's treatment was long and grueling, so she started homeschooling. The three of us didn't like being apart, not when things were so serious, so Drew and I begged our mom to let us be homeschooled too. That way, we could be with Cara and still receive an education. She finally agreed, and we never went back.

Until freshman year, I'd loved being a triplet. It set us apart and made the other kids our age think we were cool. It was like we were exotic animals at the zoo that everyone wanted to see, and we always got asked questions like whether we could read each other's thoughts or feel when one another got hurt. We always responded by putting on a show. Drew would pinch himself, and Cara and I would grab our sides and grimace as if we had felt his fingers too.

It wasn't until high school that I realized people only knew me as one of the Samuel triplets. During English class on my first day, the girl sitting next to me asked, "Are you Cara or the other girl?" as if I could only be defined by the fact that I was one of three. That was when I decided I needed to stand out from my siblings, to declare who I was and all that independent stuff. The problem was that I didn't really know how to go about doing it.

I thought about the girl from my English class. She had one of those scary nose rings that made her look like a bull, and her dread-locks were dyed purple. I was willing to bet that nobody forgot who she was—not when she looked like that. But I wasn't as daring as her.

Although my ears were already pierced, getting a nose ring scared me. On top of that, I was nervous that the maintenance required to keep all of my chestnut hair a solid blue—my favorite color— would be too much work. In the end, I settled for a single streak of aqua in my bangs and a small, sparkly stud in my left nostril to start my metamorphosis from Stella the triplet to Stella the individual.

High school was going to be my chance to break away and discover who I was, and during those first few months of freshman year, I started to. Drew, who was built like our dad, tall and thick, easily made the football team. Cara had always been the most outgoing of the three of us, so it made sense when she joined the cheerleading squad and yearbook committee. But even though we normally did everything together, I decided not to try out for the squad.

Instead, I signed up for as many clubs as I had time for—from student council, which I hated, to academic decathlon, which I also hated. Art club became my fast favorite. Not only did I love the quirky cast of kids, but there was something about imagining and shaping and creating that I found intriguing.

I packed my schedule so tightly that, during those two months, it was as if I didn't have siblings anymore because I saw so little of them.

But when Cara got sick, all of our individual growth folded in on itself, and we just became the triplets again. Sometimes I would catch a glimpse of who we could've been from those few high-school fragments that stayed with us. Cara never went anywhere without at least three different lip gloss options, and Drew always tried to make a competition out of things, whether it was beating me in a game of Scrabble or seeing who could get a better test score.

That's why I held on to photography so tightly. It was my only takeaway from a time that was supposed to be mine but never really was. One of my art friends introduced me to it, and even though I wasn't a natural, I enjoyed it enough to make an effort to improve. So while every other teenager was blundering their way through high school, experimenting and making mistakes, I was at home staying how I always had been, whatever that was—but at least I had one thing that was all my own.

Before I could dive into the details of why Bianca's work was so meaningful, I spotted a great shot farther up the sidewalk. "Oooh, look!" I said, and rushed ahead to snap a picture.

"Stella," Drew said when he caught up to me. "That's a fire hydrant. We have those back in Minnesota."

"Yeah, but look at the way the sunlight is hitting it," I said and adjusted my lens.

Drew scoffed. "Please don't tell me there's some symbolic meaning in the contrast between the light and the shadows or some artsy bull like that."

"No," I said and crouched down to get a closer picture. "I just think it's pretty."

"But it's a fire hydrant," Drew repeated, and crease lines—something my mom always warned us would become permanent if we frowned too much—formed on his forehead.

Knowing there had to be at least one good picture out of the ten I took, I straightened up and poked Drew in the side. "Sure, but it's a very *symbolic* fire hydrant."

At this, Drew opened his mouth to argue, but then decided against it and shook his head. "Come on, expert photographer," he said. "We're going to be late for the signing." He turned and continued up the sidewalk, expecting me to follow.

"All right, all right," I said, laughing before jogging to catch up with him. "I'm coming."

☆ ♭ 🎵

It only took us ten minutes to walk to the radio station, but Drew was right. We were late.

"I don't get it," I said as we took a spot at the end of a long line. "The signing isn't supposed to start for another hour."

Crossing his arms, Drew shot me a look. "Really, Stella? You're surprised that a ton of people are waiting to see a world-famous band?"

"Okay, maybe not," I admitted. "We probably should have gotten here earlier, but I didn't want to leave the gallery."

"I know," Drew said, his tone lighter. "Hopefully this won't take too long."

"Hopefully," I responded, but as I gauged the line in front of us, I had serious doubts.

Ninety-nine percent of the crowd was female—a few moms with little girls, but mainly teenagers dressed up in floral sundresses or cute tops. They made kissy faces as they posed with friends for Instagram pictures and squealed over each other's Heartbreaker merchandise.

Eyeing the girls around me, I felt like an impostor in my plain T-shirt and Converses. I patted my hair and regretted not brushing through it this morning. Instead, I had pulled it back in a sharp ponytail that showed off my bright-aqua strand. A few girls glanced at us in curiosity, and I couldn't tell if they were looking at me because I stood out like a sore thumb or if they were checking out Drew. While being distinct from my siblings was important to me, I didn't like feeling out of place. I skimmed the crowd to make sure nobody was looking before yanking out my hair band and tugging my fingers through my bangs. Nobody else had a stud in their nose or multiple ear piercings like me, but I wasn't going to take those out too.

Finally the mob of estrogen rushed forward as the doors to the station were opened. I briefly bowed my head in thanks, but my relief didn't last long. Once inside, I saw the long, roped-off line that twisted through the huge lobby. We were at the end of it.

"Are you kidding me?" I exclaimed.

Drew started to say something, but he was cut off as an uproar rippled through the crowd. Clasping my hands over my ears, I tried to block out the sudden screams of hundreds of fans.

"Ladies and gentlemen!" a man announced with a megaphone. "Please put your hands together for the Heartbreakers!"

Even standing on my tiptoes, I couldn't see the group of boys that had caused the commotion. Too many girls were jumping up and down in front of me for me to get a good view.

Another round of screaming made the room shake when a song started blasting through the building's sound system. Drew pulled his iPod out of his back pocket and put his headphones on. I groaned out loud, knowing that if I checked my backpack, mine wouldn't be there. I had left my iPod in the car, and Drew chuckled when he saw the panicked look on my face.

"Rock, paper, scissors for it?" I asked with my best puppy-dog face.

"Can't hear you, Stella," he said with a smirk. "My music's too loud."

He turned the volume up and started to head bob to whatever he was listening to. I closed my eyes in frustration. The rest of today was going to suck.

☆ ♭ ♪

My head was pounding. Between two hours' worth of cheesy lyrics, screaming, and a stuffy room, my brain felt like it was exploding inside my skull.

Cara and I were scary similar in so many ways. We both could quote every line from every episode of *Friends* like we had written and produced the show ourselves. We hated peanut butter because of the way it made your tongue stick to the roof of your mouth, and neither of us had ever had a boyfriend.

But if there was one startling difference between us, it was our choice in music. As Drew and I stood in line waiting for an autograph, I couldn't for the life of me understand how Cara enjoyed the Heartbreakers. From the look on Drew's face, he couldn't either. His iPod had died about an hour ago, so now we were both suffering.

"She's totally adopted," I muttered, which made Drew snicker.

"You're identical."

"Irrelevant," I said and shook my head. "I mean, honestly? Where did she go so wrong?"

"I think it was that girl at the hospital Cara's friends with."

"The one with leukemia?"

"Yeah, her. She made mixed CDs for all the pediatric patients."

"We should sue."

Drew laughed and rubbed his temples. "Seriously, though. I think this prolonged exposure to musical garbage is wearing on me. You'd think they'd move the line along a little faster."

"Seriously," I agreed.

The Heartbreakers' new CD was playing on a loop, but every time the song changed, another round of screams ensued. By now I could sing along with every song if I wanted.

A girl in front of me turned around. "Oh my God! This is their best song!" she exclaimed, as if we hadn't heard it a million times already today. "I love the Heartbreakers!"

I restrained myself from rolling my eyes. Every song must be their best song. Closing my eyes, I inhaled a deep breath. "How close are we?" I asked Drew for the tenth time. I still couldn't see the front of the line, but we had to be close. If we weren't…well, I didn't know how much longer I could stand this torture. Drew, who was a good foot and a half taller than Cara and me, craned his neck over the crowd and looked in the direction I assumed the band was sitting.

He smiled down at me. "Looks like it will only be ten minutes."

"Oh, thank God!" Reaching into my backpack, I pulled out a few of my sister's belongings—a Heartbreakers CD, a poster, and a tour shirt. If she didn't go crazy over this present…

As the minutes passed, we moved slowly up the line. The closer we got, the more often I could catch a small glimpse of the band through the crowd. Cameras flashed as people took pictures. Soon we were only a few people away from the front of the line. A group of girls huddled around the table moved away, and—

I could finally see the Heartbreakers. I scanned the table and my heart stopped.

There were four boys. On the far right sat a broad boy in a muscle shirt and with close-cropped dark hair. On his upper left bicep was an armband tattoo with black spirals that twisted together. Next to him was a tall, lanky guy with messy strawberry-blond hair and thick glasses. The third boy was blond as well, but his hair was styled to a T and drenched with gel to keep every strand in place. A pair of headphones hung around his neck, and he kept fiddling with the earbuds.

The final boy was the one that made my eyes pop. He had a familiar mop of wavy hair and a killer smile: the boy from Starbucks. I felt my face go red as I stared at him. He was talking with a fan as he signed a poster, and then he reached across the table to give her a hug. When she walked away, I could see the tears streaming down her face. My mind was on hyperdrive. I had been flirting with one of the boys from my sister's favorite boy band? Someone famous?

The line moved forward, and I realized I would have to talk to him again. What would he do when he saw me? Would he remember? *Of course he would*, I told myself. We'd flirted for a good five minutes and he paid for my drink! But then again, he'd probably flirted with a million girls. My palms were sweaty, and I quickly wiped them on the back of my shirt.

I didn't want him to remember me, I realized. I'd told him that I was in Chicago to see an art gallery, not to meet the Heartbreakers. When he saw me standing in front of him asking for an autograph, he would probably laugh and think I was just another crazy fan.

"They look like little kids," Drew said, startling me from my thoughts. I tore my eyes from the boy.

"What?" I responded, my heart thumping.

"The band." Drew looked at me funny. "You okay, Stella? You're kinda pale."

"What?" I said, forcing a laugh. "I'm totally fine. And yeah, you're right—little boys." My brother was still staring at me like he knew something wasn't quite right, so I continued the joke. "I mean look at the scrawny guy on the left. Can't be older than twelve."

Drew looked up at the boy I'd met this morning and cracked a smile. "I don't know, looks thirteen to me."

The girl from before turned back around again, but this time she had a sneer on her face. "Oliver is eighteen. Stop making fun of him. It's not nice."

Oliver, I thought, churning the name over in my mind. Suddenly I knew why he had seemed so familiar. He was the guy from the magazine article Cara had been reading, the one that called him a heartbreaker.

"You're kidding, right?" Drew responded, his mouth hanging slack.

She put a hand on her hip. "Does it look like I'm kidding?" When my brother didn't answer, she continued. "The Heartbreakers are the most talented band ever, and Oliver is amazing. Keep your stupid thoughts to yourself."

After a few moments of staring with his mouth open, Drew finally recovered and surprised me by apologizing to the girl. "Well, Mrs. Perry," he started, looking down at her shirt. It read: Future Mrs. Oliver Perry. "I profusely apologize for insulting you. It won't happen again."

"Don't apologize to me," she snapped and pointed at Oliver. "Apologize to him."

"Next!" one of the bodyguards called. The girl spun around, and her sneer transformed into a smile that must have bordered on painful. I blinked in surprise. During the argument, I hadn't noticed how close we had gotten to the front of the line. My empty stomach flipped over.

"Drew, I think you were right," I told him, shoving my sister's stuff into his arms. "I feel sick. I need to go to the bathroom."

"No way, Stella." My brother reached out and grabbed my shirt as I tried to run away. "You're not getting out of this one. You can puke on the band for all I care, but I refuse to go up there by myself."

I felt my arms start to shake, dread setting in. There was no way I could face Oliver. "But, Drew..." I whined.

He looked at me with hard eyes. "We are doing this for Cara."

I bit my lip. Drew was right. My sister was a billion times more important than my pride. Sighing, I hung my head. The bratty girl and her group of friends moved away from the table, and I held my breath. Hopefully the lack of oxygen would calm my nerves.

Suddenly the band stood up and headed off the stage. "Wait, where are they going?" Drew demanded.

"Sorry," a husky security guard answered. "The boys are done for today. They have to rest for their concert tomorrow."

Forgetting my embarrassment, I snapped at the man. "We've been waiting in line for hours."

"Yes, and so has everyone behind you," he pointed out. "The boys can't get to everyone. There are just too many fans. Better luck next time."

"But I'm not here for me. This is for my sister's birthday present. She—" But it didn't matter what I had to say. The Heartbreakers were already gone.

CHAPTER 3

I was spread out on my bed in the hotel, staring up at the ceiling. It was sweltering in our room, and the heat was tiresome in a way that made it impossible to move. If I did, I could feel sweat drops trickling down my neck, and every time I took a breath, my skin stuck to the fabric of my shirt. I let my head roll to the side to look at my brother, who was on his own bed.

"Could it get any hotter?" I asked.

After a silent walk back to our hotel, Drew and I had been glad to finally check in and crash for the night. Our luck, however, was still in a downward spiral, and we ended up receiving a room with a broken air-conditioning unit. Lying on the bed, I couldn't help but think that this trip hadn't been worth it. It had been fun to see Bianca's gallery, but at the moment, all I could think about was how frustrating the rest of the day had been. More than anything, I had wanted to see Cara's eyes light up when we presented her with an autograph from the Heartbreakers, and now that wouldn't happen.

My brother glanced up from the book in his hands. "Please don't jinx it," he said before returning to reading.

"We should find somewhere with air-conditioning. Wanna grab dinner?"

This time, Drew didn't bother to look up from the page. "Maybe in a little bit," he said. "I want to finish this chapter."

For the past month, Drew had been consumed with completing his summer reading list. When summer was over, he was leaving to attend school in Minneapolis. Freshman registration wasn't for another two weeks, but Drew wanted to major in English and had already picked a literature course he hoped to take. He was so excited about starting college that he'd decided to read the course material before the semester even began.

I turned away from my brother when my throat grew thick. Freshman year, before Cara was diagnosed, I'd set my heart on NYU. I'd decided that New York would the perfect place for me to discover who I was, independent of my siblings. At the start of senior year when Cara went into remission and I received my acceptance letter, things finally started to feel real. I was going to college.

By the time summer rolled around, I wasn't so excited anymore. New York was calling out to me and I wanted to answer, but at the same time, the thought of leaving was terrifying. My mom told me the flutters I felt were normal. Leaving home for the first time was a big step, and it was good to be nervous. But what I felt inside my stomach didn't feel like butterflies. It was more like killer bees.

Before I could make sense of anything, the cancer came back.

And just like that, the bees were gone. I knew I couldn't leave while Cara was undergoing treatment, so I decided to defer for a semester. It was different for Drew. Minneapolis was only an hour and a half drive from Rochester, so he could come home on the weekends to visit Cara whenever he wanted. I would be states away, completely and utterly alone. I wasn't bitter about having to put off school, but part of me wished I'd followed Drew's example and applied to a university close to home.

A drop of sweat started to trickle down my forehead. "That's it," I said and sat up.

I needed to stop feeling sorry for myself. Yes, it was disappointing that I wasn't going off to school like my brother, and yeah, I hadn't been able to get the perfect birthday present for my sister, but there was no way I could deal with this discomfort any longer. Pulling my hair onto the top of my head in a bird's-nest fashion, I decided to do something about our room.

"I'm going down to the front desk to complain. Don't have a heatstroke while I'm gone."

"You're going down like that?" Drew questioned me.

I glanced in the mirror. Okay, so I looked like hell with my sweaty bangs plastered to the side of my face, but I was way past caring. "Yes, I am, so shut up. It's not like I'm going to run into anyone important."

"Just saying," Drew said. His gaze dove back down to his book, and I watched for a moment as his eyes tore across the page. Suddenly he gasped at something unexpected. "No way," he whispered to himself.

Rolling my eyes, I left my brother to his reading and headed out of the room.

☆♭♪♫

"What do you mean, there are no more rooms left?" I complained to the concierge. He'd already informed me that the hotel maintenance man had left for the night, so no one could fix the AC.

"Sorry, miss, but everything is booked up." The man's eyes shifted around the lobby as he answered my question, almost as if he was expecting something bad to happen. I followed his gaze and noticed quite a few girls waiting around.

I placed both my hands flat on the counter. "Well, is there a manager I can talk to? I didn't pay to melt to death."

But the man wasn't listening. His face went pale and he stared past me. "Oh crap…"

"Oh my God!" someone squealed. "They're really here!"

The muscles in my shoulders went rigid, and I grabbed the edge of the counter with a grip tight enough to turn the tips of my fingers white. I'd heard a sufficient number of screaming girls for one day, and I sucked in a deep breath before turning around. Just as I was about to tell off whatever idiot had screamed, all of the girls lingering around the lobby rushed to the front doors.

"It's the Heartbreakers!"

Four boys stepped into the lobby, bodyguards swarming around them on both sides. Outside, police were manning the door so a stampede wouldn't rush into the hotel. I caught a glimpse of familiar wavy hair and my stomach dropped.

"You have got to be shitting me."

This wasn't seriously happening, was it? I mean, how was it even possible to run into the same celebrity so many times in one day? These kinds of things happened in movies, not real life.

"Ladies, ladies," the concerned concierge called out. "Please give our guests some room." His request went unnoticed.

"Xander, I love you!"

"Alec, marry me!"

"JJ, over here!"

"Oh my God, Oliver!"

The band paused to greet a few of their fans, and as I looked on, I decided that this would go down as one of my craziest days ever. Cara was never going to believe me when I told her. I continued to watch the Heartbreakers until Oliver glanced at the counter where I was standing. I quickly spun around before he spotted me.

I knew it was irrational, but I almost felt as if he'd lied to me by not telling me who he was. Or maybe I just felt stupid for not knowing. Either way, it would be awkward to talk to him again.

After a minute of negotiation with the desk clerk, I managed to get our room for free, but it wasn't much of a comfort. Just thinking about spending a whole night feeling hot and sticky made me want to yank my hair out. But there was nothing else I could do, so I headed for the elevator.

"Stupid boy band," I grumbled as I stepped inside and hit the button for the fifth floor. It was childish, but it helped to have someone to be angry with.

"Hold the door!" Glancing up, I spotted a bodyguard pointing at me. The Heartbreakers were being led across the lobby, their guards trying to hold back the growing group of girls. I jabbed the "door close" button multiple times, hoping I could escape, but no such luck. The group slipped into the elevator, the doors almost shutting on the last guy.

"Thanks so much," the boy with glasses said. "That would have been a nightmare."

"I didn't know appreciating your fans was such a chore." The words tumbled out of my mouth before my mind even registered what I had said.

Oliver's head popped up at the sound of my voice. He stared at me for a moment before breaking out into a huge grin. "Stella!"

He remembers me! My heart leaped, but for some reason I couldn't bring myself to respond, and I watched as the smile slipped off his face.

Nobody seemed to hear Oliver's comment, and the boy with glasses readjusted his frames as he tried to get a better look at me. "Say what?" he asked.

"What do you mean, not appreciating our fans?" The boy with the big muscles crossed his arms in an intimidating sort of way, and the tattoo around his bicep stretched. "We had an autograph signing today."

"Yeah, I know that," I snapped. "I waited for three hours only to get right to the front of the line and watch you all leave."

"Oh, an unhappy fan?" he asked. His expression did a one-eighty as a grin spread across his face.

"We can definitely fix that," Glasses Boy added. He pulled a Sharpie out of his pocket. "Do you have a camera?"

I let out an unattractive snort. "You think I'm a fan?" Pausing, I shot him a glare. "Not a chance in the world."

The boys glanced at each other, not sure how to respond. "I

think she might be crazy," Muscles whispered to the boy with the perfect hair, who still had a pair of headphones draped around his neck. He had yet to speak, and he only gave his friend a quick nod of agreement.

"The only thing that's crazy is that people actually listen to your music." I could feel my pulse fluttering with each word I spoke. "I was at the signing today—which was torture, considering I was forced to listen to the same CD until my ears bled—for one reason only: to get my sister an autograph. And if she weren't my sister, I'd probably disown her for listening to crap."

The band stared at me, mouths gaping.

"Anything else?" Glasses asked.

"Yeah," I added with one final burst of irritation. "You guys suck."

The elevator stopped and the door slid open.

"I think I kind of like this girl. She's got sass," Muscles said with a smirk. "Can we keep her?"

"Screw off," I told him, and then, without looking at Oliver, I shoved past the Heartbreakers onto the fifth floor.

☆♭♪♫

"Why do you look like someone just killed our dog?" Drew asked as I stormed into the room.

"Hotel's completely booked," I said, slamming the door behind me. "All I got was a refund."

"Hey!" Drew said, holding his hand out for a high five. "That's awesome."

"That doesn't change the fact that it's still stifling in here," I complained, ignoring his waiting hand. I pulled a clean set of clothes out of my backpack and stepped into the bathroom. "I'm taking a shower."

Locking the door behind me, I stripped off my dirty clothes. My whole body felt like it was on fire, and a sick feeling was gathering inside my chest. *I shouldn't have yelled at them like that*, I thought as I turned on the water. It wasn't the Heartbreakers' fault that my day sucked. Without waiting for the water to warm up, I stepped into the cold blast and closed my eyes. I stood there, hand against the tile for support, and held my breath as I waited to feel better. But the frigid water only numbed my body. It didn't do anything to ease my guilt.

Oliver probably hates you now. The incident in the elevator kept flickering through my head, replaying the moment when Oliver's smile fell. I was a jerk and he would never want to see me again. A bitter tang overwhelmed my mouth, and for a brief moment, I felt ill.

What the heck is wrong with you, Stella? I shouted at myself. *Get a grip.* Grabbing the bar of soap, I scrubbed myself with enough vigor to remove a layer of skin. There was no reason for me to be upset that Oliver Perry didn't like me. Sure, he was cute, but I didn't know him at all. From what I'd seen of Cara's magazine article, Oliver was a total player, not someone I'd want to get involved with.

Drew knocked on the door, interrupting my thoughts. "Stella, I ordered room service," he called over the noise of the shower. "Is pizza okay?"

"Sure," I answered and turned off the water. I didn't feel

completely better—I was still embarrassed that I had blamed the band for my bad luck—but I refused to be upset over a boy I'd never see again.

After drying off, I pulled on a pair of shorts and a camisole before heading out to the main room. As we waited for our food, I turned on *CSI* and braided my hair. During a particularly bloody scene, there was a knock on the door and I jumped up, happy for an excuse to avoid the gore.

"Thanks so much," I said, pulling the door open. "We're starve…" I trailed off. In the hall stood Oliver Perry.

"Stella," he said. His tone was curt.

I was staring like an idiot again, but I couldn't help it. What was he doing here?

Then I noticed his pursed lips. He looked pissed, and I realized that he probably wanted an apology. The thought made my cheeks turn pink, but I knew he deserved it. I had been pretty harsh.

I opened my mouth to apologize but choked on the words. Something entirely different came out. "How'd you get my room number?"

"Um, I gave the front desk your name," he said. My question obviously caught him off guard, but Oliver quickly recovered and narrowed his eyes at me. "Are you bipolar or something?"

"Sorry, what?"

"Well, this morning I met a girl at Starbucks," he explained. "She was completely sweet and adorable, but she seems to be MIA at the moment."

Oh, right. He wanted an explanation for my mood swing.

"You should have told me the truth," I responded, trying to defend myself.

"About what exactly?" he asked, his chin jutting forward as he spoke. He sounded irritated, but there was something about his eyes that made me think he was more hurt than anything. My throat was thickening, and I couldn't bring myself to apologize. That would be too humiliating.

"Hmm, I don't know," I said, splaying my hand across my chest, trying to hide my guilt with sarcasm. It wouldn't help fix anything, but words were flying out of my mouth again, just like they had in the elevator. "You could have mentioned who you are."

"Are you saying that you really didn't recognize me?" he asked, crossing his arms.

"Yes, I am," I said. Oliver shot me a disbelieving look, so I added, "Look, I've heard my sister talk about Oliver Perry a million times, but I didn't realize that was you when we met."

He stared at me, brows raised, as if I had just offered the answer to my own question. "That's exactly why I didn't tell you."

His response made me blink. "Okay, well, I guess I understand," I said, even though I didn't. Why wouldn't he want me to know who he was? "Now I know who you are. Thanks for stopping by." I started to shut the door.

"Hey, wait!" Oliver stuck his foot out to stop me.

"Is that the food?" Drew called out. The bed squeaked as he got up to see what was going on.

"Hey," Oliver said, poking his head into the room to greet my brother.

"Ah, hi." Drew scratched the back of his head. "Don't I know you?" After staring at Oliver for a second longer, I watched the realization wash over his face. "You're that guy from the band. Stella, what are you doing? Let him in!"

Closing my eyes, I let a sigh hiss out of my mouth. When I released my grasp on the doorknob, Oliver stepped in beside me. His arm brushed against mine just like this morning, and the contact made me suck in a sharp breath. There was a moment of uncomfortable silence as everyone stared at each other.

Finally my brother spoke up. "So no offense or anything, but what exactly are you doing here? Wrong room number or something?"

"No," Oliver said. He glanced at me before continuing. "I came to talk to your...girlfriend?"

"Sister," Drew corrected and shot me a curious look.

I watched for Oliver's reaction, but his face stayed composed. "Right, sister. Anyway, she mentioned in the elevator that you guys wanted an autograph so I thought—"

Before Oliver could finish his sentence, Drew cut him off. "Wait, you two met in the elevator?"

Dang it. Now I would have to explain everything. If Drew found out from Oliver that we actually met while I was getting coffee, he'd be beyond ticked. "Actually," I began, already regretting my words. "It was this morning."

Drew still looked lost, so Oliver clarified. "At Starbucks."

"Wait, so we stood in line all day for an autograph when you had already met him?" Drew asked, gaping at us like we were insane.

I threw my hands up in the air. "I'm not Cara, Drew. I don't have posters of the Heartbreakers hanging on my wall. I didn't realize it was him. If I'm going to listen to a band, I'll listen to a good one like the Sensible Grenade or Bionic Bones."

Okay, so Cara was right about the weird underground music stuff—of course, that didn't make her ignorance of punk-rock legends excusable—but the bands I listened to were much more talented than the Heartbreakers.

Oliver cleared his throat. "Um, okay. Low blow."

My brother looked like he was going to explode, but he took a deep breath, put a hand on my shoulder, and turned to Oliver. "Could you excuse us for a moment? I need to talk to my sister."

"Sure," Oliver said as he shrugged his shoulders. "I just came to invite you up to our room." He handed me a spare room card. "Just give this to the man in the elevator. He'll let you up."

When the door shut and Oliver was gone, Drew spun around to face me. "What the heck is wrong with you?" he demanded. "Why did you keep insulting him?"

"I'm sorry," I said, unable to meet his gaze. "I didn't mean to, but he was getting on my nerves." Well, that was somewhat true. Oliver didn't do anything that was irritating, but the sudden feelings I was experiencing around him were. He made me giddy in a school-crush sort of way, and that was mortifying.

Drew's mouth formed a thin, straight line. "We drove down here for Cara. Not you, not me, but our sister." Ashamed, I looked away from his intense glare. "Rocket..." he said, lifting my chin to face him.

It was Drew's nickname for me, short for "bottle rocket." He said it was because when I got agitated, my temper flared without warning, but the explosion was never very large, and my anger fizzled as quickly as it had been ignited. Whenever I got worked up, he used the nickname as a gentle reminder for me to cool down.

"Okay, okay!" I said, twisting away from him. He was right—I had gone all Fourth of July on Oliver and wasn't thinking clearly. "What do you want me to do?"

"Apologize," Drew said sternly.

"I'm super sorry?"

"Nice try, Stella. We're going up there to get an autograph, and you are going to apologize to Oliver."

Just the mention of his name made butterflies pulse through my stomach. I was going to have to talk to Oliver Perry. Again.

CHAPTER 4

When we stepped inside the penthouse, my stomach was a jumbled-up mess. I'd insisted on waiting for our pizza to arrive before leaving. I'd hoped the extra time would help me calm down, but instead, a watermelon-sized rock formed at the bottom of my stomach and I wasn't able to eat a bite.

"Hello?" Drew called out. The door slammed behind us, and the thud resonated through the silent suite, announcing our presence along with Drew's greeting.

When nobody answered, I hesitated. "Now what?"

"Maybe they're at dinner."

"Well, if no one's here," I said, eager to leave, "let's go." The closer I came to facing Oliver again, the worse I felt. A thick sense of dread was seeping into my veins like an injection of concrete, making my whole body feel heavy. I couldn't stop my fingers from twitching, and I had to hold them tightly to my side and resist the urge to run.

Drew clamped both his hands down on my shoulders. "But you haven't had a chance to apologize yet," he said with a wicked smile. He gave me a small push forward, guiding me down the hall until it opened up into a living room.

"Holy crap," I whispered, forgetting about my nerves. Drew and I exchanged impressed looks.

The space was massive, furnished with the sleek grays and blues of modern decor, and the far wall was a floor-to-ceiling window that framed the glimmering city below. To the right of us was the largest flat screen I'd ever seen, and it was paused on a commercial, almost as if someone had just been watching. Across from the TV was a long couch with matching armchairs, a coffee table littered with fast-food wrappers, and a pool table.

"Still no one here," I said in a hushed tone. "Can we leave now?"

Drew ignored me. "Hello?" he called out again, stepping forward onto the carpet.

It was quiet for a moment longer. Then, unexpectedly, the *Mission: Impossible* theme song blasted out of the sound system.

"Ready, *fire!*" Three boys jumped out from behind the couch, arms raised and ready. "You're going down, Oliver!"

An array of objects launched in our direction, and when something green and slimy hit my shoulder, I shrieked. I looked down at my camera, afraid that some of the mystery goo had landed on it, but it was slime free. Before I was hit by anything else, I tore my camera away from my neck. The strap was tangled in my hair, but I pulled it free just in time as a water balloon smashed against my chest and soaked my shirt through.

"Oh shit," someone yelled. "Abort mission!"

When the attack stopped, we all stared at each other—Drew and I with our eyes wide, and three-fourths of the Heartbreakers with their mouths hanging open.

"Da hell?" the muscular boy exclaimed.

Glasses scratched his head. "Well, this isn't weird."

"No, not at all," Drew said. He picked a pair of boxers off his shoulder. Besides the dirty laundry and water balloons, we had been pelted with Silly String and Cheetos. The green goo on my shirt looked suspiciously like Jell-O.

A second of uncomfortable silence passed before the boy wearing glasses jumped forward, almost as if he had been startled by the realization of what had just happened, and he rushed over to us. "Oh God!" he said, and his face was bright red as he brushed Silly String from Drew's shoulder. "I'm super sorry. We thought you were Oliver."

Drew shook his hair out, and a Cheeto fell to the floor. "Don't worry about it," he said, patting himself down to make sure nothing was caught in the folds of his clothing.

"Dammit! We had everything planned out perfectly," Muscles muttered as he chucked a Silly String can to the floor. He ran his fingers over his buzzed hair and then shook his head. Finally, he turned to Drew and me and cleared his throat. "Sorry if we scared you." He glanced down at my Jell-O stain, flinched, and added, "And pelted you with crap."

I still couldn't find the words to speak, but Drew suddenly threw back his head and laughed. "I'm sorry," he said and clutched his stomach as everyone stared at him like he was crazy. "It's just, that was probably the most eventful thing that's happened today, but nobody is going to believe me when I say the Heartbreakers ambushed me with a bag of Cheetos."

Muscles finally cracked a smile and held out his hand to shake. "JJ," he introduced himself. "I probably wouldn't believe you either."

"Yeah, let's pretend this didn't happen," Glasses said. "I'm Xander by the way, and that's Alec." He pointed at the guy still standing behind the couch. Alec hadn't said a word, but he raised his hand in acknowledgment when we glanced his way.

"Nice to meet you," my brother said and shook both of their hands. "I'm Drew, and this is my sister Stella."

The boys studied me as if there was something off-putting about my face. I held my breath and prayed they didn't remember me—if Drew found out I had verbally abused the entire band, I would never hear the end of it—but recognition flashed in JJ's eyes and I knew I was done.

"Hey," he said, pointing at me. "You're that girl from the elevator." He turned to Xander and starting whacking him on the arm. "It's the girl from the elevator, remember?"

Xander pushed his friend's hand away. "Yes, JJ. Quite clearly."

"Hang on." Drew turned to me. "You met all of them?"

"More like shouted at us," Xander clarified, "but yeah. We've met."

I didn't bother to look at my brother because I knew he was scowling at me. "Sorry about that," I said and tugged on the hem of my shirt. "I wasn't in the best mood."

"We've heard way worse," JJ said, dismissing my apology with the wave of his hand. "Right now, all I care about is getting some payback on Oliver. He filled my favorite shoes with peanut butter this morning, so he has it coming. Someone help me fill more water balloons before he shows up."

Drew glanced back and forth between the boys to gauge how serious JJ was. "You want us to help you ambush Oliver Perry?"

Apparently JJ was dead serious. "Damn straight," he said. He was already at the kitchen sink, and the hot-pink rubber of a new balloon was wrapped around the faucet. "I wanna see that sucker's face when he gets an unexpected shower. Xander, see if we have any more Silly String."

The front door banged open, and Oliver strolled into the room. "Valiant attempt, JJ. I'll give it a four out of five, but you're never going to out-prank me."

As soon as I saw Oliver, my ears started to prickle as if they'd been fried on a sunny day. I quickly stepped to the left where Drew was standing, hoping to disappear behind him.

"Aw, man," JJ groaned. He tossed the one balloon he'd managed to finish back into the sink. "How long were you out there listening?"

Oliver flopped down on the couch. "Who said I was listening?"

The way he settled back into the cushions—hands folded casually in his lap, legs spread out in front of him—made my stomach roll. This was a different person than the boy I'd met this morning.

JJ stared at Oliver, eyes narrowed. "Wait…" he said, as he slowly put something together. "You knew our plan before you left?" Oliver didn't answer, but the smirk on his face was confirmation enough.

"And then you invited them up here," Xander said, pointing at Drew and me. Again Oliver remained silent, but he tucked his hands behind his head as if he was pleased with himself.

"That's low, man," JJ said, shaking his head. "Tricking innocent people."

"I'll admit the brother was collateral damage," Oliver said, waving his hand in Drew's direction. Then he fixed his gaze on me. "But she isn't innocent." He kept his face straight as he spoke, but I could still see his anger, a raging gale captured behind his eyes. "No offense, but you had it coming. Sorry, not sorry."

I heard my knuckles crack before I even realized my fingers had curled into a fist. My blood was pumping so fast that I could feel it rushing in my ears as I took a step in Oliver's direction.

"Stella," Drew said in a warning voice. He wrapped his hands securely around my shoulders and held me in place. I knew he was only trying to prevent me from doing something I'd later regret, and I resisted the urge to shove him off.

Oliver was a complete and total ass. Admittedly, I had been harsh with my critique of the band, but while that wasn't very nice on my part, I still had the right to my own opinion. Did Oliver retaliate against everyone who was critical of the Heartbreakers? And did he really think I was going to roll over and let him get away with it just because he was famous? The fact that I still found him attractive made me seethe even more.

I was about to tell Oliver off, but then JJ cut in. "You're just pissed because she dissed your music," he said in my defense. The way JJ said "your music" sounded as if he'd eaten something that had festered at the back of the fridge for weeks. Wasn't it all their music? I momentarily forgot my anger as my ears perked up.

JJ's comment made Xander laugh, but all the air in the room suddenly felt thin and I couldn't help but tense. "You should have seen his face when we got back to the room," he said. "Just fuming! I haven't seen Oliver that pissed since he fell off the stage in Atlanta."

"I wasn't mad because she doesn't like our music," Oliver snapped.

"What is it then?" JJ shot back. Oliver stared at him, his jaw tightening as if he was trying to come up with something good to say. "Well?

"Screw you, JJ," Oliver spat out. He jumped up from the couch and bolted out of the room, disappearing down one of the suite's many halls. The slam of a bedroom door echoed back to us.

"That was a little prima donna of him," Xander said.

"Hmm," JJ replied, scratching his chin. "On a scale of humble to Mariah, I'd say he's only at diva."

Xander shrugged, and Alec wasn't even paying attention; he was lounging in an armchair with his headphones on, head moving to a beat. All three boys seemed so unaffected by what had just gone down that I wondered if they normally fought like this.

They might have been used to it, but I wasn't able to let things go so easily. "I want to have a word with him," I said, pointing in the direction Oliver had gone. I tried to keep my voice steady so I sounded civil, but everything came out choppy and sharp.

"Be my guest," JJ said. He held out both hands in invitation and gestured to the hall, the grin on his face so full it looked goofy.

"Maybe that isn't such a good idea," Drew said, but my glare shut him up quickly. It had been his idea to come up here, not mine. I would have preferred staying in our sauna of a room, sweating our asses off, but now Oliver was going to hear me out whether he liked it or not. After giving my brother one last pointed look, I nodded a quick thanks to JJ and marched off, my previous embarrassment long gone.

☆ ♭ ♫

He was out on the balcony.

After searching through a series of empty rooms, I stepped inside the master and glanced around. With the curtains pulled back, I quickly spotted him through the glass door. A surge of heat flushed through my body, making my chest and cheeks burn, and I stomped across the room, my anger refreshed.

"What do you want?" he asked when I pulled back the sliding door.

His back was to me, arms folded neatly against the railing as he stared up at the sky. I had expected him to sound furious, but all his previous anger was absent and his voice came out quiet, layered with exhaustion. It was strangely jarring, and I took a step back.

Oliver turned when I didn't answer. "Oh, I thought you were JJ," he said, a scowl flickering across his face when he saw me. "I don't want to talk to you."

I opened my mouth to snap back, to tell him he couldn't go around treating people the way he was treating me, but something over the edge of balcony caught my attention and I stepped up to the railing. Far below us on the ground, swarms of people crowded the sidewalk. They looked like specks from this high up, but I knew they were all teenage girls waiting to meet their idols. "Whoa," I gasped, unable to contain my surprise. "All those people down there?"

Oliver's gaze flickered from the stars down to the street, a distant look on his face. "Here to see us?" he said. He rubbed his arms as if he was cold. "Yeah."

I couldn't comprehend the number of girls waiting outside the hotel. The band had to deal with this every day? The thought made me dizzy.

I didn't regret my decision to be homeschooled, but sometimes being at home all the time was difficult, and I often wondered what high school was like for a normal teenager. Whenever those thoughts bothered me, I would lie in bed and stare at the walls of my bedroom to make sure they weren't shrinking around me. I often felt they were, suffocating me slowly as they closed in on all sides. It was like the cancer had trapped us and was holding us back from the rest of world. I knew Oliver's situation was completely different, but I wondered if his lack of privacy ever made him feel like a prisoner, trapped, the way I did by Cara's sickness.

"It must be overwhelming." I didn't know what else to say. There was a painful twinge inside my heart, and I pressed my hand against my chest.

"You get used to it," he said with a shrug. His answer was so full of indifference that he sounded like he was merely reciting a well-known fact. I had no answer, and he turned back to the darkness suspended above us. Only then did a calm expression soften his face, and I was reminded of the smiling boy I'd met at Starbucks, not the famous prick I had witnessed a few minutes ago.

I joined him in stargazing. "I don't think I'd ever get used to that," I finally responded.

"That's what I said in the beginning." Oliver raked his fingers through his hair and then turned to me. "Look, Stella, I'm sorry about earlier. I shouldn't have tricked you and your brother like that. But you—"

"Wait," I said, interrupting him. I didn't know why I suddenly felt the urge to apologize, especially when moments ago I had stormed in blazing with every intention of making his night as horrible as mine. It was like, in a strange way, I understood how it felt for Oliver to have the world shrinking around him. "Don't. I'm the one who should be sorry. I acted like a total bitch. You just…"

"Caught me off guard," Oliver said, finishing the sentence.

"Yeah," I said a little breathlessly. "Exactly."

We both stared at each other, and a moment passed between us that I couldn't unravel. Oliver stood unmoving, with the exception of his bangs that stirred in the wind. His face was blank, but there was something busy and full about his eyes, and it made me want to take a step closer to see if those deep blues could tell me what he was thinking.

He cleared his throat, which made me acutely aware of how loud my heart was beating, and I lowered my gaze to my feet. The temperature outside had dropped with the sun, and the breeze cooled my hot skin but did nothing to settle the nerves swirling inside me.

"So," Oliver said, his voice scratchy. "Are you really not a fan?"

His question made me cringe. "Oliver," I responded, "I was being spiteful, which was totally ridiculous because you didn't do anything to me."

"But you still don't like us, right?"

"Sorry," I said as I fiddled with my camera, "but not really. My sister absolutely loves you guys though, and she would probably die of embarrassment if she ever found out how awful I was."

Oliver was quiet as he listened to my answer, and I found the way he stared straight at me with his lips pressed together rather unnerving. He looked like a different person when he smiled, much less intimidating, and I suddenly wanted to see his dimples as his lips curled up.

I couldn't stand his silence any longer. "I completely understand if you hate my guts," I said in a rush. "To be honest, I came out here to yell at you, but then I realized you deserved an apology, so again, I'm sorry. I guess I'll leave you alone now."

As I turned to leave, I felt his fingers brush my shoulder. "Wait," he said. His touch made me jump, and he quickly retracted his hand and stared down at it like he was just as surprised by his actions as me. Too unsettled to say anything, I wrapped my arms around myself and waited for him to speak.

He looked back up at me and sucked in a breath. "Can we start over?" he asked. It was the last thing I expected him to say, and I gaped as he stuck his hand out. "I'm Oliver Perry, lead singer for the Heartbreakers."

I hesitated but then slowly slipped my hand into his. "Stella Samuel, amateur photographer." His hand engulfed mine, skin rougher than I expected, but I liked the way my fingers felt against his.

"Well, Stella, amateur photographer, it's nice to meet you." He blinded me with that face-changing smile I had been thinking about moments ago. It was contagious and I found myself smiling back.

"Nice to meet you too."

"So," he said, rolling onto the balls of his feet. "You mentioned that your sister wanted an autograph?"

"Um, yeah." I brushed my fingers against my throat when my voice jumped. "It's a surprise for her birthday."

"I'm sure the guys would agree that we'd be happy to provide you with one."

"Really?" I asked, a tentative grin slowly blooming on my face. "You'd do that?" Even after what happened? Maybe Oliver wasn't the jerk I'd imagined in my head.

He nodded. "Sure thing. Let's head back in and I'll find a pen."

CHAPTER 5

Our walk back to the living room felt longer than the drive from Minnesota to Chicago. Oliver and I had come to a truce, but at the same time, we could never go back to being the people who met at Starbucks—just a regular guy and a girl. I couldn't forget who he was, the lead singer of the Heartbreakers, and that put me on edge. My body was hyperaware of exactly where Oliver was as he walked next to me, and I made sure to keep my arms clamped to my sides so we wouldn't brush up against each other again. Even so, the hairs on my arms were prickling.

When the narrow hall finally opened to the massive living room, I let out my breath and put some distance between us. During my absence, Drew had managed to make quick friends with the rest of the Heartbreakers, and he was in the midst of an intense game of *Call of Duty* with JJ.

"I swear to God, this guy is cheating," JJ said as he died on-screen. "He's like a freaking ninja, popping up all over the place and slaughtering me."

The round ended soon after, and Drew tossed the controller aside and flexed his arms like his physical strength actually had something to do with his gaming skills. "That's right," he said, a smirk on his face. "From now on, you can call me the Slayer."

"Oh hey!" Xander called when he saw us. "You guys didn't kill each other."

"Surprise, surprise," JJ added. "We thought we'd need to recruit a new lead singer. Drew, you any good?"

"Hey!" Oliver said. "What's that supposed to mean?"

"That Stella was totally going to kick your ass," JJ responded. "Obviously."

Oliver crossed his arms and snorted. "You think I couldn't hold my own against her?" I shot him a look and he added, "What? You're like six inches shorter than me."

"Doesn't matter," JJ said, shaking his head. "She had fire in her eyes, man. You don't mess with a woman when she's angry like that."

"Jeez, thanks for the vote of confidence."

"Just saying."

"Well, if you're done knocking me, I thought you guys would like to know that I promised Stella an autograph for her sister."

"Okay," Xander said, bobbing his head enthusiastically. "Anything in particular you want us to sign?"

"Yeah, hold on." I took off my backpack, dug out the CD, poster, and shirt, and handed everything to Oliver. "Our sister's name is Cara. With a *C*." I watched as he spread everything out on a nearby table, and the boys gathered around and took turns scribbling their names.

"So how old is your sister?" JJ asked as he pulled the poster toward himself. He pressed the tip of the pen beneath his own image and produced two looping *J*s.

"Seventeen turning eighteen."

Oliver's eyebrows squished together as if my answer didn't make sense. "Well, how old are you then?"

"Seventeen turning eighteen," I said, smiling, and Oliver's frown deepened.

"We're triplets," Drew clarified.

"Bull," JJ said, straightening up so he could look at my brother clearly. "You have to be at least twenty."

Drew, who had heard the same thing many times before, had a knowing grin on his face. "Seventeen. I swear."

"Which one of you is the oldest?" Xander asked.

"Me," I said, biting back a grin. Drew coughed to cover up his laugh. The three of us always referred to the question as the stupid way of being asked which of us popped out of our mom first. *Like, hello? Do you not know the definition of triplets? It means we're the same age.* But for some reason, people always wanted to know.

From there, the typical round of triplet-based questions ensued until JJ asked, "So why didn't your sister come?"

I watched as Drew's smile dissolved and he tucked his hands neatly into his lap. "She's sick at the moment."

"Oh, that's too bad," Xander said.

Everyone got quiet, and I was afraid the Heartbreakers had picked up on our mood swing.

"Well, it's getting late. We should probably get going," Drew said, and he stood up from the couch. "We really appreciate the autographs, especially after everything." From my brother's tone, "everything" meant the way I'd treated the band.

"Wait, what? You can't leave yet," JJ said, his head jerking sharply toward Drew. "I still have to beat you in a round of *CoD*."

This brought a smile back to my brother's face, but he turned to me, seeking permission. I peeked at Oliver. His sharp eyes were on me, and when we made eye contact, I quickly looked back at Drew and nodded.

"I suppose I have time to crush you again," Drew said, reaching for the controller.

JJ leaped over the back of the couch and took a spot next to him. "Not this time, ninja man. You're going down."

☆ ♭ ♫

"I'm bored," JJ whined. He was sprawled upside down in one of the armchairs and waving a pair of drumsticks around like a band conductor. Blood rushed to his face as he hung in the seat, his shaved head almost touching the carpet. "Someone entertain me," he demanded with a flick of the wooden sticks. After losing to my brother three times in a row, JJ had given up.

"There might be a coloring book in the kitchen," Xander suggested cheekily. He grabbed JJ's legs and flipped them over his friend's head. With a crash, JJ crumpled to the floor. I let out a laugh, and even Alec, who still had his headphones in, cracked a smile. Drew and Oliver were too wrapped up in a battle to even notice.

"It's not funny," JJ complained as he sat back up and rubbed his head. He threw a punch at Xander, who ducked out of the way with a smirk. Giving up, JJ scowled in the direction of the TV. "Seriously, they've been at this forever."

"I agree," I added. As much as I loved watching Drew kick

everyone's butt, it was getting a little redundant. Besides, how long were we actually going to hang out with the Heartbreakers? Drew had made another attempt to leave when JJ quit, but Oliver quickly took his place. The band seemed almost desperate for some type of outside interaction.

"Well, what do you guys want to do?" Xander asked as he sat back down on the couch.

JJ thought for a moment before turning to me with a grin. "Strip poker?" he suggested.

I raised an eyebrow. "You want to play a game where, besides yourself, four guys might potentially end up stripping? Isn't that a little—"

JJ cut me off before I could finish. "Okay, let me rephrase that. Us guys will play regular poker, and you can play it strip style."

At the mention of strip poker, Drew spoke up. "I have no interest in seeing my sister naked. That's gross."

"Yeah, totally not happening," I agreed and crossed my arms over my chest protectively.

"Aww, come on," Oliver complained. At first I thought he was upset about my response to JJ's poker proposal, and my face turned red. But then I noticed that Drew had beaten him again, and the fact that I'd thought Oliver was talking about me made me blush even more.

"Naked Twister?" JJ asked.

I threw my hands up in the air. "How is that any better?"

"JJ, Stella obviously wants to do something a little more mature. Get your pervy head out of the gutter," Xander said.

"Fine, I can be more mature. Would the lady care for a stimulating round of Twister in the nude?"

"*JJ!*" Xander and I both shouted.

"Fine, fine," he said with a scowl. He leaned back against the armchair, deep in thought. Suddenly a slow smirk made its way over his face. "Guys, I have the best idea!"

"Why do I have the feeling that it's going to be terrible?" I asked Xander.

"Because it probably will be."

JJ didn't seem to hear. He was bouncing up and down on the seat in excitement. "Aren't you going to ask me what my idea is?"

"Depends," Xander said. "Is it something ten-year-olds would do?"

Ignoring Xander, JJ continued. "Okay, how about this?" he said as he leaned forward in the chair. "We're going to toilet paper the hotel lobby." It was silent for a moment. JJ stared at us, eager for a response.

"Um, that sounds fun and all," I started with a frown, "but I'd rather not get kicked out of the hotel."

JJ waved his hand dismissively in the air. "Don't worry, Stella. If you're with us, you won't get in trouble," he assured me.

"I don't know if that's such a good idea, JJ," Xander said, shaking his head. "Do you really want to waste all of our toilet paper? You had that chili dog for lunch."

"Oh, gross," I said and moved to the other side of the couch, hopefully upwind from JJ. "Way too much information."

"I don't see you guys coming up with any bright ideas," he snapped back.

"There's the pool," Alec said, and I jumped in my seat. It was the first time I'd heard him speak, and his voice was both deep and quiet. I had completely forgotten he was there.

"Yeah," Xander said, nodding his head in agreement. "We could go swimming."

"Skinny-dipping?" JJ threw out.

"No, JJ," we all said at once.

"Figures," he huffed, "but I guess that will work." He grumbled to himself for a little longer, even though we could all tell he liked the idea.

I looked down at my watch. "I hate to be the party pooper, but isn't the pool closed by now?"

"Yup," JJ said happily. "Nobody to bother us." He wiggled his eyebrows in my direction.

I ignored him and turned to Xander. "So we're just going to sneak in?"

"Come on, Stella. Where's your sense of adventure?"

"Um, hiding under the couch hoping not to get arrested," I told him.

They both laughed. "Touché, but you won't get arrested. There are perks to being in a band. We have a key."

"Well then," I said, turning back to JJ and Xander. "Looks like we're going swimming."

☆ ♭ ♫

"Why exactly are we ditching your bodyguard?" I whispered to Oliver as we stepped off the elevator and onto the fifth floor. This late at night, only one man was actively guarding the band, and the boys had come up with a plan to sneak away from him that involved me retrieving a swimsuit from my room. Somehow I ended up with Oliver as my escort.

He smiled at me like a little boy. "Because it's fun. Besides, do you really want him standing at the edge of the pool watching us swim?"

"No," I said and shook my head. "Not overly."

"Yeah, didn't think so."

As we rounded the corner toward my room, I glanced back at Oliver's bodyguard. He was still standing in the elevator, hands folded in front of him as he waited for us to "grab my suit," the one I had never packed. When we were out of his sight, Oliver picked up the pace and rushed right past my room.

"Wait. I want to grab a T-shirt for a cover-up," I told him.

"Not enough time," he told me as he shook his head. "Once we're gone for too long, he'll come looking for us. Then the guys will be able to sneak out."

"What am I supposed to wear in the pool?" All the guys had their own swimsuits, and JJ had offered to loan Drew one of his extras.

"Your underwear," he said like it was no big deal.

"I am not swimming in my bra and underwear. Did you hear JJ before? Your friend is a total perv."

"What's the difference between a swimsuit and underwear? They look exactly the same."

"The difference is that one is acceptable to wear in public and the other isn't."

"You're not going to be in public. It's just us guys."

"Yeah, just you guys that I met like four hours ago."

"If you're so uncomfortable, just leave your camisole on. But I don't understand why you're being so self-conscious. You look great."

I opened my mouth to argue, but then I realized the compliment he'd paid me.

"Come on," Oliver said, completely unaware of how flustered he'd made me. "If we don't hurry, he's going to find us."

Oliver pushed open the door to the stairwell, and we started taking the steps two at a time. I kept looking over my shoulder, afraid that his bodyguard was going to burst into the stairwell and attack me. Maybe he'd even accuse me of kidnapping Oliver. I could see the headline in my head: "Teenage Girl Abducts the Heartbreakers' Lead Vocalist!" As absurd as it sounded, I was starting to get nervous.

"Are you sure we won't get in trouble?" I asked Oliver.

Before he could answer, two girls opened the door to the fourth-floor landing just above us. They glanced down as Oliver tried to pull his hoodie up over his head, and suddenly I understood why he insisted on wearing a sweatshirt in such hot weather. But it was too late—the girls did a double take when they realized who he was.

Oliver looked up at them, and I noticed his hesitation, but then he grinned at me and grabbed my hand. "Come on."

We flew down the steps before the girls had a chance to shout out his name. By the time we reached the first floor, I was breathless. Not because I was out of shape, but because something about being with Oliver as he was being chased was surprisingly exhilarating. I could hear feet pounding down the stairs and a chant of "Oliver! Wait up!" but we didn't stop.

Pushing open the door, Oliver poked his head out into the hallway to make sure the coast was clear before tugging me after him. We raced down the empty hall, and I realized we were going in the wrong direction. The pool was on the other side of the hotel.

"Hey, where are we going?" I asked. "I thought we were meeting the guys at the pool."

"We're making a pit stop," he whispered to me as we crept down the hall. His eyes were scoping out possible fan girls, his body pressed up against the wall as if that might hide him. Oliver squeezed my hand as we continued to tiptoe down the hall, and I realized that our fingers were still intertwined.

I slowly looked down at our hands, not sure of what to do. A nagging thought ran through my head. *Don't get too close! After tonight, you're never going to see him again.* But it was hard to pull away. The tingles that were shooting up my arm felt too good to let go of, and Oliver didn't seem to mind.

"Bond, James Bond," he muttered to himself. With his free hand he was pretending to hold a gun as he peered around the corner. *Screw it*, I thought and smiled. I was going to enjoy tonight and worry about my heart later. "All clear," he muttered again.

We cautiously continued down the hallway like any good spy would until we reached a set of metal doors with circular windows that revealed the kitchen beyond.

"What are we doing here?"

"Dinnertime," he said and rubbed his stomach. "I've got a

surprise for you." Oliver shoved the doors and they swung open with ease. We were blasted in the face by thick, hot air that smelled of fried food.

It was well past dinnertime, but the kitchen was bursting with activity. I watched as a woman in a hairnet chopped up carrots, her knife a flashing blur. Meat sizzled on a nearby grill as a cook flipped it over. A boy with a mop and bucket zoomed right by us, water droplets spraying everywhere. He was hurrying to clean up a carton of milk that had spilled on the floor.

"Are we allowed to be in here?" I asked. I wanted to leave before someone noticed us and we got kicked out.

"Of course," Oliver said, like it was perfectly normal to stroll into a hotel kitchen. "Xander has some really dangerous food allergies. We always stay in the same hotels, and the kitchen staff learns exactly what he's allergic to. I've gotten to know everybody who works here."

As if on cue, one of the cooks shouted at Oliver. "Perry, my man! How's it going?"

Oliver grinned at me before turning back to the cook. "It's going great, Tommy," he answered. "How about you?"

I smiled and bit my lip as I listened. It was nice to see him interacting with regular people like he wasn't someone famous.

"Same old, same old. The rest of the guys coming down to see me?"

Oliver shook his head and rolled up his sleeves. "Not tonight, but I'm sure they'll be down for breakfast," he said, and I watched in confusion as he washed his hands in a nearby sink. What the heck was he doing?

"They better," Tommy joked as he turned back to stir something simmering over the stove.

When he'd finished scrubbing his hands, Oliver turned to me. "I kind of have this thing for cooking," he explained. "You're not allergic to anything, are you?"

"Um, no…" I said slowly, completely confused.

"Great," he said, cutting me off. "You just wait here. I'm going to go whip us up my favorite."

I stared after him as he made his way over to a huge refrigerator and began pulling out ingredients. Was the lead singer of America's most popular boy band about to cook me dinner?

He was.

After finding some empty counter space and spreading out the different food items, Oliver grabbed a knife and a cutting board. When he started to chop up a potato, I realized the photo opportunity I was missing and reached for my camera. As stealthily as possible, I took a few steps back and snapped some shots of Oliver working before he noticed. The potatoes went into a fryer, and while he waited, he started to slice something green. The food didn't take long, and when he was finished, he packed everything into a paper bag.

"Ready?" he asked and grabbed my hand again.

"Uh-huh."

Instead of heading toward the pool like I thought we would, Oliver led me out the back door of the kitchen. "Grab the stop," he instructed as we stepped out into the warm summer night. "The lock on the door gets jammed sometimes, and we don't want to get stuck out here."

Bending over, I scooped up the wooden block and shoved it in the door before it closed. Oliver sat down on the concrete steps, and when I dropped down next to him, he placed the food between us. I had no clue what he'd made, but a grease stain was already creeping its way up the brown bag, and I knew whatever had made it would give me a heart attack.

"So, James Bond, what do you have for us?" I could feel my stomach grumbling, reminding me that I hadn't eaten dinner, and just the smell of something fried was enough to make my mouth water.

Leaning over, Oliver unwrapped the bag and pulled out a Styrofoam box. "Why don't we start with this before it gets cold?" he said, placing it between us. He opened the box to reveal the source of the grease as steam poured out. It looked like french fries, but they were covered in a white sauce with shredded cheese sprinkled on top. "I had this in Dublin during our European tour. Now I can't get enough of it."

"What the heck is it?" I asked, feeling less hungry. I wasn't normally a picky eater, but whatever it was looked disgusting. Maybe I shouldn't have let Oliver cook for me—just because he enjoyed it didn't mean he was any good.

"Garlic cheese chips. You're never going to look at a fry the same way again." Oliver picked up a loaded fry, shoving it into his mouth before anything fell off. A piece of shredded cheese stuck to the corner of his mouth.

"Um," I started, not sure how to tell him. "You got something right here…" I used my thumb to brush the edge of my mouth.

"Oh." Oliver licked his lips. "Did I get it?" Momentarily, my gaze lingered on his mouth and I wondered how it would feel if he pressed his lips against mine. "Stella?"

"Huh? Oh yeah. It's gone," I said, directing my attention to the fries as my heart rate picked up. "So what exactly is the white stuff?" I could already hear the "that's what she said" joke, as if JJ were sitting next to us.

Grabbing another crispy fry, Oliver dunked it in the goo. "Maymays favor ith galic owder," he said with a full mouth.

I looked at him and laughed. "Never heard of that before."

Oliver swallowed. "It's mayonnaise flavored with garlic powder."

I wrinkled my nose. "I like ketchup."

"Figured that," he said and pulled a handful of packets out of the bag. As I reached for the sugary tomato sauce, he pulled away, keeping the ketchup just out of reach. "If you want it, you have to try this first."

"Come on, Oliver," I said, staring down at the sloppy mess. "That looks gross."

"Nope. You gotta try one."

"What if I said I'm allergic?" Oliver lifted both hands to his face and covered a sneeze. "Bless you," I said on reflex.

"Thanks," he said. "I'm allergic to bullshit."

"Hey," I complained and whacked him on the shoulder. "That's not funny."

Picking up another fry, Oliver cupped his other hand underneath to catch the droppings. "Just close your eyes," he told me. I clasped my hands together and blinked. *He wants me to do what?* When I didn't react, Oliver frowned as if it were perfectly normal to hand-feed the girls he hung out with. "Stella, just do it."

Unsure how else to respond, I did as he said, but not before grabbing my water bottle from my backpack in case I needed to wash down the fry. Oliver brought the food up to my mouth, and his finger grazed my lip as I slowly opened up.

"Well, what do you think?" he asked, as I chewed tentatively. It was a masterpiece of cheesy, salty heaven. I was too stubborn to admit that out loud, so instead I picked up another fry and shoved it in my mouth.

"That's what I thought," he said with a bemused smile. We finished the rest of the fries quickly and fought over the last one before continuing with the next course.

"Ready for round two?" he asked me. Wiping my greasy fingers on a napkin, I nodded my head. "Okay, this is something my grandma used to make me when I was a kid." Oliver pulled out another container. He opened the lid and revealed a weird, pink-and-green food.

"Is that…ham and pickles?" I asked, raising an eyebrow.

He nodded his head. "And cream cheese. It holds it all together."

"You eat the weirdest food ever," I said. Oliver had spread cream cheese over slices of ham, placed a pickle in the middle, rolled it all up, and cut them into to bite-sized pieces. Truthfully, I wouldn't have been surprised if he had pulled out a rainbow eggplant dipped in chocolate and told me it was his favorite food.

He cradled the box against his chest. "Don't insult the pickle rollups. They're delicious."

I held back a snort. "Sorry, I didn't know pickles had feelings."

"They do."

"If I try one, will they forgive me?" I asked, as I covered a grin with my hand. The pickle rollups didn't sound appetizing, but they looked much safer than the garlic cheese chips. The first dish had surprised me, so why couldn't this one?

Oliver glanced down at the food in consideration before looking back up at me. "I suppose so."

I picked up a pickle rollup and took a bite. "Pretty good," I told him. The cream cheese actually brought the combination of foods together nicely.

"You mean pretty damn good," Oliver corrected me.

"Of course," I said and picked up another. "My bad."

Giving me a nod of approval, Oliver grabbed a pickle thing and popped it into his mouth. As he chewed, a smile spread across his face. He looked like a kid who had just been told he could eat dessert for the rest of his life. I chuckled as I grabbed another roll-up, one that had a little more cream cheese than the rest.

"Has anyone ever told you that you're a bit crazy?" I asked, licking some excess cheese off my finger.

Oliver shrugged. "I'm a rock star." The way the words rolled off his tongue made me stop, pickle halfway to my mouth. He swiped it out of my hand before I could protest, shoved it in his mouth, and lounged back on the steps. "People like me are allowed a little bit of craziness."

"Are you now?" I asked and shifted away from him. His comment made me uncomfortable because it reminded me of exactly whom I was sitting with.

71

"You know it, babe," he said with a lazy smile.

"Don't call me that," I said. I had no problem with pet names, but when guys used them in such a casual way, they came off as demeaning. Appetite gone, I pushed the box of pickles and ham away from me. Maybe coming out here with him had been a bad idea.

Oliver froze, the smug smile wiped off his face. "Sorry," he said, sitting up straight. "I didn't mean anything by that."

"It's fine," I told him, even though it wasn't. For a moment, I had forgotten that I was sitting with the leader singer of the Heartbreakers. Oliver's goofy personality had made me bubbly, but now I only felt deflated. And with my disappointment came the realization that I actually kind of liked Oliver—that was, when he wasn't being pretentious.

Unable to hold his piercing gaze, I focused on my nails. The black polish was chipped in places, my left pinkie completely free of paint.

"Stella?"

"Hmm?"

"You okay?"

"Yeah, fine. Why?"

An almost silent sigh hissed out of his mouth. "Nothing."

Thankfully, my phone buzzed. "It's Drew," I said, glancing down at the text. "We should head to the pool. He's wondering where we are."

Oliver studied my face. "You're right," he said, his expression unreadable. Then he stood up, brushed off his jeans, and held open the door. "After you."

CHAPTER 6

The door to the pool was unlocked, and when we stepped inside, I inhaled a deep breath of chlorine. I scanned the room quickly, looking for the guys. There were deck chairs and white plastic tables, a towel rack, and a sign that read: WARNING! No Lifeguard on Duty. Someone had dumped a cell phone, car keys, and a T-shirt on the nearby table. I recognized them as my brother's stuff, but I didn't see the boys anywhere.

"Where are they?" I asked and turned to Oliver. He smiled and pointed to the deep end of the long, rectangular pool. All four guys were sitting at the bottom under the bright blue water. "What the heck are they doing?" I asked, as air bubbled up and broke the surface.

As the words left my mouth, one of the dark shapes on the bottom shot up. Xander gasped when he reached the air. "Dang it!" He wheezed and slapped his fist across the water. "I always lose."

"Oh! A breath-holding contest," I said with a laugh. "They don't stand a chance. My brother used to be on a club swim team."

"You need to cheat!" Oliver shouted across the room.

Xander turned around in the water at the sound of Oliver's voice. "But I did!" he complained when he spotted Oliver. "I waited almost fifteen seconds after they went under, and I still can't hold my breath long enough. Oh God, I think I need my inhaler."

As Xander made his way over to the edge of the pool, Alec popped up, followed by JJ. "There you guys are," JJ said. "We were starting to think you didn't get away from Aaron."

"Aaron?" I asked, turning to look at Oliver.

"Our bodyguard."

"You know, the one without hair?" Xander added when he reached the table. He grabbed his inhaler off the table and sucked in a deep breath as he sprayed it.

Drew finally shot to the surface and inhaled a deep breath of air. "I am the champion, my friends!" he sang in victory. Alec and JJ responded by splashing him in the face.

"Hey, don't be sore losers." Drew grinned and splashed them back.

"Maybe someone shouldn't be such an obnoxious winner," I teased.

Drew's head snapped up at the sound of my voice. "Stella." The grin on his face disappeared, and he raced to the edge of the pool. After pulling himself out of the water, he stormed over to me. During his approach, Oliver took a hasty step back. I didn't blame him; my brother could be intimidating sometimes.

"Where were you?" he demanded. Both of his hands gently grasped my shoulders, and he looked me up and down to make sure everything was okay. "You were only supposed to be gone for ten minutes."

I rolled my eyes. "We stopped for some dinner. I'm fine, promise." Knowing that this interrogation still wasn't over, I planted my feet firmly on the concrete and crossed my arms.

"Well, what took so long?" Drew asked. He eyed Oliver suspiciously.

"Oliver was cooking."

Drew blinked and turned to Oliver. "You were?" His reaction mirrored what mine had been, and Oliver nodded his head. "Well, that's...unexpected."

"You didn't make anything for me?" JJ asked. The rest of the guys had joined us at the table, still dripping wet from the pool. JJ was frowning. "I didn't eat dinner yet."

"You had two Quarter Pounders on the way back from the signing," Oliver responded.

"So?"

"Do you want to die of a heart attack?"

"I'm a growing boy, Oliver," JJ said and pointed at his muscles. "Sorry that's something you and your scrawny arms will never understand."

"Lean, not scrawny," Oliver corrected him. The two continued to bicker as JJ tried to explain the importance of daily McDonald's runs.

"So," Xander said as the rest of us tuned out the stupid argument. "You guys have any problems ditching Aaron?"

"Nope." There were the two girls from the stairwell, but I didn't think they were worth mentioning.

"Good," Xander said. "I don't remember the last time we ditched our bodyguard. I was afraid Oliver might be out of practice."

"You've done this before?" Drew asked.

"We used to, loads," Xander said. He looked like he was going to say more, so Drew and I waited, but then a loud yell and splash filled the room, echoing off the walls.

"Jerk," JJ complained when he broke the surface of the water. Oliver was standing next to the edge of the pool with a guilty smirk on his face. JJ pulled back his arm and sent a spray of water in his friend's direction.

"Dude, what the hell?" Oliver yelled and jumped back. "I still have my clothes on."

"Good," JJ said and continued to splash a wall of water in Oliver's direction.

Alec turned silently to Xander before glancing back at Oliver. Xander smirked as if he knew exactly what Alec was thinking. "You take the left side. I'll get the right." Alec nodded before both boys dashed toward Oliver. They grabbed his arms, lifted him up, and threw him into the pool, clothes and all. Everything happened in a split second, and all I could do was blink in surprise before Oliver resurfaced. He sputtered for a moment and then pushed his bangs, which were plastered to his face, out of his eyes.

"You're both assholes," he said.

Xander and Alec gave each other a high five. "That's for giving my phone number to that crazy chick in Dallas the other weekend," Xander told him. JJ was laughing so hard he had to clutch the metal ladder for support.

"Very funny," Oliver grumbled as he swam over to the side, waterlogged clothes weighing him down. "You two better sleep with your eyes open the next few nights."

Drew nodded in the direction of the pool. "You coming in?"

"Yeah, hold on a second." I quickly stripped off my shorts and camisole, folded them up, and placed them on the table where they wouldn't get wet. I turned back around to find my brother glaring at me. Putting a hand on my hip, I snapped at him. "You didn't pack a swimsuit either! What did you expect me to wear?"

As much as I wanted to keep my cami on, I needed something to sleep in at night. Drew muttered something under his breath, picked his T-shirt up off the table, and handed it to me.

I crossed my arms. "Do you want me to drown?" I asked, refusing to take it. The shirt was an extra large and would fall well past my knees.

"Stella," Drew hissed, "you're about to go swimming with a bunch of famous, probably horny guys…in your underwear!"

"What difference does it make that they're famous?" I questioned him and put a hand on my hip. "Do boy bands suddenly have the ability to impregnate girls with devilish smolders?"

"You know that's not what I meant." Drew sighed, clearly unimpressed with what I thought was a rather funny remark. "They are probably used to getting whatever they want."

My face turned red at his words. "Are you suggesting I'm easy?"

"No!" Drew snapped, and threw his hands up in frustration. "All I'm saying is that your outfit might give someone the wrong idea."

Suddenly, I found myself repeating Oliver's words. "What's the difference between this and a bikini?"

"Stella, you are wearing a lacy bra!" Drew bent over and hissed in my ear.

"Are you guys coming in or what?" JJ shouted from the pool. I glanced over to see that all of the Heartbreakers were in the pool. Oliver had pulled off his wet clothes with the exception of his swimming trunks and left them in a sopping pile on the edge. They were waiting for us to join them.

"Don't worry, Drew. With you around, I'm going to be stuck a virgin until I'm thirty." With that, I left my brother by the table, strutted over to the pool, and plunged in.

The water had a sharp bite, and I felt the hairs on my arms stand up as I sank effortlessly. Bubbles rushed up around me, making it feel as if I had jumped into a fizzy bottle of champagne. I floated at the bottom for a moment with my eyes shut tight before pushing off and springing toward the surface. The tight pressure on my lungs released when I gasped for a deep breath.

"Surprise attack!" someone shouted, and I was dunked back under the water as quickly as I had popped up.

After I struggled back to the surface and pulled the hair out of my eyes, I found a smirking JJ in front of me. "Jerk," I said and splashed him in the face. He just smiled, looked down at my bra, and then winked at me. He was lucky that his back was facing Drew, who was trying to demonstrate that looks could kill.

Then an idea popped into my head. I swam closer to JJ and trailed a hand down his bicep, my nail digging into his skin. "You have such big muscles," I told him, and JJ's mouth slowly dropped open in disbelief. I moved closer and slid my arm around his neck. Leaning in, I whispered in his ear, "But my brother's are even bigger and he'd love to kick your ass."

Before JJ knew what was happening, I wrapped both of my hands around his neck and shoved him under the water with all my strength. When he came back up, coughing on water, he was greeted by a room full of laughter. "Surprise attack," I told him innocently.

I looked over at Drew, who was now smiling ear to ear. He swam over to me and pulled me into a headlock. "Have I ever told you that I have the best sister in the whole world?" he asked as he gave me a noogie.

"Ow! Drew, stop!" I shouted, trying to squirm away from his knuckles. Chuckling, he let me go.

JJ, who had finally stopped coughing, turned to me. "You're sneaky," he said with a smile, "but I can totally take your brother."

"Just like you beat him at *CoD* and Xander beat him in a breath-holding contest?" I asked.

"Hey!" Xander protested. "Asthma over here!"

Shrugging his shoulders, JJ responded. "We just lost to save your brother the embarrassment."

Xander looked horrified. "Wait, that's not true! I never said—"

But Drew wasn't paying attention. "Is that a challenge?" he asked, his eyes lighting up.

"Damn straight it is. Chicken fight. Best two out of three."

"I won't need three tries, but okay," Drew agreed. "If I win, you have to admit that I am stronger, better looking, and overall more talented than the Heartbreakers," he said, grinning. Alec raised an eyebrow at him. "Minus Alec, of course," Drew apologized to him. "He's cool."

"Fine," JJ said, nodding his head in acknowledgment. "But if I win, I get a kiss from Stella."

I let out a snort, knowing that Drew would never agree to that.

But then one shocking word left his mouth. "Deal," my brother said and held out his hand for JJ to shake.

"Hey!" I shouted angrily and sent a spray of water in Drew's direction. "You can't offer me up like a piece of meat. I'm not kissing him!"

My gaze darted to Oliver for a split second, and my heart thumped when I noticed that he didn't look happy with the situation either.

"You won't be kissing him," Drew said confidently, "because we won't lose. Now get up here." Water rushed around his neck as he sank down so I could easily get up. Suddenly, a very fun game turned deadly serious.

Grudgingly, I swam over to my brother and situated myself on his shoulders, just like little kids do with their fathers. Drew stood, and I was raised up out of the pool, streams of water droplets cascading off me.

"If we lose," I warned him, "you're paying for my therapy sessions."

My brother grabbed my legs and held on tight. "Stella, when do we ever lose?" he questioned.

"Never," I responded and ground my teeth.

Alec, who was almost the same size as JJ, was too big for his friend's shoulders, and Oliver refused to participate, so Xander faced me in the air a few moments later.

"No biting, nail digging, hair pulling, or cheap ball shots." Xander recited the rules as I stared him down.

"No grabbing my sister," Drew added quickly.

Xander flushed red, but JJ complained. "What is he supposed to do? Not touch her? Topple her over with a huff and puff?"

"Can we just get this over with?" I intervened.

"I know I'm a sexy beast, Stella, but you need to be patient," JJ said and blew a kiss in my direction.

Ignoring him, I focused my attention on the best possible way to beat Xander. He was so skinny, and without his glasses, he might not be able to see as well. But he had long fingers, which would make it easier for him to hold on to my wrists in a death-like grip. It seemed best to go for a quick shove to the chest before he could get his hands on me.

"Someone say 'go' already," Xander demanded. "Stella looks like she's going to kill me."

"On your marks, get set, go!" Alec said in a loud, clear voice. If I weren't so focused on crushing Xander and JJ, I might have been shocked by the number of words that came out of his mouth.

Drew and JJ circled one another, neither making the first move.

"How long do you think this will take?" Drew asked me. I could tell that he was grinning. "Two minutes? One?"

I glared at JJ. "Ten."

"Ten?" Drew asked, confused.

"Seconds," I replied confidently. I dug my heels into his sides, like one would a horse, and my brother lunged forward in response.

My hands darted out and connected with Xander, slamming into his chest before he had time to react. I watched gleefully as his arms flailed and he and JJ collapsed into the water. *One down, one to go...*

"Xander, what the heck was that?" JJ sputtered when he resurfaced.

"Sorry," Xander muttered as he tried to wipe the water from his eyes.

"Well, just don't let it happen again," JJ grumbled as he sank under the water so Xander could get back on his shoulders.

Alec directed the start of round two with a smile on his face. When he said "go," JJ charged forward and the clear, blue water rippled away from his waist, creating a small wake.

Even though his face was pale with nerves, this time Xander was ready to counter my attack. As I shoved my hands against him, trying to knock their tower over, his fingers coiled around my arms, forming an unbreakable grip. I tried to rip free, but his hands stayed firmly clamped.

"Damn, you're a lot stronger than you look," I admitted to Xander as I tried to wiggle my way out.

"Thanks."

"Concentrate, Xander," JJ growled below him.

With newfound confidence, Xander furrowed his brows and tightened his hold on me. Then he started to pull.

"Come on, Stella," Drew said, his voice rising in alarm. He moved forward, trying to find his balance so I wouldn't slip forward off his neck.

A wicked smile spread across Xander's face before he yanked me to the left with all his might. My stomach dropped and I hit the water with a splash. It happened so fast that Drew didn't even fall over. Xander had pulled me right off the top of him.

"And that's how it's done, boys," JJ gloated. Xander reached down and fist-bumped his friend, his lips turned up in a half smile.

Sighing, I peeked over at Oliver, who was sitting on the edge of the pool. He was glaring holes in the back of JJ's unaware head. I cleared the hair away from my face again and swam back over to my brother.

"Anyone have any breath mints on them?" JJ called out.

Drew and I both ignored him. "What happened?" he asked.

"Xander has suction cups for hands. I couldn't get free," I answered. A knot started to form in my stomach. Whoever took the next battle would win overall, and I had no clue how to best Xander. I had already taken him by surprise during the first round, and I couldn't think of any other strategies.

"I have an idea," Drew said. He bent down and whispered in my ear.

When he finished telling me his plan and pulled away, a look of doubt crossed my face. "Are you sure that will work?"

"Just trust me, okay? I won't let you fall." Drew squeezed my hand, and reassurance flooded through me.

"Can you losers hurry up?" JJ taunted us. Even with Xander on his shoulders, he was hopping from foot to foot in anticipation. "I'm tired of waiting. Do you want me to die of old age over here?"

"Your insults are improving by the minute," Oliver said dryly as he rolled his eyes in JJ's direction.

Drew ducked under the water, and I climbed back on, determined to win. Out of the corner of my eye, I saw Oliver slip into the pool and swim closer for a better view.

Alec repeated the countdown. "Ready, set, go!"

JJ attacked again quickly, but Drew was faster and moved a step back. We continued to dance away from JJ until he was exceedingly frustrated.

"Would you two stop being such pussies and actually fight us?" he demanded and slapped the water with both of his hands.

"I take offense at that," I said, looking down at him.

"And I'll take my kiss," he said, his eyes laughing at me.

"Never going to happen," Drew said.

"JJ," Xander added, "I think you'd make a wonderful super villain."

"That would make you my evil sidekick," JJ responded. Xander frowned in response.

My brother tapped my ankle as if to ask, *You ready?* I squeezed his arm, *Yes.*

Drew moved forward to collide with Team Evil, and Xander's hands swiftly found their way around my wrists. I pretended to fight him for a moment before Drew let go of my left leg and wrapped his free arm tightly around my right leg. I kicked out and my free foot slammed into Xander's chest. My wrists slipped free from his hold, and he splashed into the water with a cry of surprise.

"Cheater! You can't kick anyone," JJ shouted and pointed at me. "I win by default."

Oliver swam over to his friend and slinked his arm around JJ's shoulder. "Actually," Oliver said as he tried to hide his grin. "Kicking was never included in the rules. They covered balls, breasts, teeth, nails, and hair. Any questions?"

JJ turned to Alec, who only shook his head and shrugged. "I still don't think it's fair," JJ complained.

Drew let me slide off his shoulders and pounded on his chest in triumph before pulling me into a hug. "Told you we wouldn't lose."

"Yeah, yeah," I grumbled, but I smiled at him anyway. Then I turned to Xander. "Hey, you okay? I didn't hurt you, did I?"

Xander grinned and shook his head. "Not at all, but you did scare the crap out of me."

It took a few minutes of Drew pestering JJ to get him to hold up his end of the bargain. When the words finally left JJ's lips, they came out in an embarrassed mumble, and Drew almost died of laughter.

However, once that was done, JJ seemed to relax and returned to his happy-go-lucky self. "I have to admit," he said, turning to me, "that was one hell of a kick. I almost fell over!"

"Thank you," I said as I bobbed up and down in the water, "but it was all Drew's idea." My brother flourished his hand and took a deep bow.

"You guys might be jerks," JJ said, and for a moment I thought he was actually mad at us, "but this is the most fun I've had in the longest time." He displayed a wide grin, and I instantly grinned back. Surprisingly, I felt the same way.

"More chicken fights?" Xander suggested.

"Definitely more chicken fights," JJ and Drew said together.

CHAPTER 7

When we stepped off the elevator, Aaron gave Oliver a disapproving look. "Where have you been?" he demanded. Oliver and I had gotten tired of the chicken fighting, so we'd left the boys and returned to the suite.

"Sorry, Aaron. We got lost," Oliver said with a smirk.

"Where? In a lake?" Aaron asked sarcastically as he took in our wet appearances.

"It was huge," Oliver said and spread his arms wide to indicate the size. "I mean, it was probably as big as the ocean. We got stuck in the middle, and there were a killer octopus and poisonous seaweed. I almost drowned when I got a side cramp, but Stella pulled me to shore. It was an amazing rescue, although unfortunately there was no need for mouth-to-mouth resuscitation."

"Poisonous seaweed?" was Aaron's only response as we headed inside the penthouse and Oliver shut the door.

"Won't he go looking for them at the pool?" I asked, turning to Oliver.

He shrugged. "Yeah, probably."

"So they'll have to come back up?" I asked, feeling guilty. "I didn't mean to ruin their fun."

Oliver threw his wet towel onto a nearby chair. "Just because he knows they're in the pool doesn't mean he'll be able to get them out," he said.

"You sure?" I asked, running my hands up and down my arms to keep warm. I had left my clothes at the pool, and I suddenly remembered that I was in my bra and underwear with only a small towel wrapped around me. It was cold.

"I promise," Oliver reassured me. Then he pointed down the hall in the direction of what must have been his room. "You need something to change into?"

I was freezing, and a small pool of water was collecting on the hardwood floor from my still-dripping hair. "That would be perfect."

When Oliver came back, he was wearing a pair of athletic shorts and a plain, white T-shirt. He handed me an identical pair of shorts and a ratty, black cutoff tee. I raised an eyebrow at Oliver as I held up the shirt.

"Sorry," he said, a small blush tingeing his cheeks. "It was the smallest shirt I could find."

"I suppose I can't be a chooser," I said and shrugged. When I dropped my towel to pull the shirt over my head, Oliver looked away. Jamming my arms threw the holes, I quickly put the shirt on. Even though he said it was small, it still hit me way below the waist. Taking a deep breath, I inhaled Oliver's scent: laundry detergent and cinnamon. It was a weird combination, but it still smelled good and I smiled to myself. Oliver coughed, a silent question as to whether I was done.

Embarrassed, I yanked up the shorts and rolled the waistband a few times. "All right," I said as I pulled my tangled hair out from the collar of the shirt. Oliver turned back around and stared at me as I stood in his clothes. "What?"

He shook his head. "Nothing," he told me. "So, what do you want to do?"

"I don't know." I took a step toward the couch, right into the patch of water that had pooled beneath me. As my legs slipped up, my stomach jolted.

"Whoa!" Oliver's arms shot out, and he pulled me against him before I lost my balance. Adrenaline was still rushing through me, and I stood frozen as I waited for my heart to calm down.

"You okay?" he asked, pulling away slightly so he could look down at me. Both of his hands were still on my arms, and suddenly all I could focus on was the lack of space between us, our chests inches apart. Oliver must have noticed, because he quickly let go and stepped away from me.

I rubbed the sore part of my arm where he had grabbed me, and I looked away. "I'm fine," I said, and then I took a quick breath. "Talk about a death grip though. You're like the Hulk."

This made him grin. "Awesome. The Hulk is my favorite superhero."

"The Hulk? Really?" I asked. "Why him?"

"'Cause he turns green and explodes out of his clothes. Pure man right there."

"Personally," I said, "I don't like my men green."

"Fine. Who's your favorite superhero?"

"Superheroes. I like Scooby-Doo and the gang."

"They aren't superheroes. They don't have any powers."

"Neither does Batman, but he still counts," I countered. "Besides, Scooby-Doo always catches the bad guy."

"Which is pretty amazing, considering they're a bunch of stoners."

"Oh my God, Oliver! Take that back!" Nobody insults Scooby-Doo.

"Come on, that show was right out of the seventies. Look at the Mystery Machine. Total hotbox, and Shaggy and Scooby always had a serious case of the munchies."

I plugged my ears. "You are ruining my favorite childhood TV show!"

Oliver's laugh was loud and full, and he clutched his stomach with both hands. "Sorry, sorry," he said as he slowly calmed down. "I'll stop."

"Too late," I told him and slumped down onto the couch. "Damage already done."

"Let me make it up to you," he said, sitting down next to me. "We can watch your favorite movie."

I nodded. A movie was an acceptably easy activity. "Okay, but nothing scary. I hate horror movies."

Oliver laughed. "Yeah, I totally pegged you as a chick-flick type of girl."

"Oh really?" I asked, raising an eyebrow.

"Yeah," he said and scooted closer to me. "I bet I can name your top three movies."

"Let's hear it then," I said and crossed my arms over my chest.

"First, *The Notebook*. Every girl loves *The Notebook*. It's a no-brainer." Oliver confidently stretched and draped his arm around my shoulder.

"All right, next," I said without letting him know if he was right.

"Next, *Titanic* because Jack represents the kind of guy that every girl wants."

"Why's that?"

"Because he shows that if you truly love someone, you'll do anything for them. I mean, he knows he can't have a relationship with Rose, yet he never stops fighting for her and eventually dies for her. Not to mention that he's played by Leonardo DiCaprio."

"Got the hots for Leo?" I teased and poked him on the chest.

"He's a bit old for me."

"All right," I said with a laugh. "Final movie."

"Definitely something Disney," Oliver said, stroking his chin. "Girls love Disney. I'm guessing *Cinderella*."

"Oh yeah?" Oliver was wrong on all accounts, but his explanations were funny.

"Because you girls like that Prince Charming, knight-in-shining-armor crap," he said and shook his head, dismissing it as nonsense.

"I see," I told him and hide a smile.

"So, how did I do?" He perked up in his seat, waiting to hear that he'd gotten them all right.

"I've never seen *The Notebook*. *The Goonies* is my all-time favorite."

Oliver frowned for a second before he replaced that look with a certain smile. "Okay, so I got two out of three, right?"

"My second favorite is *Interview with the Vampire*. Brad Pitt is way hotter than Leo, and besides, he's a real vampire. None of that sparkly shit."

Surprisingly, Oliver didn't seem upset when I told him he'd guessed another movie wrong. Instead, he perked up when I said "Brad Pitt" and "hot."

"So who's your celebrity crush?" he asked, changing the subject.

My forehead wrinkled as I contemplated the question. It was hard because there were so many good-looking guys. "Ohhh!" I finally said, getting excited. "Joe Manganiello. Two words: mus-cles! He played a totally sexy werewolf on *True Blood*."

"What?" Oliver said, putting a hand to his heart. "A werewolf? How about your friendly, teenage heartthrob?"

"If you are referring to yourself, then no," I said and choked back a snort.

"Fine, whatever," he said and crossed his arms. "What's the last movie?"

"Well, if I have to pick a Disney movie, I'll go with *Hercules*. Oh, or *Mulan*. She's badass," I said.

Oliver shook his head. "Jeez, I don't stand a chance with you, do I?"

"Why do you say that?"

"Well, your ideal man is a vampire-werewolf hybrid who's as swift as the coursing river and mysterious as the dark side of the moon."

I giggled. "And the son of Zeus," I added, but I supposed Oliver deserved some credit for being able to quote *Mulan*.

He ran a hand through his hair. "And here I thought being in a band counted for something…"

☆ ♭ ♫

In the end, we settled on watching *Skyfall*, which Oliver said was his favorite movie. When we first started watching, there was a good foot of space between us, but somehow it slowly disappeared, shrinking to a half foot, a few inches, and then nothing. I didn't remember either of us moving; it was more like the couch dwindled between us.

I didn't really pay attention to what was happening on-screen— Oliver's knee was touching mine, and I was hyperaware of the contact. Tingles shot up my entire leg.

He must have been distracted too, because twenty minutes in, he cleared his throat and asked, "So where are you from?"

"Minnesota," I said, tilting my head so I could see him. For the first time since starting the movie, I was able to relax back into the cushions, because talking took my mind off how close we were sitting. "Minneapolis originally, but my family moved to Rochester a few years ago."

"We just had a show in Minneapolis."

"Yeah, my sister really wanted to go," I said, and then I realized that Oliver might ask why she couldn't, so I quickly returned his question. "What about you? Where are you originally from?"

Oliver's eyebrows shot up, like he couldn't believe I didn't actually know the answer to my question, but there was an excited gleam in his eyes. *His fans must know everything about him,* I realized. *He probably doesn't have conversations like this very often.*

"JJ, Xander, and I are from Oregon," he said. "We grew up together and formed a band in high school." Oliver smiled to himself at a funny memory. "We called ourselves 'Infinity and Beyond.'"

"I really like that." If I ever stumbled across a band with that name, I would definitely check them out. "That's cooler than the Heartbreakers." As soon as the words left my mouth, I realized what I'd said and winced.

"We didn't pick that," he said, his mouth twisting slightly. "That was all the record label's idea. Apparently we needed to 'appeal' more to teenagers." He used air quotes around "appeal."

I stared at the TV as I processed what Oliver had said. I had always been so critical of the Heartbreakers, and my cheeks got warm as I wondered if I had been too harsh. From what Oliver had just told me, the band didn't seem to have any control over its own image.

"Well, I suppose it worked," I said. There was no denying that the record label had known what they were doing when they renamed the band. The Heartbreakers had cast a spell on millions of teenage girls.

"Maybe," Oliver said, a grin slowly creeping onto his face. "But I've always liked to think that my adorable smile won everyone over." He winked and I rolled my eyes.

"So if you three grew up together, how did you meet Alec?" I asked, changing the subject before Oliver's cocky side could make an appearance.

"Alec is actually how we got our record deal," he said. "He's from California and his dad is the CEO at Mongo Records. Alec always wanted to perform, but his dad didn't think he had the right personality to be in the industry.

"That's when JJ got an email from Alec saying he liked our music.

He found us on YouTube and promised he could get us in to see a producer if we didn't mind adding a fourth member to the band. So we—"

"Wait," I interrupted. "Let me get this straight. Alec emailed total strangers and asked if he could join your band?" There was no way. I hardly knew Alec, but I could already tell that he was way too shy to ever do something so assertive.

Oliver nodded his head. "Surprising, huh? I think his love of music outweighed his fear."

"Wow, good for him."

"Right? Well, anyway, we were totally excited about Alec's email, but we didn't really know what to think about him joining the band. I mean, we didn't even know if he could sing. So we told him that we wanted to meet and see what he could do. Alec was on a flight to Oregon the next day. Not only could he sing, but he played bass, which was perfect since Xander and I both play guitar and JJ's a drummer. Everything just fell into place," Oliver said, finishing his story.

His gaze was focused on the TV, but I could tell by the half smile on his face and his glazed-over eyes that he was in a different place, reminiscing over memories. After a few seconds, he shook his head and looked down at me. His lips tweaked up into a grin, and then he reached out and pulled me against his chest.

It was a bold move, something only a guy with real confidence could do, and Oliver didn't hesitate in his execution. My back and shoulders grew rigid, and suddenly I could feel the rise and fall of each breath he took. Resting my head on his chest felt so personal, like something only a real couple would do, but I couldn't make myself pull away.

"Do you ever miss it?" I asked, trying to distract myself again. My breathing hitched, and I hoped he hadn't noticed.

"Miss what?"

"I don't know, like, before everything?"

"You mean my anonymity? Sure." Something in Oliver's voice sounded off, and I craned my neck to look up at him. He was staring past me, deep in thought, and then a scowl crossed his face. "But I would never go back. Ever," he added fiercely.

The skin covering his knuckles turned white as he tightened his fist, and I bit my lip, not sure what to say. I didn't think he was mad at me, but something had upset him.

"Sorry," I told him. "I didn't mean to pry."

"No worries," he said, sounding much softer than before.

But Oliver seemed to be done talking, because he turned his attention back to the movie. And without our conversation, my nerves crept back up. I realized I was holding my breath when he started moving his thumb in small circles on my arm. For some reason, I found the sensation calming. Bit by bit, my breathing returned to normal and I nestled down into his side.

Just as I finally relaxed and turned my attention to the movie, Oliver chuckled at something 007 said, and I felt him shake beneath me. Tilting my head back a few inches, I looked up at him through my lashes. There was a dusting of pink on his cheeks, and his eyes shone as he laughed.

He must have felt my gaze, because his eyes snapped down and found mine. His lips slowly parted as he stared down at me, and my whole body flooded with warmth. Someone was shouting something crazy on-screen, but I was too preoccupied with Oliver to turn toward the TV. The way he was looking at me made me want to press my body farther up against him, and the thought made me blush.

Embarrassed by my own thoughts, I suddenly needed to look away, to focus on anything but him. But as I turned, Oliver gently grabbed my chin. He held my head in place until I made eye contact, and then, once he knew I was watching, he dipped his head and brushed his lips against mine.

The small bit of contact was all I needed. Something flared up inside me, and instead of waiting for Oliver to deepen the kiss, I wrapped my arms around his neck and pulled him closer. I'd kissed boys before, but I had never felt like I did in that moment—crazy and wild and losing control. When Oliver yanked me onto his lap, my mouth left his and I started kissing down his neck. His head rolled back against the couch, and he groaned, yanking at his shorts with his free hand as he tried to readjust.

The front door banged open. "Stella? Oliver? Are you guys up here?"

When Xander's voice rang through the apartment, Oliver pushed me off and shot to the other side of the couch as if I suddenly had a contagious disease. Sitting up straighter, I patted down my hair.

"There you guys are," Xander said when he entered the living room.

"Oh hey," Oliver said.

He put on a wonderful performance. First, he casually glanced up at his friends like he hadn't heard anyone enter the penthouse. Then he yawned and stood up to stretch as if his muscles were cramped from watching the movie. *If he wasn't a singer*, I thought, *he would make an excellent actor.* Grabbing the remote, Oliver flipped the movie off just as Aaron ushered the rest of the guys into the room. Then a woman with short, blond hair stepped inside after them.

"Aaron called Courtney," Xander said, his lips tightening.

Oliver narrowed his eyes at his bodyguard. "Traitor."

"Aaron did the right thing," said the lady I presumed was Courtney. "We have an interview tomorrow morning and a concert tomorrow night. You should have gone to bed hours ago."

"We're not kids, Courtney," JJ complained. The way he rolled his eyes made him look exactly like a little kid, and I covered my laugh with a cough.

"Really?" she responded and put a hand on her hip. "Could have fooled me. Aaron shouldn't have to call me in the middle of the night to make you behave. I'm your manager, not your babysitter." So this Courtney chick was the band's manager.

"Okay, we get it," Xander grumbled. "We'll behave. You can go back to bed now."

"I will," Courtney said, "but your friend has to leave." She pointed at Drew.

"Friends," Drew corrected her. "My sister is coming with me." He shot me a look that said, "No way in hell are you staying here alone."

Courtney's eyes flickered over to the couch when my brother looked in my direction. She sighed before turning to Oliver. "Your friend has to leave as well." The way Courtney dismissed me made it seem as if she had done it many times before, almost like it was a normal occurrence.

"Okay," Oliver said calmly. For a moment, nobody moved.

"Well, are you both coming?" Courtney asked as she nodded in the direction of the door.

A gut-wrenching feeling washed over me as I stood up. I turned to Oliver, but he wouldn't meet my eyes. Okay…why was he acting so strange all of a sudden?

Alec spoke up. "It would be nice if we could say good-bye to our friends." Courtney raised an eyebrow as if she were waiting. "Privately," he added and crossed his arms over his chest.

The boys' manager pursed her lips together before responding. "Fine," she agreed, "but don't take too long. I'll see you four in the morning." Taking Aaron with her, Courtney backed out of the room. It remained quiet until the door clicked shut.

"That went well," Oliver grumbled to himself. He stuck his hands in his pockets and looked around awkwardly.

Drew started our good-byes. "It was great to meet you all." He actually looked a little sad as he gathered Cara's belongings from the table. "Thanks again for signing everything. It will really mean a lot to our sister."

"Oh! That reminds me," Xander said before disappearing into one of the back rooms and returning with another poster.

"Good call," JJ said when he saw it.

"It's going to be in next month's issue of *Tiger Beat*," Xander explained to me as he held it up. It was a picture of all the guys jazzed up in suits. My eyes went straight to Oliver, who had his hands raised to form a fake gun. His eyes twinkled in amusement as they stared up at me from the glossy page. Bond, James Bond.

"Nobody has it yet," JJ added. He took the poster from Xander, flattened it out on the table, and wrote a message for Cara in the top left-hand corner. It read:

Happy Birthday, Cara!

Sorry we missed you, but we hope you have an awesome day.

—the Heartbreakers

All four boys signed it, the letters in their names dipping in and out in impressive loops. I was always jealous of celebrities' signatures because they looked so perfect and special. Mine looked like a two-year-old wrote it.

When they were done, Drew rolled up the poster and tucked it underneath his arm. He lifted a hand and carved it through his hair, holding a bunch at the back for a moment before letting go and shaking his head. "I don't know what to say," he said. "Thank you so much."

I knew exactly how he was feeling. No words could express how happy Cara would be when she saw her gift, and there was nothing more Drew and I wanted. This would be unforgettable for her, and we would never be able to properly thank the Heartbreakers for that.

"No problem," Oliver said and smiled at Drew. It was one of those million-dollar smiles, just like the one that threw me off guard at Starbucks, and I gritted my teeth and looked away.

Oliver held out his hand for Drew to shake, and before I could get upset about having to leave, Xander pulled me into a smothering hug. He was so much taller than me that my face collided with his chest. "I'm glad we met," he said as he squeezed the air out of me. "Even though you did scare the shit out of me in the elevator."

I pulled away. "I scared you?"

Xander pushed his glasses back into place and nodded his head. "You were quite formidable."

Next it was JJ's turn to say good-bye. "Do I get a kiss now?" he asked me. I laughed and shook my head no. "Fine," JJ said before quickly pecking me on the cheek. "I'll just have to steal one."

Then came Alec. I didn't exactly know what to say to him, but I didn't need to worry about it. He spoke first. "Can we talk privately for a moment?" His face was completely blank, making it impossible to know what he was thinking.

"Um, sure?" I said, cocking my head. What did Alec want to talk to me about that was so secret?

He led me into the kitchen where no one could overhear us. "Sorry," he said then. "It's just that I wanted to ask you a personal question."

I shrugged, trying to hide my sudden apprehension. "Shoot."

"You always have your camera with you," he stated, pointing down at it.

My shoulders instantly relaxed. Of all the possibilities that had run through my head, my camera was not what I'd expected Alec to be curious about, but I didn't mind. I could talk about photography all day long.

"Yeah," I said and picked it up from where it hung around my neck. I ran my thumb over a row of controls.

"Why?" There were two little indents between his eyebrows as he frowned. His face was filled with concentration, like he was trying to solve a puzzle.

"Because I like taking pictures?" My response came out sounding like a question since I wasn't completely sure what he was trying to get at.

His mouth turned up into a grin, and even though it was only a small one, it was one of the first I had seen from him. It lit up his face and made his normally stormy gray eyes look blue. "I know that," he said as he studied me, "but I can tell that it means something more to you. It's like…" Alec trailed off, trying to think of a way to explain what he meant. "I'm having a hard time thinking of a good example, but for instance, some people always wear a specific piece of jewelry and never take it off. It isn't just an accessory, but a source of strength. You know what I mean?" As he explained, he twisted the cord of the headphones hanging around his neck.

I blinked, completely taken aback. From the start, I'd recognized that Alec was a quiet observer, the type of person who noticed everything. What I hadn't realized was how perceptive he was. His guess was right on the money, so I decided he'd earned an explanation.

"I got into photography right about the time Cara got sick," I told him, trying to find the right place to start. "I had to be strong for her, but that was really hard. One day I was a normal teenager and the next my sister was dying. The whole thing knocked me off balance, you know?

"I was a wreck on the inside because I was angry and afraid and all these other feelings I didn't understand, so then I just started taking more and more pictures of, like, everything. But Cara was always my main subject. It was like I was trying to capture every single moment we had together in case—" I stopped, not wanting to finish my sentence.

But my story was spilling from me like a gushing fountain, and I started up again. "I don't know. I guess it was just easier to hide behind the lens of my camera. Having it with me has become such a habit that I just feel weird without it."

A silence passed between us. Alec looked at me funny, and then I realized what I'd just said. My hand flew to my mouth as a small gasp escaped my lips. I hadn't meant to tell him that. It was like the words had left my mouth without me knowing.

But Alec didn't have that sad look in his eyes that I'd become accustomed to over the past few years. Instead, he held my gaze with a look of understanding, almost as if he'd expected the truth all along. He'd figured out the puzzle.

"Thank you," he said. His voice was low and quiet, and I knew he wouldn't broach the subject again. "Can I ask you one more question? I promise it's not as nosy as my first."

"Okay," I said and grabbed on to my camera.

"Could you send me the pictures you took tonight?" He held up a small piece of paper with what appeared to be an email address scribbled on it. "I'd like to have my own copies."

"Oh," I said and loosened my tight grip on my camera. I took the paper from his hand. "Of course. I'll edit them and have them to you by the end of the week."

Now Alec offered me his first full smile. "Thanks," he said. "I'd really appreciate it."

"Stella?" Oliver popped his head into the kitchen and smiled when he saw me. "There you are."

"Tell your sister happy birthday for me," Alec said and then moved out of the way so I could say good-bye to Oliver. Even though I hadn't really been able to get to know him, I could tell that Alec was a genuinely nice guy.

"I will," I told him, and then he was gone, leaving Oliver and me alone.

We were both silent as we studied one another. Finally, he reached up and tucked a piece of hair behind my ear. "I'm glad you yelled at us."

"I—what?" This was a strange and confusing good-bye.

"In the elevator," he clarified. "I can't ever forget you now, can I?" My mouth opened, but I didn't know what to say. A quarter-sized lump formed at the back of my throat, so I closed my mouth and didn't say anything.

"Can I have your phone?" he asked suddenly.

"My phone?" I asked, but I pulled it out of my pocket anyway.

Oliver took it from me and started typing something in. "Here's my number. Please don't sell it to the tabloids for hundreds of dollars," he joked.

"Your number?" No guy had ever given me his number before.

"I want you to call me, okay?" He handed it back after he finished punching his information in. "You promise to call?" I nodded my head, still unable to mutter a word. Oliver grasped both of my hands, his skin warm against mine. He rubbed his thumb in circles on my palm, just like he had when we were watching the movie.

"God, I don't want to say good-bye to you." He sighed as he looked down at me.

"Then don't," I finally said, wrapping my arms around his waist and pulling him into a hug. His hands snaked around my back in response, and I buried my face in his shoulder, my nose against his shirt. We stood there for a long moment, neither of us talking, and then someone cleared his throat behind us. I turned to see my brother standing in the kitchen doorway, and we detangled ourselves quickly.

"You ready, Stella?" he asked me.

"Yeah," I responded, even though I was nowhere close to ready. When I turned to follow Drew, Oliver grabbed my wrist and pulled me back.

"You remember what I said?"

"Sell your number to the highest bidder?"

"Please call."

"Okay."

CHAPTER 8

There was a knock on my door, and my dad pushed it open. "Hey, kiddo," he said and leaned against the door frame.

"Hey," I replied before flopping back on the bed. For the past hour, I had been moping around my bedroom.

"You sound tired." Even though I couldn't see his face, I could picture the frown lines etched into his forehead. My dad had developed the habit of being perpetually worried when Cara first got sick.

"Didn't sleep well," I told him.

Last night, when we got back from our trip, our parents told us the good news—Cara's white blood cell count was doing better, and she was being released from the hospital. After that, I went straight to bed. Even though I was worn out, I had stared at the ceiling until early morning, unable to fall asleep. A certain boy had been on my mind.

"Too excited about Cara coming home?" he asked.

"Yeah, something like that." I picked a spot on the ceiling and studied it, hoping that my dad wouldn't hear my lie.

Oliver was the reason I couldn't sleep, not Cara. He'd given me his number and asked me to call. Was today too soon? Would it make me look desperate? Maybe I should hold off for a few days. But if I waited too long, would it look like I wasn't interested? Calling or not calling was all I could think about.

Was I a horrible sister because I was focused on Oliver Perry and not Cara? Yes, I was excited that she was coming home, but it didn't mean her cancer was gone. She was still sick. And if there was one thing that I truly wanted, even more than a chance to spend more time with Oliver Perry, it was for my sister to get better.

"Well, your brother and I helped her into the kitchen. Mom is making breakfast."

"Mom is cooking?" I sat up on the bed. My mom wasn't much of a chef. She could make Easy Mac and PB&J, but normally family meals were my dad's responsibility.

"Attempting to. I should probably go help her before the pancakes turn into a scrambled mess." Cara could live off pancakes, so it was no surprise that my mom wanted to make them. Syrup was practically a food group in our house.

"Scramcakes," I said with a smile.

"Yeah, we don't want that," he said, laughing.

As my dad turned to leave, Drew stuck his head into the room. "Hey, Stella, Cara keeps asking where we were the last two days. Can we just give our present to her now?" He was bouncing up and down, and I could tell that he couldn't wait to see her reaction.

"Sure thing," I said and got off the bed. "Let me just get everything together."

"Okay. There are some birthday gift bags in the hall closet if you want to wrap everything up."

After grabbing a gift bag covered in glitter and tucking all the signed merchandise inside, I headed to the kitchen. My mom and dad were by the stove, and the smell of breakfast filled the room.

"Stella!" Cara called and patted the chair next to her. She was at the table with Drew and they'd started playing Rummy 500, our family's favorite card game. Dad had taught us how to play when we were little, and we'd been perfecting our own personal strategies ever since. Drew was the best out of the three of us, but I hated playing with Cara the most. Over the years, she'd earned the nickname The Scooper, because of her infuriating knack for scooping up the discard pile just when you wanted it the most.

"Hey, you," I said and smiled back. Cara was always buying wigs, and today she was sporting an edgy pixie cut. "Looking sassy today."

"You like?" She fluffed up the fake hair. "I think it brings out my rebellious side."

"Since when do you have a rebellious side?" Drew asked and shot her a skeptical look. It wasn't that Cara was a goody two-shoes, but with her illness, she didn't have the opportunity that normal teenagers did to break the rules.

"Well, for starters, I've already looked at your hand twice. It would be really nice if you laid down the queen of hearts," she answered innocently.

I burst out laughing and sat down.

My mom turned when she heard me. She had flour in her hair and on her face. "Morning, honey," she said with a smile. "Want a pancake?"

"I don't know," I said, trying not to laugh. "Did you make them?"

"No," my mom grumbled and waved the spatula at me. "Your dad took over. He was mumbling something about scramcakes."

"All right, I'll take one."

"Thanks for the love and support," my mom said. Nevertheless, she took a plate down from the cabinets and held it out for my dad to scoop one perfectly golden cake onto. The syrup and orange juice were already on the table, so she only grabbed a fork before setting the breakfast in front of me.

"Thanks, Mom," I said happily and dug in.

"Who's that for?" Cara asked when she finally spotted the gift bag.

"Yum, this is great, Dad," I told him through a full mouth. When I swallowed and set down my fork, I turned to Cara. "Possibly for a nosy sister."

"Ohhh!" she exclaimed and wiggled her eyebrows in excitement.

"It's your birthday present," Drew added.

"Is the nosy, yet completely charming sister allowed to open her present?" she asked.

"I suppose so."

"Yay!" Cara gushed and clapped her hands together. When I pushed the bag across the table to her, Drew scooted away in caution. Cara was about to flip.

Cara pulled out the tour T-shirt first. When she unfolded it, she smiled. "Aww, thanks, guys. I love the Heartbreakers." I could tell that she was trying to be nice, since she thought we had gotten her a T-shirt that she already had.

"You're welcome," I said. "When did you get a hole in the armpit?"

Cara shrugged. "Oh, it's been there since—" She stopped suddenly and then flipped over the sleeve to see if it really was her own shirt. Frowning, Cara looked back and forth between the two of us. "I don't get it. You're giving me my shirt?"

"Your new and improved shirt," I told her with a smirk.

She looked confused for a moment before something finally clicked in her head. "No way!" she said in disbelief and flipped the shirt over to inspect it. There in black Sharpie were the boys' names.

"Oh my freaking God!" Cara screamed. "This is amazing. No, this is better than amazing. This is like Christmas on steroids!" She was so excited that she didn't know what to do with herself. First she squeezed the shirt to her chest before deciding to pull it on over the one that she was already wearing.

"Thank you guys so much," Cara said, looking at both of us. She acted like she was going to cry. "You totally win best birthday present this year."

"You haven't even finished opening it yet," I pointed out.

"There's more?" She tore into the rest of the bag, squealing with glee each time she pulled out another one of her signed belongings.

"I don't remember this one," Cara said when she unrolled the poster that Xander had given us.

"It's not out yet," Drew told her. "Xander said it's going to be in the next issue of *Tiger Beat*."

"He gave this to you?" Cara exclaimed, her eyes practically popping out of her head. "You say that like you know him."

For a moment, I think Drew forgot that we were talking to Cara, a.k.a. the crazy Heartbreakers stalker. "Well, yeah, we hung out with them Saturday night."

Cara spent the next few hours interrogating us about the Heartbreakers. After Drew mentioned that we had hung out with the band, my sister made us share every detail about our trip. As a punishment for his slip, I made Drew do the retelling. While he told the story, I let Cara flip through my camera. I had recorded most of the night. There were a few pictures of Oliver cooking, shots from the pool, a video of one of the chicken fights, and of course the pictures I had taken of Oliver at Starbucks.

"So, who has the prettiest eyes?" Cara asked as she watched the chicken-fight video for the tenth time.

Drew raised an eyebrow. "You're really not asking me that, are you?"

Cara set the camera down before resting her elbows on the table and propping her head up in her hands. "In my opinion it's JJ," she said dreamily.

"I don't know," Drew said and rolled his eyes. "I was leaning more toward Alec."

"What do you think, Stella?" Cara asked as she continued to stare off into space. My thoughts went immediately to Oliver, but I wasn't going to tell her that. After years of trying to convince me that the Heartbreakers were "so hot" there was no way I would admit to Cara that she had been right all along.

Drew smirked at me. "No contest there." Then he traced a heart in the air with his fingers.

"Shut up!" I hissed and gave him a hefty kick to the shins under the table.

"What the heck, Stella?" he complained and rubbed his sore leg. "That hurt."

Cara snapped out of her daydream and turned to me. "Huh? What are you guys talking about?"

"Absolutely nothing," I lied and looked away so she couldn't see the pink forming on my cheeks.

"Bullshit," Drew coughed.

"Do you want another kick?" I threatened.

"Okay, you have to tell me now," Cara said and clicked her manicured nails across the table impatiently. I glared at my brother, daring him to say something. "Stella?" Cara asked.

I kept my mouth shut, and Drew and I continued our silent staring contest. Finally he looked down. I thought I had won and for a moment I silently celebrated a victory, but then he smiled wickedly.

"OliverPerrygaveStellahisnumber!" He spoke so fast that his words blended together. I almost didn't understand, and by the time I did, Drew had jumped out of his chair and well away from my foot.

Cara giggled. "No, really. What are you guys talking about?"

"'Please call me, Stella,'" Drew mocked.

I gritted my teeth together. "I am going to kill you, Drew!"

"Oh. My. God," Cara said slowly. She looked back and forth between us. "He wasn't joking?"

When neither of us said anything, Cara had the confirmation she wanted. "Holy shit! Oliver Perry gave you his number? You're such a lucky bitch. Oh my God, can I see it?"

For someone who wasn't very mobile, Cara was adept at launching herself toward my pocket where my phone was tucked away.

I pulled my cell out of my jeans, and she snatched it away before I could blink. While Cara was searching through my phone, I flipped Drew off.

"Where is it?" Cara demanded. "You guys weren't lying, were you?"

"No," I said as my cheeks turned red. "It's under 'Starbucks boy.'"

Cara eagerly flipped through the numbers again until she found Oliver. "Wow," she said slowly. "That's really it?"

"Yeah," I answered, feeling slightly uncomfortable. Cara was staring at my phone like it was a miracle from heaven.

"So have you called him?" she asked. I could tell she was doing everything in her power to keep from hitting the call button.

"No," I muttered.

"Oh my God. Okay, so when you do, you need to tell me everything. Do you think it would be weird if I said hi? I know he doesn't know me, but come on. You know I'm like the Heartbreakers' biggest fan," Cara gushed.

"Sure, no problem," I said quietly.

Sensing my discomfort, Drew switched the subject as he sat back down at the table with another plate of pancakes. "Okay, moving on to something way more important than a phone number. What do we want to do for our birthday on Friday?" *Thank you*, I mouthed to Drew even though it didn't make up for him being a jerk.

For our birthday, I wanted to do something simple so we wouldn't have to worry about Cara. Last year had been perfect since we spent the day on the beach. Our aunt and uncle own a cottage on the ocean in South Carolina, and my entire family flew out to visit them for a whole week.

We played sand volleyball and Frisbee with our cousins—Cara cheering from the side—and swam in the cool water. For breakfast, lunch, and dinner we munched on fresh watermelon and sipped lemonade. When it got dark, we built a bonfire in the sand and roasted marshmallows as the waves crashed against the shore in a soothing nighttime song.

"We could go to the movies," Drew offered and shrugged his shoulders.

"That's so boring," Cara whined as she spun my phone in circles on the tabletop.

As much as I agreed with Cara, I couldn't think of something to do that was a perfect combination of safe and exciting. "A movie could be fun," I said slowly. "Didn't that one thriller just come out?"

"I don't like thrillers," Cara complained. She turned to Drew. "Besides, didn't you say that you would never go to the movies with me again?"

"What?" he asked.

"Oh yeah," I said and snorted. "Remember the *Twilight* premiere?"

"Oh God," Drew said and buried his face in his hands. "Don't remind me."

Cara had been so excited about the opening of *Twilight* that she dragged Drew to the midnight showing with her. But that hadn't been the worst of it. She dressed up as Alice and forced Drew to be Edward. After the movie, he had run into his crush from school, his face covered in sparkling glitter.

"We looked so perfect," Cara said, remembering the event fondly.

"You put powder on my face," Drew said, irritated. "I looked like an idiot."

"And that's different from any other day?" I said. "I think I have a picture of you on my computer somewhere."

"Okay, never mind," Drew grumbled. "We're not doing a movie."

CHAPTER 9

I wasn't expecting a call.

A week had passed since my adventure in Chicago, seven full days since Oliver and I said good-bye. Dad had taken time off from work for Cara's homecoming, and we'd spent most of our time curled up in the living room watching classic movies or sitting at the kitchen table playing cards. For our birthday we went to a local park, enjoyed a picnic, and watched the fireworks for the Fourth. It wasn't a beach day in South Carolina, but it was still nice.

My life reverted to the boring routine that had existed before my path collided with the world's most famous boy band.

Or so I thought.

Today, it was just Cara and me—Mom and Drew were in Minneapolis for his class registration, and Dad was back at work. Cara had dozed off some time ago to *E! News*, but I refrained from changing the channel to something I actually liked. Instead, I was skimming through one of the books my mom checked out of the library for Cara when my ears perked. A small part of me was hoping to hear anything about the Heartbreakers or Oliver.

I had made the decision not to call him. It wasn't that I didn't want to; I did, but I also knew that nothing was ever going to happen between us. He was a world-famous musician, and I was just normal, boring Stella. I'd had my one Cinderella night, and I didn't want to ruin its magic with a letdown. By not calling, I was figuratively closing the door on Oliver Perry.

It wasn't working very well. Despite my best efforts, I couldn't stop thinking about him or how I'd felt when he kissed me.

When my phone rang, the book flew from my hands and hit the floor with a flutter of pages.

"Hello?" I answered in a whisper, not wanting to wake Cara. I slipped out of her room, carefully closing the door behind me.

"Is this Stella Samuel?" a man asked on the other end of the line.

"Speaking." I settled onto the worn couch in our living room.

"Darling!" he exclaimed, and I had to hold the phone away from my ear so I didn't go deaf. "I'm so excited to finally talk with you."

"Sorry, but who's this?"

"Oh, how silly of me. My name is Paul Baxter. I'm the Heartbreakers' publicist. I wanted to speak to you about some photographs you took of the band." My back instantly straightened. Why was the Heartbreakers' publicist calling about my pictures? When had he even seen them? "Stella? Hello?"

"Yeah, sorry." I cleared my throat. "Um, you mentioned my photographs?"

"Yes, yes! Alec showed me the shots you took a few weekends ago."

"Oh, right," I said, remembering the email I'd sent to him.

"You're quite talented with a camera. There's this quality about your pictures that I can't put my finger on. It's like—" Paul paused as he tried to explain himself. "I suppose this sounds cheesy, but you have a knack for capturing the energy in a moment."

For at least three full seconds my mind was completely blank. Paul's praise was so unexpected, so unbelievable that nothing he said registered in my mind. But there was warmth flowering in my hands and feet, the feeling growing and spreading through my body like a vine, and finally my brain jolted out of its lag. *The Heartbreakers' publicist likes my work?*

"Stella, are you still there?"

"Yes," I said, my voice squeaking. "Sorry. My head's all jumbled up right now. I don't even know what to say. You really like my stuff?"

I could hear Paul smiling into the phone. "Cross my heart and hope to die. You're phenomenal, and that's why I'm interested in working with you."

There was a flutter of lightness in my chest and head, and I didn't know if I was going to pass out or float away. Was this a joke?

I'd always hoped to make a living from my photography, but I also knew it wasn't the most realistic career in the world. That's why I'd decided to go to college before pursuing my real interest. Maybe I'd get a degree in advertising or marketing and somehow spin that into a commercial photography gig. Or maybe by the time four years were up I'd have discovered a completely different passion, and photography would fade into a high-school hobby.

But Paul's offer could change everything. Suddenly a dream was in the foreground of my life, closer than it had ever been before. How was that even possible? I was proud of my work because it meant so much to me, but I never considered it good. Not like Bianca's. Did Paul really want to hire a teenage girl with no professional training?

He dove right into his proposal. "My job with the band is to generate and manage the Heartbreakers' publicity. Think of me as a bridge between the boys and the public. Now, it's no secret there are rumors about the Heartbreakers splitting up. Some say there's tension between the boys, and others talk about too much pressure from the label. Regardless, it's my job to squash those rumors—they're poisonous—but the more I try to quiet the buzz, the louder it gets."

Paul sighed into the phone, and even though I'd never met him, let alone finished our first conversation together, I felt bad. The stress in his voice was evident, all his earlier cheerfulness gone, and the rumors seemed to be poisoning him as well.

Why in the world is he telling me all of this?

"Sounds frustrating," I said carefully, "but I'm a little confused. Is there something you think I can do to help?" As I spoke, I shook my head, struggling to believe the words coming out of my mouth. A lot had changed since my trip to Chicago—one week ago I would never have offered to help the band I disliked so much.

Paul sighed again, this time in relief. "As a matter of fact, there is. None of my normal strategies are working, so I've been toying with an idea that's a bit unorthodox. Tell me, do you have any experience with blogging?"

"Not really," I admitted. I'd thought about posting some of my pictures on Tumblr in the past, but I'd always chickened out.

"Don't worry about it," Paul said quickly. "For this project, I want to turn my focus away from the rumors. Instead, I need to concentrate on showing the world that the Heartbreakers are stronger than ever."

"Okay?"

"You managed to capture the band when they were goofing off and being themselves."

"We were just hanging out. I'm still not sure what you're asking of me."

"Stella, I don't remember the last time I've seen the boys look that happy," he said, "and I want more of that—it's gold. What's I'm proposing is that you run an official photo blog for the Heartbreakers. You'll take pictures of the band, shots of them doing everyday things like hanging out and having fun."

"So more pictures like the ones I took the other weekend?" I asked.

"Exactly like those. You'll also be responsible for the actual blogging. With each picture you post, there should be a short description of what's happening. Talk about your time with the band so fans feel like they are there experiencing the moment with you."

I paused. "But how will I take more pictures?"

"From what I've heard, you made fast friends with the boys. All you have to do is hang out with them. I'm positive you'll get plenty of material to work with."

"Hang out with them? Like on a regular basis?" How the hell was that going to work? The Heartbreakers were in a new city every other day.

"Yes, of course. You'll join us on tour. I've never done something like this before, so it will be a learn-as-we-go experience for both of us, but I really think an out-of-the-box approach could be successful. What do you think? Are you interested?"

I took a deep breath. "Truthfully, this is all a bit overwhelming."

"Completely understandable," Paul said quickly. "I threw lots of information at you, and I'm sure it's a lot to process. Why don't you take a few days to think things over and then we can talk?"

"That sounds like a good idea," I told him.

Paul gave me his number in case I had any questions, and we made plans to speak at the end of the week. After hanging up, I collapsed back into the couch.

My head was spinning. I'd just been offered the opportunity of a lifetime, the type of job people killed for. An uncontrollable grin tugged at the corners of my mouth.

"Stella, professional photographer," I said. The words made me giggle, but saying them out loud made it feel real. Someone wanted to hire me as a photographer. Scratch that. Not just someone. The publicist for the Heartbreakers wanted to hire me. "Oh my God, I have to tell Cara!"

Jumping up, I shoved my phone in my pocket. As I raced back down the hall I somehow felt taller, bigger, stronger—ready to take anything on. The feeling didn't last long.

When I reached the door to Cara's room, I stopped. She had decorated it with pictures of the three of us. It was a collage of our childhood: Drew, Cara, and I in matching outfits as babies, the first day of kindergarten, standing outside Cinderella's castle at Disney World, waiting at the bus stop in high school. The more

I studied the pictures, the more I was overwhelmed with a sense of dread.

I'd wanted an opportunity like this for so long, a chance to go off on my own, and this job was more than I could ever hope for. But instead of being ecstatic, I felt a slow, paralyzing coldness cascade from my head to my feet. I didn't know why I suddenly felt so terrible, but I couldn't let Cara see that I was upset. Before I could talk to her, I needed time to think about Paul's offer.

Using my sleeve, I wiped away the water building in my eyes before I opened the door. When I stepped inside, Cara was awake and sitting up in bed.

"Hey," she said. "Where'd you disappear to?"

"The living room," I said. "Mom called." The smile I'd forced onto my face quivered, and I hoped Cara didn't notice.

"Is everything okay?" she asked, her eyes narrowing as she squinted at me.

"Yup," I said in the most cheerful tone I could muster. "Why wouldn't it be?"

"Because you're lying to me."

"What? Am not!" I said quickly, but I could feel the color rising in my cheeks. "Why would I lie to you?"

"Well, considering I just got off the phone with Mom, I know you weren't talking to her," Cara said, crossing her arms. "So I don't know, Stella. You tell me."

Shit. There was a sudden ache in the back of my throat, and with each passing second, it grew harder and harder for me to swallow. What was I going to tell Cara now? There was no way she'd drop the subject. And once she found out what that was, I wouldn't even be given a chance to consider my options. Cara would want—no, she'd demand that I take the job.

"Cara," I said, taking in a shaky breath. "Can you please just let it go? I don't want to talk about this right now."

"Maybe if you'd just said that from the start, sure. But you lied to me, Stella. And the only logical explanation for why you'd do that is because you don't want to tell me something," she said, her nostrils flaring. Then in a much quieter tone she added, "What could possibly be so bad that you're afraid to talk to me about it?"

In that moment Cara sounded so dejected and lost that it felt like all the energy was suddenly wrenched from my body. I slumped into the armchair by her bed and gave in. "The Heartbreakers' publicist called me today," I said, staring down at my hands as I clasped them together in my lap. "He offered me a photography job working for the band."

At first Cara didn't say anything, but then she exploded. "Shut up! Are you serious? That's amazing, Stella. It's like the perfect job for you and—" She stopped gushing. "Wait. You don't look excited. Why don't you look excited?"

I didn't have a plausible explanation. She was right; I should be over the moon. But when I let myself imagine how amazing it would be to go off with the band, to turn my passion into a potential career, there was a horrible feeling in my stomach, like it had frozen solid.

And that's when I realized why I didn't want to tell Cara about the job—not because I needed time to think it through, but because

I'd already made my decision. A long, low sigh whistled from my mouth, and my hands went limp. "Because," I said finally, "I don't think I'm going to accept."

Cara blinked. "Are you crazy?" she exclaimed seconds later, leaning away from me as if I'd said something unforgivable. "You love photography."

"I'd have to join the band on tour, and I can't leave," I said, shaking my head. It didn't make sense, but there was a fluttering in my lungs, the level of my anxiety escalating the more I thought about leaving. "You're in the middle of your treatment and—"

"Don't you dare finish that sentence," Cara said in a deadly voice. Her sudden mood change was startling, and I leaned away as she bared her teeth at me.

"What?" I asked, my voice jumping up an octave. "Why are you mad?"

"You're making this about me."

"Of course not, Cara," I said in an attempt to soothe her. "I'm just prioritizing, that's all. There's nothing wrong with that."

"Prioritizing?" she snapped. "Stella, you're putting your entire life on hold."

"I think you're being a little dramatic."

"Really?" she said, throwing her hands in the air. "If that's the case, why'd you defer school?"

I scoffed. "You didn't actually expect me to leave when you're sick again, did you?"

"Drew is."

"That's different and you know it," I said, my eyes flicking up so I could glare at her. "He'll only be an hour and a half away. I'd be in a completely different state where I would never get to see you guys."

Cara's head dropped, and she closed her eyes as she took a moment to compose herself. Three long seconds passed before she looked back up at me. "Is that really so bad?" she asked, her voice a half whisper.

My chest hitched. "Don't—don't you think so?" How could Cara be okay with me leaving?

"No, I don't," Cara said. "News flash, Stella. We're not always going to be together, and you need to stop acting like it. The thought of you passing up such an amazing opportunity because of me..." She shook her head. "There are no words."

"You have to understand. If I leave and something happens—"

"*Stop!*" Cara finally shouted. "You're not listening to me. Do whatever you want, but if you turn down this job and end up regretting it, that's on you. I'm done being your excuse."

"Cara, please don't be like this," I said. I wanted to beg, to get down on my knees and will her to understand that I couldn't do this. Not when just thinking about it made me feel so awful.

"Can you just leave?" she said, looking away from me. "I want to be alone right now."

I stared at her, trying to understand how things had suddenly gone so wrong. "Yeah, sure," I finally said, my voice cracking.

Then I picked up the book I'd been reading and was gone.

CHAPTER 10

Nothing could drown out the sound of Cara's voice, how it had been laden with anger, but the scream of Bionic Bone's front man, Freddie K, blaring from my stereo came pretty close. Since our fight, I couldn't stop thinking about what she said.

"*Stella!*"

There was movement at the edge of my peripherals, and I glanced up to see Drew. He was standing in the doorway of my bedroom, waving his hands to get my attention. He looked exasperated, and I wondered how long he had been standing there before I noticed him.

"*What?*" I shouted over the music. Drew's lips moved as he said something, but I couldn't make out his words. "*What?*" I yelled again.

Rolling his eyes, Drew stormed across my room and paused my iPod, cutting Freddie K off midshriek. "Why do you listen to that stuff?" he asked, grimacing as he twisted his finger in his ear.

I was sitting cross-legged on the floor, a year's worth of old photos spread out on the carpet around me. When we moved to Rochester, I had dumped everything into boxes, and now I was sorting through the mess, organizing by date as a way to distract myself. "I find it calming," I said, looking back down at my work. "How was orientation?"

"It was fun. Took a tour of campus, figured out my schedule. That sort of stuff," Drew said. "What about you? How was your day?"

My back stiffened when he changed the subject to me. "It was fine." I picked up another photograph and took a moment to examine it so he wouldn't notice how uncomfortable I felt. "Nothing exciting. Ate lunch with Dad. Binged on Netflix."

"Stella," Drew said. "I already spoke with Cara."

"Oh." Setting the picture down on a stack of black-and-whites, I sighed. "And she told you everything?"

Drew crossed his arms as he leaned against my dresser. "Pretty much."

"So you're here to yell at me?" When I'd decided to defer from school, Drew had made his disapproval quite clear. He liked to remind me every time an opportunity presented itself, and I had a feeling this would be one of those occasions.

"Why would I yell at you?"

"I don't know." I shrugged. "Because you think I'm being stupid?"

"I don't think you're stupid, Rocket."

"But?" With my siblings, there was always a "but."

"This is what makes you happy," he said, gesturing at the collection of memories that blanketed the floor. "I'm struggling to understand why you would turn down a job where you can do what you love."

I didn't have a response, at least not one he wanted to hear, so I lowered my gaze. "Being here with Cara is more important."

"No," Drew said, and the force in his voice made me glance back up. He pushed away from the dresser and crouched down next to me. "I'm not saying Cara isn't important, but forget about her for a second. Pretend she isn't sick. Would you still turn down the job?"

His question bore down on me, and I closed my eyes as if it would help me avoid answering. "Why does that even matter?"

"Because you're asking the wrong question."

"Yeah?" I said, my eyes snapping open. "And what question should I be asking, Drew?"

"Ask yourself what you're so afraid of."

His response shut me up, and I pressed my face into my hands as I shook my head. "How do you expect me to answer that?"

"You should take the job," he said. "Otherwise you're never going to figure that out." He squeezed my shoulder and then left me with my thoughts.

☆♭♫

I looked at my alarm clock. "Ugh, come on," I groaned.

Grabbing my pillow, I fluffed it up and flipped onto my other side, trying to find a comfortable position in bed. It was past midnight and I was trying to sleep, but my mind wouldn't slow down or allow me to drift off.

Since our fight, I'd avoided Cara. I knocked on her bedroom in the morning to try to patch things up, but she refused to talk to me "unless," she said, "you're here to tell me you accepted Paul's offer." In fact, she was so mad that she threatened to never speak to me again unless I took the job. I hadn't, but I hadn't declined either. Regardless, she kicked me out.

Three full days later, and I was no closer to knowing whether I should stay or go. All I needed to do was choose, and even though I'd never been an indecisive person, any attempt to make up my mind seemed futile. Decision-making had always been so straightforward for me: yes or no, black or white, Pepsi or Coke. Maybe that was because I was impulsive, jumping into things headfirst and listening to my heart. But what was I supposed to do when my heart wanted two conflicting things?

Ask yourself what you're so afraid of.

Drew's question kept swimming through my thoughts, and as hard as I tried to drown out his words, they refused to sink, instead choosing to tread the turbulent surface of my mind with fierce determination.

"Dammit!" I said and threw off my covers when I realized sleeping was pointless. As I climbed out of bed, I stepped on something sharp—probably a hair clip—and a colorful string of swear words erupted from my mouth.

My room had fallen into neglect over the past three days, and I was sick of it. I flipped the light on, squinting as my eyes adjusted, and then started cleaning at random. My collection of post-hardcore CDs, which normally lived in a stack next to my stereo, was strewn across my desk. I had yanked them out while searching for Bionic Bones the other night. It took me a few minutes to order them the way I liked, all-time favorites to least, and then I moved on to my clothes. It looked like my dresser had vomited onto the floor. Not knowing what was dirty, I sniff-tested everything I picked up, folding some items and chucking others into the hamper.

I worked in a heated sort of manner, tearing around my room like a Happy Meal wind-up toy that would lose steam at any moment. When I'd finally burned through my frustration, there was a slick layer of sweat on my forehead, but my room was restored to its normal organization.

"Stella?" Drew pushed open my bedroom door, blinking as he adjusted to the light. He didn't bother to cover his yawn. "What are you doing?"

"Crap. Did I wake you?" I glanced at the clock again: 2:17 a.m.

He nodded. "You were slamming drawers and stuff."

"Sorry. I went on a midnight, can't-sleep-for-the-life-of-me cleaning spree."

"That's chill. I thought maybe—" Drew stopped and lifted an eyebrow. "Stella, are you…packing?"

"Packing?" I repeated with a frown. "No." But then I looked at my bed and saw what Drew did.

Five neat piles of clothes covered the basics: shirts, shorts, underwear, and so on; my camera bag was packed with all my equipment, camera resting beside it; a colorful collection of eye shadow and lipstick was inside my zebra-print makeup bag; and last was a Ziploc bag full of my favorite jewelry. All I needed now was a suitcase.

"I-I…" I was more than speechless, so I just stood there feeling my heart slam repeatedly into my chest. How had I done all this without realizing?

Drew noticed my sharp mood shift and took a step toward me. "Hey, it's okay," he said quickly and held up his hand. "I didn't mean anything by that. I was just curious."

"It's not okay," I exclaimed and pointed at the stuff on my bed. "How can it be okay when I didn't even realize I was doing that? My head is all over the place, Drew. The more I try to make up my mind, the more anxious I get, and I can literally feel my heart stressing itself out."

"I'm sorry," Drew said and pulled me into his arms. "Just take a few deep breaths."

So I listened to him. In and out I breathed. The first few lungfuls were shaky, and it took me a few minutes to calm down, but with my head buried in Drew's shoulder, I could hear the *thump-thump* of his heartbeat and I focused on that.

Finally, I worked up the courage to mumble into his shirt: "How am I supposed to do this?"

"Do what?" he asked and pulled away so he could see me.

"Leave," I said, my voice cracking. "Be on my own."

Drew tilted his head as he worked out what I meant, while I looked away. I'd missed a sock while cleaning. It was poking out from under my bed, and I concentrated on its crumpled form instead of my embarrassment. Drew probably thought I was being silly, because what eighteen-year-old was afraid of leaving home?

"You know," he said, sitting on the end of the bed and pulling me down next to him, "I'm nervous too."

I swallowed and turned back to him. "Nervous?"

"About going to college."

"You are?" What did Drew have to be nervous about? He would only be a quick drive away from home, and we would see him every weekend.

"How could I not be?" he said. "I mean, what if I'm not smart enough, or my roommate is a weirdo? And what will happen if I don't make any friends and miss home too much?"

"So don't go," I said, even though I knew I was being ridiculous.

Drew laughed. "I'm excited to leave," he told me. "The nerves—that's all part of the experience. You just gotta trust that the good will make up for the scary."

This made sense, but something still wasn't sitting right with me. "I was excited when Paul first called me," I admitted, "but then I thought about being away from you and Cara, and I panicked. It's always been us, together."

Drew smiled. "The Three Musketeers."

"Exactly."

"It'll still be the three of us," Drew said, bumping his shoulder into mine. "Being in different places won't change that."

"I know," I said, staring blankly ahead of me.

"Even if you were on the moon." He held out his pinkie. "I promise."

Drew was right. The nerves I felt about leaving home were just that—nerves. Which would be manageable except for the awful, nagging feeling that I just couldn't shake.

It was like this: I'm standing on the shore looking out at the ocean. It's all a bit familiar, maybe because I'm reminded of the coast in South Carolina. The sun's beating down on me, and the more I start to sweat, the more I want to peel off my clothes and dive in. But there are all these signs posted along the beach warning swimmers of deadly rip currents. Sure, the water looks peaceful enough, but even though I can't see the danger below the surface, it's still lying in wait to sweep me away.

That's how I felt about accepting Paul's job offer. I couldn't put my finger on what was bothering me so much—it was a blind spot, the danger under the calm. But I knew it was there, and I was terrified of drowning in it. Then again, taking a photography job wasn't comparable to swimming in treacherous waters. Doing something for myself wasn't going to kill me.

I'd asked myself what I was so afraid of, but I drew a blank every time. And that was almost as terrifying as the thought of leaving. So even though it felt wrong, there was only one thing left for me to do—take another piece of my brother's advice. Because if I didn't accept the job, I'd never figure out what really was lurking below the surface.

I slowly wrapped my pinkie around his. "I think I should call Paul."

"You should," Drew said and laughed, "but you might want to wait until morning. I doubt he'd appreciate being woken up in the middle of the night."

CHAPTER 11

I had no clue what Paul looked like. We'd only spoken on the phone three times: once when he called to offer me a job, another when I called to accept, and the final time to make arrangements for me to fly out and join the band when they were in Miami. In spite of that, I knew exactly who he was when I stepped into the hotel lobby. He was sitting on one of the many lounging couches and speaking animatedly on the phone. His hair was a deep red, and he was wearing a lime-green shirt that, amazingly, managed not to clash. It was the way he was smiling and waving his free hand that identified him; somehow his mannerisms perfectly matched the voice I remembered from our conversations.

As I approached, he must have recognized me too, because his eyes lit up and he snapped his phone shut. "Stella, darling," he exclaimed, rising from his seat to greet me. "It's so nice to finally meet you."

"You too." I set down my suitcase. "I'm excited to be here."

"Wonderful, wonderful," he said, clapping his hands together. "We have loads to talk about, but I bet you're starving after your flight. Why don't we sit down and have something to eat?" Paul gestured in the direction of the hotel restaurant.

I'd been too nervous to eat breakfast, and the complimentary peanuts on the plane were stale and crumbly, so I'd thrown them out even though I was hungry. Now my stomach was protesting the neglect. "That'd be great."

We were seated quickly, and after looking over the menu, I decided on breakfast for dinner. I ordered a plate of Southwest scrambled eggs, bacon, wheat toast, and a large glass of orange juice, while Paul went with chicken dumpling soup. I was starting on my last triangle of toast when he pushed his bowl away and pulled a folder out of his briefcase. My name was written across the top in bold letters.

"Let's see," he said, mumbling to himself.

Inside was a collection of papers. Paul emailed me the information a few days earlier, but he went over it again to make sure everything made sense. First, he detailed my job responsibilities and what was expected of me. Then he explained my pay. Not only would I received a salary, but Paul would purchase each picture I used on the blog. When I first saw the number in his email I thought it was a mistake, but here it was again and I tried not to gawk—I could pay my way through college if I continued to work for the band.

There were pages of paperwork to read through and dotted lines to sign. By the time we finished, it was nearly nine, and I could hardly keep my eyes open. It had been a long day.

"Sorry to keep you so long," Paul said, shuffling everything together and stuffing it back inside the folder. "But now that all the boring stuff is out of the way, you can focus on the fun part. Are you excited about tomorrow?"

"I'm a bit nervous actually," I admitted.

It wasn't an official work day, but Paul had arranged for me to shadow the band. He wanted me to get a sense of what a typical day on tour was like. I didn't even have to take pictures if I didn't want to. All that was required was for me to show up on time and go along for the ride. Even so, my stomach wouldn't settle.

Yes, I'd decided to accept the job, but I was still nervous about starting something new without Cara and Drew. On top of that, there was Oliver. Would things be weird between us? The thought of seeing him in the morning made the food I'd just eaten slosh around in my stomach.

"Don't worry," Paul told me. "Knowing the boys, they'll make you feel right at home."

I didn't find this very reassuring—one of those boys was the reason why I felt nervous. Not sure how to respond, I smiled and agreed. "I don't doubt it."

After that, Paul provided me with the information I needed to check in to the hotel. Twenty minutes later, I was unlocking the door to my room. Flipping on the lights, I dropped my suitcase and kicked off my shoes with a sigh. My feet ached and I was beyond exhausted, but I wanted to be prepared for the morning, so despite the fact that the gigantic king bed was calling my name, I forced myself to take a quick shower, set out my clothes, and— even though I didn't need it—pack my camera bag. I wasn't going anywhere without it. Only then did I set my alarm and climb under the covers.

Every muscle in my body ached from a long day of travel, and I'd thought I would drift off instantly. Instead, I stared at the ceiling. Alone and without any distractions, my mind wouldn't stop thinking, spinning, fearing, because tomorrow I would see Oliver again.

We'd left off on a beautiful note.

In Chicago, when our paths crossed, I'd spent one exciting night with Oliver. It had been dazzling and so completely unexpected that it made me see stars. Then we parted ways, like I always knew we would, and in the morning the stars cleared from my vision. I was a little sad at first, especially when I wondered what things would've been like if Oliver was a regular guy and we'd met under different circumstances, but I wasn't going to be unrealistic. We both had our own lives to live, which were on two completely different paths. I didn't know if I'd upset him by not calling, but I had to do what was best for me.

Now, by some seriously comical twist of fate, my path had moved in his direction again. Our lives were suddenly intertwined, at least for the next two months, and I had no idea what to expect. Would things be like before, or had our time together only been exciting because we'd thought it was limited?

Either way, I was about to find out.

☆ ♭ ♪♫

I was exactly two minutes early. Paul had told me to meet the band at six o'clock, and as I stepped off the elevator, my phone flashed "five fifty-eight." My aim was to arrive ten minutes early since it was my first day, but I'd ended up changing twice when I had an outfit crisis.

Anyone who was sane was still sleeping, so the lobby was relatively empty. To be precise, three other people were present—the front-desk receptionist who was typing something into the computer, a janitor emptying the garbage, and a woman who was reading on the couch where I'd met with Paul last night.

None of the Heartbreakers or their employees were present, and my empty stomach rolled. I knew it was just nerves, but part of me worried that I'd somehow messed up the time and the band was already gone. I checked my phone again—now it was six. *Get some caffeine and chill out,* I told myself and headed toward the continental breakfast. *They're probably just running late.*

As I stepped inside the small sunroom connected to the lobby, I twisted my nose stud between my fingers and took deep breaths. On the far wall was a service station with pastries, cereal, hard-boiled eggs, and a basket of assorted fruit. Ignoring the food, I went straight for the coffee machine. I was so focused on pouring my drink that I didn't notice who was sitting at one of the tables behind me. When I turned back around, I nearly dropped my coffee.

He was reading something out of a magazine, and whatever it was put a scowl on his face. Next to him were a plate with an untouched glazed doughnut and a to-go cup with a tea bag dangling over the side. His wavy brown hair was messier than I'd last seen it, like he hadn't bothered to brush it when he got up, and there were circles under his eyes.

"Oliv—" My voice cracked, so I cleared my throat and tried again. "Oliver."

His head popped up. He blinked at me a few times, his mouth

parting slightly, almost as if he wasn't quite sure what he was seeing. After three long seconds, he scrambled to his feet.

"Stella, hey!"

"Hi yourself," I said and offered him a tentative smile.

He smiled too and slid his dog tag back and forth on its chain. "It's good to see you." Then, before I knew what was happening, he wrapped his arms around me. It was the world's quickest hug, but it still made me grin.

"Yeah," I said, hiding the small smile with my hand. "You too."

Before either of us could think of something else to say, someone shouted my name—or at least a very strange version of my name.

"Stella Ella Bella Bear!" JJ called out. I easily spotted him across the empty room, waving his hands as he tried to catch my attention. "You're finally here!"

Xander stood next to him, his red-blond hair matted in the back—a style my brother called "pillow syndrome." He yawned and removed his glasses to rub his eyes.

"Hey, guys," I said, and when JJ reached me, he pulled me into a hug that lifted me clear off the ground. I couldn't help but laugh. His friendly welcome helped ease some of the nerves that were making me jumpy.

"Like the nickname I've been working on?" JJ asked. "Now that you're an honorary member of the band, I thought you needed one."

"Um, it's a little long," I told him.

"I thought that might be a problem," JJ said and shook his head like he knew better. "All right, just Bear then."

"Since when do we have nicknames?" Oliver asked before I could tell JJ I preferred that he call me Stella. The only people who had pet names for me were Cara and Drew, and I didn't want to get homesick already.

"Since always," JJ said, smirking at Oliver.

"How come I don't have one?"

"Oh, you have plenty. Tubsy Malone and Asshat are my personal favorites, but there's Turd Burger, Douchenozzle, and Butt Nugget," JJ said. Xander's shoulders shook as he tried not to laugh.

"Don't forget Dipshit," Alec said, materializing behind Oliver. I nearly choked when I heard his voice—I'd never heard Alec openly insult any of the guys—but Oliver was unfazed and flashed his friend the middle finger. "Courtney's waiting for us," Alec continued, gesturing over his shoulder with his thumb. "Time to go."

Oliver grabbed his tea and gave JJ the untouched doughnut, but he left the magazine sitting on the table. For a split second, I eyed it up as everyone followed Alec into the lobby. I was curious to know what had upset Oliver, and before I could change my mind, I snatched it off the table and shoved it inside my camera bag.

"Stella!" Paul said when he saw me. He was standing by the revolving front door with a tall, blond woman I recognized as the band's manager. "You're already here, wonderful. There's someone I'd like to introduce you to. Stella, meet Courtney. She's the Heartbreakers' very lovely, very hard-working tour manager. Courtney, this is Stella. She's the new photographer I hired to work on the blog I was telling you about."

Courtney turned to me, and her eyebrows slid up when she saw me. "I remember you," she said with an amused smile.

"You two have already met?" Paul asked.

"In Chicago, but I don't think I've properly introduced myself." Courtney tucked the clipboard she was holding under her arm and extended her hand. "I'm Courtney Stiller, the band's make-shift mom."

"Nice to meet you," I said as she shook my hand.

"You too," she said, and then she was back to business. "Is that everything then, Paul? I'll make sure to take good care of Stella today, but we really do need to get moving."

"That's fine," he responded. "I was just here for introductions. I have a meeting in fifteen. Stella, you have my number in case you need anything. Boys, you better be nice to my new girl or else."

"I'm hurt, Paul," JJ said, placing a hand on his heart after he shoved the rest of the doughnut in his mouth. There was a bit of glaze left on his lip, but he quickly licked it away. "When have we ever been anything but nice?"

Paul gave JJ a look, but then his phone was ringing and he was gone.

"Okay, crazies," Courtney said. "Move out."

The boys grumbled and made a fuss, but they actually listened to Courtney's direction. I was seriously impressed—this woman had the command of a drill sergeant. She got everyone outside quickly, and then we all piled into the town car waiting at the curb. I was the last to climb in, and there were only two spots left: one by Oliver on the other side of the car and the other next to the door. The car started to move and my decision was made for me. I toppled into the seat next to Xander.

"Breakfast," Courtney said, producing four bananas from her tote bag. She gave me an apologetic look. "Sorry, Stella. I completely forgot you were joining us today."

"No worries," I said, waving her off. "I'm not much of a breakfast person."

"That's not healthy, you know," Xander told me as he meticulously peeled away the yellow skin. "Eating breakfast gets your metabolism going."

"Amd it's belicious," JJ said, half the banana already shoved in his mouth.

Courtney immediately started reviewing the day's schedule. I tried to pay as close attention as I could, but I could feel Oliver watching me. When the car came to a stop at an intersection, he got up.

"Scoot over," he told Xander and squeezed in between us. Once he clicked on his seat belt, he passed me his banana. "Here," he said. "Who knows when we'll eat lunch today. You might need it."

"What about you?"

Oliver shrugged. "Never been much of a potassium fan myself. I'll be fine."

"Okay, thanks." I tucked the piece of fruit into my camera bag where it wouldn't be crushed, and tried not to smile. I knew it was only a piece of fruit, but I couldn't help but feel like it was a sign of what was to come, as if we were meant all along to have more time together than just one night.

"—and after the radio interview, we're heading across town for the sound check. If I remember correctly, a group of contest winners will be there to listen, and you'll have to do a quick meet-and-greet. But then it's straight to hair and makeup. Show starts at nine. Am I forgetting anything?"

"Yeah," JJ said. "Do you enjoy being a slave driver?"

Courtney didn't miss a beat. "I live for it. Anything else?"

"About the radio interview," Alec said, and I turned to watch him. "Is there a list of questions? So we"—he paused and his gaze flickered to me—"um, know what to expect?"

"Oh yes! I have it here somewhere." Courtney dug around in her tote again and retrieved a piece of paper. "After what happened last time, I insisted on reviewing the questions beforehand, and I also made it clear that you four will not be answering any questions about breakup rumors—" She stopped.

I felt Oliver tense beside me, and everyone got quiet. I had a feeling that my presence was the reason everyone was suddenly uncomfortable, because as I looked around the car, nobody would meet my gaze. Obviously I was missing something; everyone knew I was missing something; and nobody wanted to tell me what that was. I shrank back into the leather seat, focused on my hands, and tried to be as invisible as possible.

Alec cleared his throat. "Thanks," he said, taking the sheet from his manager.

Even Courtney seemed affected by the sudden hush, and she didn't say anything as the list left her hands. She blinked a few times before shaking her head and snapping back. "You're very welcome, Alec. Make sure everyone looks it over. We also have to go over the…"

Courtney kept talking, but I stopped listening.

"Hey," Oliver whispered, his elbow gently bumping mine. "You okay?"

My head snapped up. "Am I okay?"

"Yeah. You got quiet."

I couldn't tell if Oliver was joking, or if he was really going to pretend that I was one who was acting weird and not everyone else. "*I* got quiet?"

"Yeah," he said slowly. "Are you just going to repeat everything I say?"

So he was going to pretend. I didn't want to push Oliver since things seemed to be going well between us, so I dropped the subject and smiled. "Are you just going to repeat everything I say?"

"Okay, you're a jerk," he said. "I so didn't miss you."

"Yeah," I said, biting my bottom lip. "I so didn't miss you either."

CHAPTER 12

By the time we arrived at the radio station for the interview I was starving, and I had already eaten my banana. Oliver was right—there was no time for lunch.

But I didn't care. I was too engrossed in my surroundings to be concerned about my complaining stomach. I'd never been inside a radio station before—unless you counted the autograph signing in Chicago, and that was only the lobby. Being here with the band, I got the chance to go behind the scenes and see how everything worked, and I found all the computers and buttons exciting.

The boys were in the middle of their interview. They were sitting in the studio with the two radio hosts, Jack and Kelly, and everyone was crowded around a circular table that had microphones sprouting from the middle. JJ was telling a story about how the band had been locked out of their dressing rooms during a show in Toronto, and I was watching the entire discussion through the long, rectangular window that looked in on the room.

My stomach was being loud, and I knew I should go hunt down the vending machine we passed during our tour of the station, but I couldn't tear my eyes away. The Heartbreakers were captivating. During the short time we'd hung out together, I'd gathered as much, but this was different. With the attention on them, the boys turned up the charm and were charismatic in a way that made it impossible to hate them. While I was listening, it occurred to me that this was why the boys were able to wiggle their way into millions of girls' hearts. They had star power.

"...and so then Oliver was running through the halls in his boxers, and he ran smack into a fan who'd managed to sneak backstage," JJ said, finishing his story. Everyone laughed.

"She must have had the surprise of a lifetime," Jack said, still chuckling. "I bet she didn't expect to find one of her idols gallivanting around the halls in nothing but his underwear."

"She practically jumped me," Oliver said. "Security had to pry her away. I had nail marks on my shoulders for a week!"

"So it seems you're quite popular with the ladies," Kelly said then.

Oliver lifted both his shoulders, shrugging in an attempt to seem casual, but he had a knowing smirk on his face. "I suppose."

"Is all the attention hard to deal with?"

"It can be overwhelming at times," Oliver said, "but it helps to have three other people who know exactly what I'm going through. If I'm stressed, I can turn to them."

"None of us would be able to do this on our own," Xander added. "We're each other's support system."

Oliver was nodding his head. "These guys are my family. I don't know what I'd do without them."

"You four have accomplished so much together," Jack said. "I bet it's impossible to imagine it any other way."

"Exactly," JJ answered.

"That's incredible," Kelly said, shaking her head as if she truly was impressed with everything the band had told her. "Now, we're almost out of time, but before we wrap up, I want to take this conversation back to girls. Oliver, have you ever dated a fan?"

"I'm not saying that I wouldn't date a fan, but I'm not one to date in general," he responded. "It's just too hard when we're on the road all the time."

"So there's no special girl in your life right now? Not anybody?" Oliver paused and I held in a deep breath. I felt JJ's gaze flicker in my direction, so I quickly looked down at my phone and pretended to be reading a text.

"Oliver?" Kelly prompted, and I peeked back up.

Pushing back his bangs, he offered her a devilish smile. "Maybe," he said, and my heart started to flutter like the wings of a hummingbird, light and quick.

"Ooh," Kelly said, her eyes sparkling as she leaned in. "Someone we've heard of?"

He continued to smirk. "Definitely," he said, and his words shot the hummingbird right out of my chest. Oliver was seeing some other celebrity?

"Is she an actress? Maybe a model?" Jack asked. "Give us some sort of hint."

Oliver shook his head as his lips twitched in amusement. "I'm not saying anything else."

I looked away from him and swallowed hard. I'd known nothing was going to happen between us, so why had I let myself think otherwise? No doubt because Oliver had been so charming today.

Then again, he probably made every girl he talked to feel special. My brows pinched together in a frown, but I wasn't angry at him. I was annoyed with myself. How could I possibly feel disappointed when I'd known this would happen from the start?

Kelly said something about Oliver being too secretive, and I was pulled back into the conversation.

"I wouldn't say secretive, per se," he responded, "but I try to keep my love life private."

"Really? 'Cause you're not very good at it," JJ said. "Terrible, really."

"'Try' was the important word," Jack said and chuckled. "You should know by now that we media folk are professional detectives."

Everyone laughed, but the way Oliver's eyes crinkled up in amusement made it hard not to grin. I instantly realized I was in trouble. Major trouble. Regardless of his lack of interest in me, I still liked him, and the feelings I was starting to have were dangerous. We couldn't keep flirting, and he most definitely couldn't keep charming me with tropical fruit.

The next time a private moment presented itself, I would talk with Oliver. Even though he'd obviously already forgotten our shared kiss, I had to make it official that, moving forward, we would be strictly friends. Maybe then my good senses would return, and I would stop feeling light-headed and silly whenever he glanced in my direction. After all, I wasn't here for Oliver. I was here for myself.

"Hey, Stella?" I tore my eyes away from Oliver and found Courtney standing over me. "May we have a word?"

"Sure," I said, shooting out of my seat. I was eager to get away from the interview and Oliver, so I dumped my camera bag on the chair and followed her out of the room. We made our way down the empty hallway until we were out of earshot.

"You having fun so far?" she asked. She rolled forward onto the balls of her feet, and I could tell she was trying to be friendly before broaching whatever topic she really wanted to talk about.

"Loads," I said, which wasn't a lie, but it wasn't the truth either.

"Good," Courtney said and nodded. "I wanted to talk about the privacy policy you signed with Paul. I'm sure he covered this, but I have to reiterate how important it is that while you're working with the band, you don't divulge any privileged information that you may hear. Does that make sense?"

"Yes, of course," I said quickly. I would never do that, not only because this job was important to me, but also because the boys were becoming my friends. I had a feeling this little chat was prompted by what I'd overheard in the car earlier today. At the time, the conversation was confusing, but later that morning I slipped off to the bathroom and paged through the magazine Oliver was reading. I found a short article about how the Heartbreakers appeared on a talk show, and when the host asked some direct questions about the breakup rumors, the boys were so caught off guard that the interview was cut short.

"Wonderful," she said, letting out a deep breath. "Glad that's sorted out. Turkey or ham?"

"Huh?"

"My assistant is running out to pick up some sandwiches."

"Oh. Turkey works," I told her, but I wasn't really feeling hungry anymore.

☆♭♫♫

My first day with the Heartbreakers could only be described as a whirlwind, especially considering their concert hadn't even started yet, and all I wanted to do was crash. Thankfully, around half past eight there was a short break in the storm. As fans poured into the arena, chanting the boys' names and singing their songs, silent anticipation swept over the group while we waited in the backstage dressing room. All four guys retreated into their own worlds, so I took a spot on one of the empty couches and gave them space, content with merely observing as they readied themselves.

JJ seemed the most nervous. He was pacing back and forth with his drumsticks moving in a blur as he twirled them between his fingers. Every once in a while he'd fumble and one of the wooden sticks would clatter to the floor. Xander was sitting on the counter-top in front of the long wall of lighted mirrors. He had his inhaler clutched in his hands, and even though he'd already administered the medicine, he turned the plastic device over and over as if it would bring him luck. Like usual, Alec had his headphones in. He was leaning against the far wall, his foot tapping along to whatever song he was listening to.

And then there was Oliver. He was sitting cross-legged on the floor, eyes closed as he meditated. His outfit was plain—a black V-neck and skinny jeans, combat boots, and the always-present dog tag that hung around his neck—yet somehow in its simplicity, he managed to look both seductive and mysterious. Like the bad boy at the back of class who could make any good girl want to be bad with one smoldering stare.

I couldn't help but study him—the way his long lashes brushed against his cheek, the fullness of his lips, the sturdy line of his jaw—and I wished he didn't have such an effect on me.

My gaze must have lingered too long.

Oliver cracked an eye open. "What?" he asked, looking directly at me.

I felt my ears heat up and started winding the cord of my back-stage pass around my fingers. "Nothing," I said, wishing the couch could swallow me up.

"You were staring at me."

"And you were sitting scary still," I said, throwing out the first bullshit excuse I could think of. "I was trying to decide if you're petrified with fear or if you'd actually turned into a statue."

"Petrified?" He scoffed and gestured at himself. "Pure confidence right here."

I rolled my eyes but secretly agreed. Oliver seemed nothing short of composed. Although Paul said I didn't need to take pictures today, I reached for my camera on the coffee table. "You don't ever get stage fright?" I asked as I focused the lens. He smirked and I snapped a picture.

"Never," he said, and then he returned to his meditation. As I took a few more shots, Xander flopped down on the couch next to me.

"He's a liar," Xander said. I turned my camera on him and found him in the viewfinder. "We all get nervous before shows."

"I can imagine," I said and took a few rapid-fire pictures. "There are like a bazillion people out there." Pulling away, I hit the playback button and chuckled. Because of my proximity, Xander's glasses made him look bug-eyed.

"Mind if I look? I never got to see the pictures from the other weekend."

"Sure."

For the next few minutes he scrolled through our night in Chicago, grinning and laughing at the memories we'd made. He reached the last picture and, not knowing it was the end of the footage, continued to scroll. Cara flashed onto the tiny screen.

"Oh, sorry," Xander said when he realized he'd gone too far, but then he was squinting down at the photo.

It was from the day Cara and I had made up. We spent the afternoon playing Rummy 500, and I'd captured her at the perfect moment—she had been looking over the top of her hand, cards splayed out like a fan, and then she stuck her tongue out at me.

I brushed my hair off my shoulder and braced myself for the questions I knew would come.

"It's okay," I told him and gently took my camera back.

Xander cleared his throat. "She isn't you."

That much was obvious. Since her diagnosis, Cara's once-tan skin had faded to a dull wash of gray. Even more noticeable was how the cancer had carved away her face, leaving behind sharp cheekbones and deep-set eyes.

"It's my sister," I said, my voice soft.

"She's sick." He said it as a statement, but I knew he was asking.

A lump started to swell inside my throat, but I forced it back down. "Cara has lymphoma. Non-Hodgkin's."

Xander pulled the glasses off his face and pinched the bridge of his nose. "When you said your sister was sick, I thought you meant the stomach flu or something."

So he hadn't heard. I peeked up at Alec. He was still standing against the wall with his headphones in, but now his gaze was focused on Xander and me. His foot had stopped tapping, and I knew he was listening to our conversation.

"You didn't say anything," I said, looking Alec dead in the eye. "Why not?"

Alec looked hesitant about answering, but he took a quick breath and said in his deep voice, "That's your story to tell. Not mine."

"Wait? How'd he know?" Xander asked as he squinted at his friend.

In spite of myself, I smiled. "Accidentally. He asked about my photography and it just sorta slipped out."

Xander bobbed his head. "No surprise there." Then he leaned in and whispered so Alec couldn't hear us. "People always seem to tell him their secrets. I think it's because they know he'll never say anything."

"Yeah," I agreed. A short stretch of silence passed, and then a sigh escaped my lips. "Well," I said, clasping my hands together in my lap, "now you know the real reason why Cara didn't come to the autograph signing."

Instead of saying he was sorry, Xander wrapped an arm around me and pulled me to his side, our shoulders bumping against one another. It was a surprisingly forward gesture, but a comforting one.

"You two look freaky similar," he said after a quiet moment.

"That's because we're identical twins." Well, identical except for the fact that she was sick and I was healthy.

"But you're also triplets? How does that work?"

"We're dizygotic triplets," I said. I'd explained this so many times before that now I probably sounded like a textbook. "It's when two separate eggs are fertilized, and one subsequently divides into two."

"So that makes Drew your fraternal twin?"

"Yeah, and Cara's."

"Okay," Xander said, frowning and scratching his head. "That's way confusing. No more science talk."

"Fine by me." Talking about Cara and Drew made me think of home, and thinking of home made me feel a whole range of unwanted emotions. I hadn't even been gone two full days, but my stomach churned with a pang of homesickness, and I blinked a few times to keep my eyes from watering.

Before either of us managed to change the topic, Courtney swept into the room. "You lot ready?" she asked, one hand on her hip, the other clutching the clipboard she always had with her. "It's showtime."

It took another fifteen minutes before the Heartbreakers actually stepped onstage. Before leaving, the boys huddled in a tight circle and Oliver led a quick prayer. Then Courtney ushered them out of the room and I tailed behind, receiving a crash course lesson on the who's who involved with running a concert.

It was amazing how many people were actually required for the operation. There was Dan, the production manager, who ran the technical crew that dealt with the movement and setup of equipment. Fred, who the boys called Smiley, was the stage manager, and his job involved controlling the band and crew's movement both onstage and off.

He directed the boys to their preshow spots, and then the back-line crew, who were in charge of the instruments, handed Oliver and Xander their guitars and Alec his bass. Ritvik was the sound engineer, and then there were Barry, the monitor engineer; Mr. P, the lighting operator; and dozens more employees whose names I couldn't remember.

When it was finally time, the lights in the arena were brought down. The audience reacted instantly, the screams of thousands of girls melding together to form one giant roar, and the sheer volume made the hair on my arms rise.

"Excited?" Courtney shouted over the noise as a crew member handed us headsets to counter the sound of the show.

"Strangely nervous," I admitted. As I pulled on the headset, I peered out at the crowd. It was a glowing, flashing mass of cameras and cell phones, and the thought of stepping onstage made my stomach drop.

"Just between you and me?" she said. "I always get preshow jitters."

Her confession made me feel better, but I never got the chance to thank her. The stage lights flashed back on, revealing the Heartbreakers to the crowd. Cheers tripled, but the sound was suddenly overtaken by the band's opening song as it blasted from the arena's assembly of speakers.

The jitters, as Courtney called them, fell away the moment my eyes found Oliver. I sucked in a sharp breath, and for the next three and a half minutes I couldn't look away.

"Thank you everyone for coming tonight," Oliver shouted when the song ended and the crowd noise finally died down. "We're so happy you could join us!" The thundering response of the audience made my head rattle, but the boys seemed unaffected. Oliver looked back at the rest of his bandmates. JJ nodded his head and raised his drumsticks over his head.

"Ladies and gentlemen," Oliver said. "We are the Heartbreakers."

"A one, a two, and a one, two, three, four!"

☆ ♭ ♫

"Stella Bear, don't be such a party pooper."

The concert had finished a half hour ago, and we were back in the dressing room. The boys were trying to convince me to go out and celebrate with them. Apparently there was an after-party at some dance club downtown, but I declined their invite.

"Are you trying to kill me my first day on the job?" I asked JJ. "I'm exhausted. I could curl up on the floor right here and sleep for the next week."

It was both the truth and an excuse. My entire body ached. The band's never-ending schedule wore me out, but that wasn't the real reason I didn't want to go to a party with the boys.

Today was my freebie, the one day I had to acclimate myself to the boys' busy lifestyle. Now it was over and tomorrow was the real deal—I wouldn't just be hanging out with the guys and goofing off. I had a job to do, and Paul expected me to produce results. The realization made my throat tight, and for the first time in my life, I worried that I wouldn't be able to get a good enough shot.

What I needed now was to go back to my hotel room where I could decompress and try to prepare myself for tomorrow.

"Have a shot or two," JJ said, swiping a bottle of whiskey off the counter and offering it to me. "Then you'll be ready to go." He'd pulled the dark-brown liquor out when we first returned to the room, and the boys were taking turns chugging straight from the mouth of the bottle.

"I better not," I said, declining his outstretched hand. "Tomorrow is my official first day of work, and I don't want to chance a hang-over." I didn't mention that I'd never actually drank before. It wasn't that I was a Goody Two-shoes, but with Cara's cancer, partying was never on my priority list.

"Pretty please?"

"Give it a rest, JJ," Alec said, turning away from the mirror. He'd spent the past ten minutes restyling his hair. I didn't know he'd been listening, but I was thankful he had.

"But we're—" JJ started to say.

"There'll be plenty of other parties for her to go to," Alec said and cut him off with a stern stare.

The two boys glared at each other, a silent battle of wills, but then JJ sighed and looked away. "Fine," he said and crossed his arms. "But only if Stella promises to come out with us next time."

Everyone turned to me to see if this was okay. "Deal," I said, nodding my head like an excited bobblehead.

"I'm going to hold you to that," JJ said, waving a finger in my face.

I quickly started to pack my equipment before he changed his mind. First, I popped the lens protector in place and then tucked my camera into its bag. Courtney was leaving for the hotel in a few minutes, and I wanted to catch a ride with her.

"Hey, has anyone seen my sunglasses?" I asked, turning around in a slow circle as I scanned the room.

"Right here." Oliver was sitting on the arm of the couch, my sunglasses clutched in his hand. A half grin tugged on his lips as he watched me.

"Thanks." When I reached out to take them back, his fingers wrapped around my hand and he pulled me forward, close enough that his knees brushed against my thighs.

"So, you sure you don't want to join us tonight?" he asked in a whisper. "It will be a blast." He was still clutching my hand, and the way he ran his thumb over my knuckles made it hard to focus on anything more than the sensation.

I hesitated. It would be fun to go to a party with Oliver. Maybe even more fun than our night in Chicago. But thinking of Chicago and our kiss reminded me of the radio-show interview this afternoon, which reminded me of my decision. I liked Oliver, I really did, but I was skeptical about his feelings. And on top of that, to be good at this job I needed to focus my attention. If I was constantly worrying about Oliver, then he'd only be a distraction. A very hot distraction, but a distraction nonetheless.

"Don't worry about me," I said and gently pulled my hand from his. "Go have fun. I promise I'll come next time, okay?"

His shoulders dropped, but I couldn't tell if he was actually disappointed because the smile never left his face. "Yeah, okay," he said.

"Well, I should probably get going." Oliver nodded and handed back my sunglasses, and then I turned to face the rest of the group. "Have fun tonight, guys."

"Night, Stella," Xander said. "See you tomorrow."

"Dream about me tonight," JJ said with a wink, and I shot him a dirty look in response.

Alec already had his headphones back in, so I mouthed him a silent thank-you before turning to leave. I could still feel Oliver's eyes on my back, so I called one final good-bye over my shoulder and hurried out the door. If I looked back at him and he hit me with one of my favorite smiles, I might just change my mind.

☆ ♭ ♪♩

I was almost at the lobby when I heard him shout my name.

"Stella, wait!" Glancing back, I saw Oliver jogging to catch up with me. When he reached me, he pulled his fingers through his brown waves. "Hey," he said.

"Um, hey." Had I forgotten something?

"I thought maybe I could walk you out," he said, smoothing out his shirt as he spoke.

"Oh." For an instant, a small part of me was hoping he'd chased me out here to try to convince me one more time to go to the party, because he wanted me there. "Yeah, sure. That'd be great."

We walked in silence, Oliver with his hands shoved in his pockets and me with my fingers clutching the strap of my camera bag. *Come on, Stella*, I thought. *This is the perfect chance to talk to him.* But my stomach was so full of butterflies that I could feel them moving up my throat, making it hard for me to speak.

Oliver beat me to it. "So," he said, dragging out the word as if he wasn't sure what he was going to say next. "I wanted to talk to you about something."

There was a sudden rushing feeling inside my chest, but I resisted the urge to look at him. "Yeah, me too," I said before I could do any second-guessing. It was now or never. If I didn't put up a wall between the two of us, some kind of line that I knew I couldn't cross, I wouldn't be able to resist his charm in the future.

He smiled in a way that was both curious and nervous. "Okay," he said. "You first."

Shit. I didn't know where to start, and I couldn't think right. It felt like my brain had been sucked out, and I was searching for words that I could no longer remember. *Just say something*, I shouted at myself.

"Um, well," I said, my words all tangled up. "It's about the other night."

"What about it?"

I tugged on my collar. "You know, when we watched the movie?" I asked. I was trying to make this as un-awkward as possible but was failing miserably. Talking out loud about what had happened was mortifying, and I knew that my face was as bright red as a flashing stoplight.

This made Oliver smirk. "You mean our super-hot make-out session?"

"Yeah, that." I looked down at my feet. "I, um, had fun and all, but"—I paused, and then the last part came tumbling out—"I don't think it should happen again."

Oliver stopped midstride. "Huh?"

Taking a breath, I forced myself to slow down. "Now that I'm working for you guys, we can't do that anymore. It's not professional."

"And by 'that' you mean...?"

"We should just be friends," I said, watching him closely. There was this weird, punch-drunk look on his face, as if I'd smashed him over the head with my camera bag. For the smallest millisecond of a moment, I thought that maybe Oliver was upset. That he didn't want to just be friends. But then he slowly nodded.

"Friends," he repeated, still nodding. His temple was wrinkled in a half frown, like the whole thing was a strange concept he was trying to wrap his head around.

"Is that...okay?" I asked.

He ducked his head in thought. When he looked at me again there was a smile on his face. "Yeah. Totally fine."

"Awesome," I said, even though in that moment I felt anything but.

CHAPTER 13

Seven hundred and sixty-two. That was the number of pictures I'd taken by Wednesday afternoon. You'd think there'd be at least one decent shot somewhere in the lot, but no. All garbage.

Tonight the boys had an appearance on some late-night show, so I decided to use the rest of the day to assess my work thus far. After downloading the files onto my laptop, I started sifting through the images, hoping to separate out anything worth using for the blog. I was meeting with Paul on Friday—he was going to review the pictures I'd taken and show me how to work the blog—and I wanted to present him with my best work. But as I clicked through a never-ending series of terrible, if not atrocious, photos, my lungs started shrinking, one small breath at a time.

Who did I think I was, accepting a job that should be done by a professional photographer? And what was Paul thinking in hiring someone with no experience? This was the kind of stint Bianca Bridge should be doing, not some eighteen-year-old who didn't even have a clue who she was. Professionals like Bianca went to school for photography and traveled the world perfecting their skill. All I'd done was graduate from high school.

Photography had become my comfort, my distraction, my

crutch. Sometimes it was even my hope. So when Paul offered me the job, I thought it might become my future as well, but clearly I was wrong. Loving something didn't make me good at it. And if I wasn't meant to be a photographer, than what was I supposed to be doing with my life?

Pushing my computer away from me, I buried my face in my hands to hide my stinging eyes. In that second, I felt just as lost as when I'd found out Cara had cancer. One moment I was standing safe on shore, my path clear in sight. The next, my feet were swept out from under me, and that rip current of self-doubt was dragging me out into a dark, murky sea with no hope of rescue.

"Stella?" When I heard his voice, I forced myself to look up. Alec was standing over me, leaning forward on the balls of his feet, one hand half raised as if he thought I would bolt like a deer.

"Hey, Alec," I said. "What's up?"

He narrowed his eyes and looked me over, as if considering how upset I was and whether or not he was needed. Finally, he must have come to the conclusion that something was definitely wrong, and even though he wasn't much of a talker, now wasn't the time for his silent, brooding complex.

"I was going to ask you the same thing," he said. "What's wrong?"

I knew the "nothing, I'm fine" routine wasn't going to work with Alec. He wasn't the type of person to pretend to care by faking concern, only to take the first out that was offered. He might be quiet, but that was because he used his words thoughtfully and with deliberate purpose.

"Can I ask you a question?" I said, instead of responding to his.

He nodded and placed his hands on the back of the chair in front of him. "Why'd you show my pictures to Paul?"

Cocking his head, Alec stared at me as if I'd asked him to explain the basics of breathing. "Because," he said, his brows crinkled up, "they were worth showing."

"But how can you know what's worth showing?"

Alec shrugged. "I don't know much about photography or what qualifies as good or bad. But I do know what I like, and I figured if I enjoyed your work, then why wouldn't someone else?"

As he said this, I thought about how simple he made it seem. Like I'd made a whole big fuss in my head, and over what? A few photographs? Well, more than a few, but that's wasn't the point. Was I really stressing myself out over something that I shouldn't worry about? Or was Alec off base?

"My turn to ask you something," he said before I really had time to consider the answers to my questions. He pointed at my computer. "Do you have any work you can show me from before we met?" Obviously I had stuff I could show him—there was an entire hard drive worth of pictures—but why did he want to see it?

"Please?" he added when I hesitated.

"Yeah, okay." I thought for a minute, tapping the side of my chin as I tried to decide what to show him, and then suddenly I was hit with an oh-duh revelation.

Ninety-nine percent of the time, when it came to her disease, Cara was the most positive, hopeful person in the world. The doctors told her she had cancer, and she smiled, nodded her head, and told them that she would get better before her first prom.

One of the only times I saw Cara truly angry was when she first lost her hair during chemotherapy. I remembered walking into her room and seeing her staring at herself in a compact. She wasn't crying, but one look at her red-rimmed eyes told me she'd been bawling all night. Then she saw me standing in the door and smashed the mirror against the bedside table, raining silver shards onto the floor. In that fleeting instant of raw, unbarred grief, I was inspired to start a new project.

My sister needed to understand that just because she was sick didn't mean she wasn't beautiful. Her struggles with cancer and determination to get better only made her a stronger person. And there is so much beauty in strength. So I photographed everything that made Cara a tough person on the inside—the number of pills that she had to take each day, her collection of hospital wristbands, the needles and tubes that sprouted from her body every time she got sick—and the pictures I took turned into my first real portfolio.

It took a bit for me to find the file, but after pulling it up, I passed my laptop to Alec. He pulled out the chair and sat down next to me, and then took his time sifting through the different photos. When he finished, he gave a satisfied nod and handed my computer back without a word.

I waited to see if he was going to say anything, and when he didn't, I asked, "So…why'd you want to see those?"

"Because I can tell you're nervous," he said, as if those few words were explanation enough. I frowned at him, unsure of what he was saying, so he continued, "I don't know if it's because you're worried about impressing Paul or our fans, but honestly, you could take a picture of us staring at a wall and everyone would love it. The reason I wanted to see something else, something not related to the band, was to make sure I was right. This stuff here," he said, pointing at the screen, "confirms that. You're good at this, Stella. If you just trust yourself, this job is going to be a piece of cake. I promise."

It was the longest speech I'd ever heard Alec give. And as for the cake part? I really hoped he was right.

☆ ♭ ♪♫

He might not be the most social person in the world, but Alec was a sweetheart. After our conversation, he took me out to lunch to cheer me up. At first I feared it would be awkward because I didn't know what to talk to him about, but one on one, he was surprisingly good at holding a conversation.

As soon as we finished, Alec had to meet the rest of the band to rehearse for their show tomorrow night, and to keep my thoughts from wandering back to my nerves, I decided to tag along. When we arrived at the arena, security showed us into the main floor. What was normally a basketball court had been converted into a huge theater, with a stage set up at the far end of the room. The space looked strangely empty without anyone filling the thousands of seats.

"Everyone should be over by the stage," Alec told me as we crossed the large room.

I spotted JJ first. He was already standing onstage, pacing back and forth, and twirling his drumsticks in both hands. Alec waved, and when JJ saw us, his eyes went big.

"Hey, Stella," he called out. His voice was loud. Too loud. "I didn't know you were coming to watch our rehearsal."

"I didn't have anything else to do so—" I stopped midsentence when I saw Oliver.

He was leaning against the side of the stage and some girl was pressed up against him, her arms wrapped around his neck, her fingers buried in his wavy brown hair.

"Oh, Ollie," the girl said and giggled.

I forced myself to look away. My mouth was hanging wide open, the shock on my face clearly displayed for Alec and JJ to see, but I didn't even care because my brain was still trying to register what I'd just seen. Oliver wasn't kissing her, but they looked cozy enough to make me wonder if they already had. It seemed the magazine article Cara had read about him was true—Oliver Perry was a player.

I knew I had no right to feel hurt, but there was a biting ache in my stomach, so I pushed my fist against it, trying to force the pain away. Oliver was free to kiss whomever he wanted, especially considering that I'd told him I only wanted to be friends, but for some reason a tiny painful feeling of betrayal wrapped itself around my heart.

What I should have felt was relief—if I'd let things carry on between us, I could have ended up with a hurting heart—but all I wanted to do was kick myself for loving that adorable, yet clearly deceitful smile. I bet it was his favorite weapon of choice. One small upward tweak of the lips, and he could have any girl—even a sensible one that didn't like his shitty music.

JJ clearly saw the look on my face because he chucked one

of his drumsticks in Oliver's direction. "Hey, idiot!" The stick missed his head by inches and ricocheted off the stage with a resounding clatter.

"What the hell?" Oliver demanded, looking up from the girl. Alec cleared his throat and raised his eyebrows at Oliver before glancing at me. A look of pure confusion crossed his face when he saw me. I couldn't tell if it was because he didn't get why he was being interrupted or if he was surprised to see me standing here. I hoped the second.

The room was silent as we stared at each other, both of us waiting for the other one to make a move. Finally he pushed the girl away from him and took a step forward. He opened his mouth like he was going to say something, but I didn't want to hear whatever he thought would make this entire situation less uncomfortable.

"Hey, Oliver," I said cheerfully, forcing a smile on my face and hoping he wouldn't pick up on how upset I was. My stomach turned like I had eaten something rotten as I said his name. All I wanted to do was scream. At him. At the stupid girl standing next to him. At myself.

How could I be so stupid? I had known from the moment Oliver tricked Drew and me that he was trouble. He was the lead singer of America's most popular boy band, for Christ's sake! How could he not be a heartbreaker?

"Stella—um, hi," he started to say, but then Courtney appeared from backstage, Xander trailing behind her.

"Is Alec here?" she asked, looking around the room, and then she spotted him. "Perfect. Let's get started, boys."

☆ ♡ ♫

Cara picked up on the first ring.

"Stella! Oh my God. I'm so glad you called," she blurted out before I even had a chance to say hi. "How's Miami? Wait, are you even in Miami anymore? What about your new job? Is it everything you thought it would be? Are you having fun? And ooohh! How are things going with Oliver?"

I hadn't wanted to call Cara yet—I mean, I did, I desperately did, but I hadn't even lasted four days before needing to talk to her. My plan was to call home on Monday after I had a full week of work under my belt in hopes that, by then, my homesickness would be curbed. But seeing Oliver with someone else had the opposite effect. It messed with my head, and now there was a dull aching in my heart for home.

"God," I said, half laughing, half crying. "It's so good to hear your voice." I didn't even care that Cara had bombarded me with questions the instant she picked up.

"You sound upset," she said, her voice getting soft. "Are you okay? You're not thinking about coming home, are you?"

"Not really," I said quickly, even though the thought had crossed my mind. "I just feel so stupid."

"Oh, Stel," Cara said, and I could almost see the way her lip jutted up when she frowned. "How come?"

"It's Oliver."

"Uh-oh, that doesn't sound good. Tell me everything from the beginning."

"Okay, well, I was super nervous about seeing him again," I

started. "Like, so nervous I didn't sleep at all Sunday night. Things went well in the morning. It was a bit awkward at first, but Oliver gave me his banana for breakfast, which was incredibly sweet. But then we went to this radio interview and Oliver started talking about some girl, which made me realize he didn't like me." I paused before finishing my story, trying to work up the courage to tell Cara everything. "I-I didn't want to get hurt, so I told him that we should just be friends. Now he's—"

"*You did what?*"

I flinched. "We're working together now," I said, trying to defend myself. For some reason, saying this to Cara sounded ten times stupider than when I'd said it to Oliver. Maybe that was because I knew she'd called me on it. "I thought it would be for the bes—"

"No, just no," Cara said, refusing to listen to my explanation. "That's a load of bull. Why in the world would you tell him that? How do you know the girl he was talking about in the interview wasn't you?"

I opened my mouth to tell her otherwise but stopped. During the interview I'd assumed that Oliver was talking about someone famous, someone Kelly had "heard of" to use her exact words, but Cara had a point. Kelly had met me when we arrived at the station, which meant he could have been referring to me.

But it didn't matter—not after seeing that girl at the band's rehearsal. Even if he had been talking about me, that would mean Oliver's interests had an exceptionally fast turnover.

"He. Doesn't. Like. Me," I said slowly.

The line was silent for a moment, but then Cara sighed. "You're such an idiot, Stella," she said. "He gave you his freaking number."

"Yeah, sure," I said, letting my breath out in a quick huff. "He gave me his number because we had fun for a night," I told her, "but that's all. I was just another random girl to him, and if Paul hadn't offered me this job, Oliver never would've thought about me again."

"Do you really think Oliver Perry goes around handing out his number to 'random' girls?"

I could easily have ended this discussion by telling her the truth—that I'd seen Oliver cozying up to someone else. That was why I'd originally called her, but now, just thinking about admitting what had happened made me feel sick, like my ribs were squeezing in on all the organs trapped between them.

"It doesn't matter. I'm not going to let myself like him, Cara. I don't want things to be awkward—*I* don't want to be awkward. All I did was uncomplicate things."

Cara heaved a sigh. "If you think it's for the best, do what you want. But you can't chalk it up to Oliver dismissing you if you're going to do the same thing to him."

Maybe she was right, but the damage was already done. I couldn't revoke my friends-only request without Oliver thinking I was completely jealous and pathetic.

"Can we just forget about this?" I asked, suddenly regretting my decision to call.

"Sure, Stella." I knew from the way Cara said my name that she thought I was making a mistake, but for once she let it go. "What else do you want to talk about?"

I did my best to push Oliver out of my thoughts and focused on another of my mounting problems. "Well, on Friday I have my first blog post."

"Ohmygee!" Cara gushed, her mood changing in an instant. "Totes exciting. Are you super-pumped?"

"Not exactly," I told her. Alec's reassurance had helped settle some of my insecurities, but that didn't mean my nerves were completely gone. "I know I'm being ridiculous, but I'm scared Paul's going to take one look at my work and realize my pictures from the other weekend were just a fluke."

Cara scoffed. "Yup. Totally ridiculous. He's going to like them, Stella. Stop stressing yourself out."

"But how can you be positive?"

There was a long pause in which I assumed Cara was giving me a look, even though I couldn't see it. "Because I know you, Stella," she finally said, "and I know what you can do. I also know that you overthink everything, which tends to induce pointless panic."

And Cara was right. About both things actually—the pictures and the panic.

By the next morning, I'd chewed my fingernails down so far that, if I kept going at this rate, all I'd have left would be bloody stumps. As I sat down with Paul at a café a few blocks from our hotel, I made a conscious effort not to bite them anymore. But without a diversion, my fingers started to twitch.

"Let see what you've got so far," Paul said with a smile. I slid my computer across the table to him, and then I tucked my hands under my butt to keep them from moving.

"Wow," was the only thing Paul said as he clicked through the gallery.

Wow? Was that a good wow or a these-are-so-bad-I'm-shocked wow? My heart was hammering, and I felt like it was expanding inside my chest, leaving my lungs with no room to function.

"These are all seriously impressive, Stella."

"I'm so sorry," I said in a rush, but then I stopped. "Wait. You—you think so? Because if this isn't what you're looking for, I can try to get some better stuff tonight." His praise was exactly what I needed to hear, but I still couldn't believe him. Part of my brain was convinced that I just wasn't good enough.

"New stuff? Heavens no!" he said and laughed. "I'm more concerned that we have too much material. How am I supposed to narrow this down when it's all so amazing?"

"Really?"

"Really, really."

In the end we picked fifteen group shots, leaving out all the individual pictures I'd taken of the boys. Paul wanted the initial blog post to be simple, but there were at least twenty more pictures he wanted to use, so I already had material for next week. After showing me how to use the blog website and its different features, we added the images and spent an hour writing goofy captions.

"Looks good," Paul said, scanning the page one last time. "I think it's ready."

I looked to him for instruction. "What should I do?"

He pushed the computer back over to me. "Hit the publish button, Stella. This is your blog. You should be the one to bring it to life."

"Okay," I said.

Okay, okay, okay. I repeated the word to myself to incite some courage as my finger hovered over the mouse. My whole body was buzzing—I was excited and hesitant at the same time. I'd never put myself or my work out in the world like this before, and once I clicked "Publish," there was no going back.

"Stella?"

I cracked my neck. "Let's do this," I said, and then I slammed my finger down. I probably used more force than necessary because the mouse skipped across the table, but I didn't care. A rush of adrenaline had flushed through my veins, and I couldn't keep my knees from bouncing. It took five seconds for the file progress bar to go from empty to the bright blue of fully uploaded, and when it did, a new box popped up on-screen. It read: *"The Heartbreak Chronicles" has been published.*

I beamed at Paul. The blog—my work—was finally live.

"Take the weekend off," he said. "You deserve it."

CHAPTER 14

"Hey, Cara," I said, when her phone went to voice mail. "I was just calling to tell you the blog is up, and that you were right. Paul loved the pictures. Give me a call when you get this. Love you. Bye."

I hung up and tucked my phone away, my lips pressing together in a thin line. The first thing I'd done when I left the café was call my sister. When she didn't pick up, I called Drew. He didn't answer either, and after the thrill of posting my pictures, their silence was a letdown. I wanted to share my high, to let them know that I was starting to believe that accepting this job was the best thing for me, but what was the point of doing something exciting if I didn't have someone to celebrate with?

Back at the hotel, I found the band in their suite.

"Stella! Get over here. Someone needs to tell these idiots that Thai food is ten times better than ordering boring pizza," JJ complained.

"Oh hell no," Oliver said. He snatched the Thai menu from JJ's hands.

"Why not?" I asked, sliding into a chair next to Alec. "I could totally go for some pad thai right now."

"Don't get me wrong," Oliver said. "I love Thai food. It would totally hit the spot right now, but last time we ordered it, JJ stank up the plane with his poisonous gas. It reeked of spicy butt noodles."

"Besides," Xander added, "there's not much I can order from a Thai place, allergies and all."

I wrinkled my nose in disgust. "You guys order what you want. I think I just lost my appetite."

"Fine, how about Mexican?" JJ suggested.

Oliver shot him a look. "How is that any better?"

In the end, the guys decided on subs, much to JJ's dismay. When the food was delivered, we all sat at the kitchen table to eat. I'd ordered a sandwich, even though I wasn't in the mood; I knew my stomach would grumble as soon as I saw the guys eating.

"Tuna-fish melt," I said, reading off the order scribbled on the outside wrapping. Alec held up his hand and I passed it to him. Next I pulled out the salad, which I knew was Xander's before he said anything. Then I grabbed another sandwich. "California club?"

"Right here," Oliver said, raising a finger. He reached across the table to grab his sandwich, and our hands brushed as he took his food. I quickly yanked back. Ever since Wednesday, things were weird between us. We avoided being alone together in the same room, and all of our conversations were forced, like distant relatives who had nothing to talk about but were trying to be polite.

Looking away from him, I dug back into the bag and pulled out the final sub. "Meatball melt," I announced and handed it to JJ. He muttered something under his breath about the injustice, but took his food without further comment.

"Are there any napkins?" Alec asked as he tried to cut his sub in half with a plastic knife.

I dumped out the remaining contents of the bag. A wad of napkins fell out, along with a stockpile of little red packets. "What's with all the ketchup?" I asked. It looked like the sub shop gave us enough tomato sauce to make it through the year.

"For my sub," JJ said, as if it was the most obvious answer in the world.

Xander made a face. "It's totally gross. He puts it on everything."

"Really?" I asked as I took a packet for myself. "That's funny. Me too."

JJ gave me a nod of approval. "Ketchup should be its own food group."

"I used to eat it with a spoon when I was a little kid," I admitted. For the first time since we shot down his Thai food idea, JJ grinned. "I used to do that too! We should be ketchup buddies!"

"Just thinking about that makes me want to throw up," Xander said. "Do you know how much sugar is in one of those little packets?"

"I've never met anyone who likes ketchup as much as me," I told JJ, ignoring Xander.

"Well, I doubt that you like it as much as *I* do," JJ said and puffed out his chest.

"Wanna bet?"

He leaned across the table and narrowed his eyes at me. "You're on."

Fifteen minutes later, Oliver and Alec returned to the room with two economy-sized containers of ketchup from the hotel kitchen.

Oliver set one down in front of JJ, while Alec put the other next to me. Xander went to the kitchen to get two spoons.

"All right," Oliver said, sitting down between us. Something about the competition seemed to lighten his mood, like he'd forgotten about the tension between us. "Here are the rules. Whoever can eat the most ketchup wins and will be declared the biggest ketchup fan. This is not a race. Contenders will eat equal amounts of ketchup until someone gets sick and gives up. Are the rules clear?"

JJ and I both nodded, but I was worried that since he was bigger than me, he'd be able to eat more. The only advantage I had was that JJ had already finished his entire sub while I was starting on an empty stomach. "All right, ketchup lovers, grab your spoons."

I picked up my utensil and dunked it into the thick, red goo.

When JJ and I shoveled the first spoonful into our mouths, Xander's face turned green and he gave the rest of his salad to Alec. "That's disgusting," he said, trying not to gag.

After a few spoonfuls, JJ frowned. "This tastes funny." I raised an eyebrow in response. Tasted fine to me.

"It's a brand-new container of ketchup," Oliver said. When he looked away, I saw his lips twitch.

Four spoonfuls of ketchup later, JJ reached for his soda. "Why is it so hot?" he asked, but he continued to keep pace with me. Soon JJ had finished his entire coke and his upper lip was glistening with a layer of sweat. Finally, he pushed his tub of ketchup away. "Someone tampered with this." He looked at Oliver in suspicion.

"Are you giving up?" Oliver asked. He had a guilty smirk plastered across his face.

"No, I'm saying this wasn't a fair competition. My mouth is on fire."

"Sounds like an excuse," Oliver said. "You're too embarrassed to admit that a girl is going to beat you."

This shut JJ up and he pulled the ketchup back over, but he only managed a few more spoonfuls before drops of sweat were running down his face. "I need water," he gasped, pushing away from the table and rushing into the kitchen.

"Thank God," I sighed and let my spoon clatter to the table. I loved ketchup, but I could barely manage another bite myself.

"And Stella Samuel is the winner!" Oliver said, shouting out my victory like a sports announcer. "The crowd goes wild!" Alec and Xander both cupped their hands around their mouths and imitated the roar of a packed stadium.

"What was in the ketchup?" I asked. JJ was bent over the sink with the faucet running, mouth wide open as he gulped down as much cold water as possible. Oliver pulled something out of his pocket, placed it on the table, and smirked. It was an empty bottle of hot sauce. I laughed. "You're evil."

"No, I'm an opportunist. I could never pass up the chance to mess with JJ." The dimples from his smirk made me smile up at him for the first time since rehearsals, but then my phone buzzed.

Scrambling out of my seat, I pulled it from my back pocket in hopes that it was a text from Cara. But it wasn't. I'd received a message from the bank informing me that a transfer had been made to my account—my first payment from Paul. I heaved a sigh and dropped back down into the chair.

"Hey, what's wrong?" Oliver asked. He squatted down so we were at eye level with one another and fixed his sparkly blue gaze on me. After two days of acting distant and stiff, his abrupt change to the funny, caring guy I met in Chicago made me pause.

"I—it's nothing," I said, turning my cell phone over in my hands.

Oliver shot me a doubtful look, but his eyes were tender. "It doesn't seem like nothing."

"I'm fine," I said and forced a smile. "Just a little homesick, that's all. I uploaded my first post for the blog today, and I wanted to tell Cara and Drew about it, but neither of them are answering."

"Homesick, huh?" Oliver ran a finger back and forth across his lips as he thought. After a few seconds he said, "I think I have a solution."

"Yeah, what's that?"

Unless Oliver could suddenly make my siblings appear, it was highly unlikely he could actually come up with something that could pull me out of this mood. However, it was sweet, if not totally unexpected, of him to want to do something to make me feel better.

He grinned at me then, and it was the type of smile that made me fear what was going to be said next. "A party." His delivery was filled with the type of excitement I'd come to expect from JJ when he came up with a really awful idea.

"A party," I repeated. I could write an entire book on why that was a bad idea.

"Yeah, to cheer you up." He lightly touched my shoulder, and I was so amazed by the gesture after his cold attitude that I looked down at his hand. He pulled away quickly and added, "You should be celebrating."

The word "no" was perched on my lips. I wasn't in a party mode, and there was no way loud music, a crowded room full of people I didn't know, and alcohol were going to change that. Before I could tell him that, Oliver stood up and turned to the rest of the guys, who were still discussing the ketchup-eating contest.

"Hey," he shouted and clapped his hands to get their attention. "What do you guys think about throwing a party to celebrate Stella's first blog post?"

Xander, Alec, and JJ looked back and forth at each other before simultaneously nodding their heads in agreement.

"I think one of my good DJ friends is in town," Alec said and pulled out his phone. "Let me see if he's free."

"We need champagne!" Xander said, pushing his glasses up in place on his nose. "Lots and lots of champagne!"

"Guys," I said, "I don't need a party."

JJ pointed a finger at me. "Don't even try talking yourself out of this one, Stella. You promised, remember?"

He had me there. "I'm not much of a party person," I said anyway. Of course, I'd never been to a real party so I didn't know for sure.

"I have a solution." JJ disappeared into the kitchen. He returned a minute later with a bottle of something clear and two shot glasses. "You need to loosen up."

"I don't know," I said hesitantly. Was his solution always booze?

"Come on, Bear. Tonight will be a blast if you let it be," he said as he poured a drink for both of us.

Again, I was about to say no, but then I thought back to my fight with Cara; she wanted me to take this job so I could live my life, have fun, that sort of thing. Maybe this was my chance to make up for all that lost time in high school that I always wanted but never really had.

"Fine," I said and gave in, "but I better not regret this."

JJ only grinned and picked up his shot. "To a night we will never forget," he said, clinking his glass to mine.

"A night we'll never forget."

☆ ♭ ♫

I cracked open my eyes, and the bright morning sunlight blinded me.

"What the hell?" I grumbled, sitting up in bed. My head was pounding; my hair was a knotted mess; and my mouth tasted like alcohol. I tried to remember what had happened last night, but all I could come up with was a big black blank. When someone groaned and rolled over next to me, I yelped and grabbed a pillow for defense. Lying at my side was a boy, and he had the familiar brown waves of Oliver Perry.

"Holy shit." I scrambled out of bed.

Am I still dreaming? For the next minute I stood by the nightstand in hopes that, if I opened and closed my eyes enough times, Oliver would disappear.

No such luck.

Eventually I accepted that I was, in fact, awake, and my heart stopped racing. Then I realized that Oliver wasn't wearing a shirt, and my heart jumped right back to pounding. I wanted to run, but I couldn't look away from the dip of spine between his shoulder blades and the lean muscle of his back.

Then a horrible thought crossed my mind and my eyes went wide. *I didn't sleep with him, did I?* Thankfully, I was still wearing all my clothes from the other day…but what about Oliver?

"Please don't be naked. Please don't be naked," I chanted as I lifted the sheets. I let out a sigh of relief when I spotted jeans with a bit of boxer hanging out over the top. Hopefully that meant we hadn't done anything. There was no way that I wanted to lose my virginity to a rock star. How clichéd would that be?

So what did happen? If I slipped out of the room before Oliver got up, I could save myself the embarrassment of trying to answer that question, but I also knew that I would have to face him sooner or later. Better to rip off the bandage now. Leaning over the bed, I poked Oliver on the back.

"Hey." He didn't move, so I poked him harder. "Hey, Oliver. Wake up."

"Not now, JJ. I'm watching *The Vampire Diaries*!" he muttered, clearly still asleep.

"Wow, that's embarrassing."

Oliver rolled over again, and I burst out laughing. Someone had drawn a pair of round glasses around his eyes and a lightning bolt on his forehead. Scribbled across his bare chest were the words "Harry Perry, the boy who passed out."

"Stella?" he asked, my laughter finally rousing him from his sleep. He rubbed his eyes, which smeared the marker on his face, giving him what looked like two black eyes. "What's so funny?"

I bit back a smile. "Nothing, Harry Perry."

"I don't get it," he said.

"Maybe you should go look in the mirror."

Oliver frowned at my response and climbed out of bed. Wanting to see his reaction to his reflection, I followed him, and when he pulled open the bathroom door, a white blur flew at our heads. We both ducked.

"What the hell!" I exclaimed. "Was that a… chicken?" I glanced around the bedroom wondering if I was still drunk, but sure enough, one very large bird was flapping around on the bed.

"Yup," Oliver said as he grinned. "Must have been a killer party."

As if *that* could explain the farm animal in the hotel room.

We found JJ curled up on the floor in the bathroom. He was wearing a bra over the top of his shirt, and his arms were wrapped around a life-sized cardboard cutout. I stepped over his legs to get a better look. It was a cardboard cutout of himself.

"Oh God, where's your camera?" Oliver asked. "This is priceless."

"Honestly, I'm not sure," I said, which was a little worrisome. I had no clue where my camera was *or* what happened last night. Before I could give it much thought, my foot connected with something solid and I almost tripped. It was a glass bottle, and it rolled away, clinking across the tiled floor until it hit the far wall.

"What's with all the champagne bottles?" I asked when I noticed a collection of them resting at the edge of the bathtub.

Oliver didn't answer. He walked over to the tub and peered over the edge. Inside was a bubbly, light-yellow liquid. "Brilliant," he said, shaking his head in amazement. "Just brilliant."

"You're not going to think that when you look in the mirror," I said, but to my surprise, when Oliver saw what had been scribbled all over him, he let out a deep laugh. I looked at him in disbelief. If someone had done that to me, I would be fuming.

"It's pretty clever," he told me.

"It's going to be a pain to get off," I pointed out.

He shrugged. "As long as I can scrub it off in a bath full of champagne, I'll be happy."

We tried to shake JJ awake, but he swatted our hands away and refused to open his eyes. Leaving him on the floor, we decided to inspect the rest of the penthouse to see the extent of the party's damage. Out in the hallway, the floor was littered with red Solo cups, and it looked like a disco ball had exploded. Glitter covered everything.

I gasped when we walked into the living room. If I hadn't known about the party, I would have guessed a bomb went off. Most of the furniture was tipped over, and a pair of pants was hanging off the ceiling fan. Someone had TP'd the place with different-colored party streamers, and one of the walls was splattered with a red substance that looked like blood, but I had a hunch it was ketchup left over from our contest.

And in the middle of it all was Xander.

"Finally," he complained when he spotted us. "Can you guys help me? I've had to go to the bathroom for like an hour." He was sitting on a chair, and someone had duct-taped him to it. It must have taken a whole roll of tape, because his entire shirt was hidden underneath the gray.

Oliver was on his hands and knees laughing so hard that he was crying. "Best. Party. Ever," he managed to get out between laughs.

"Shut up, Harry Perry," Xander said. "I'm seriously going to pee on myself."

I rushed to Xander's side to help him, but before I could peel back a single strip of tape, the front door slammed open, and the entire penthouse shook. A beer bottle toppled off the bar and shattered on the floor. The clicking of heels filled the now-silent suite, and we all stared as a very angry-looking Courtney stormed into the room.

"Oh shit," Xander said.

A cheerful whistle filled the air. "Morning, guys," Alec said as he strolled into the living room. He looked freshly showered and dressed for the day, not like he'd partied all night long. When he spotted Courtney, he spun back around, attempting to escape before she noticed him.

"Don't you dare move a foot, Alec," Courtney hissed. "You boys were supposed to be down in the lobby half an hour ago. What the hell is going on here?"

"Well, we had a party," Xander started to explain.

"*Clearly*," she said, her impatience obvious.

"It wasn't supposed to be a big one," Oliver said, "but then—"

"Honestly, what's gotten into you boys lately?" Courtney said, cutting him off. She shook her head a moment later. "Never mind. I don't think I want to hear the answer to that question. Someone go find JJ right now. You four have ten minutes to meet me downstairs." Then Courtney was gone, the door slamming behind her.

"Oh my God," I said, slumping down onto the couch. "This is all my fault, isn't it? I'm so sorry, you guys." At first nobody said anything, but then Alec started laughing. When Oliver and Xander joined in, my mouth fell open. "What? Guys, this isn't funny!"

"This is not your fault," Oliver said between laughs. "Don't apologize."

"But you threw a party for me, and now Courtney's pissed."

Alec shrugged. "You know what? I'm glad."

I gaped at him. "What? Why?"

Oliver nodded. "Me too. When was the last time we did something that pissed her off this much?" he asked, as if making Courtney angry was some kind of accomplishment he'd been missing out on.

"I can't remember," Alec answered. The boys considered this for a moment before grinning at each other like dorks.

"You're all psycho," I said, shaking my head. "Completely psycho."

"Hey, guys?" Xander said then. "I still have to pee."

CHAPTER 15

It took nine of Courtney's allotted ten minutes to get the duct tape off Xander. Then the boys freshened up and were out the door in another five. I had no idea what their schedule was for the day or when they'd be back, but I didn't care because my plan was to sleep for the next twenty-four hours.

That didn't work out so well.

As soon as I lay down, I started thinking about this morning and waking up with Oliver. Thinking turned into worrying, and soon I was in full-out panic mode. Exactly what had happened between us? I prayed it was nothing. Maybe we were both so drunk that we accidentally passed out in the same bed. Maybe. But the evil part of my mind jumped to the worst possible explanation—what if I'd thrown myself at him?

Unable to sleep, I tried watching a movie, but nothing could distract me from my thoughts. When I couldn't take it anymore, I went back to the boys' suite to see if they'd returned. Nobody was there, but I decided to stick around because I knew Oliver and I had to talk. I spent the next hour practicing what I was going to say. The minute he walked through the door, I was going to march over to him and tell him that whatever happened last night was an accident, which was definitely the tequila's fault, and that it would never happen again.

"Ugh, this is ridiculous," I exclaimed and pulled at my hair.

Shaking my head, I sunk down on the couch. The more I rehearsed my speech, the more I thought talking to Oliver wasn't such a good idea after all. Most of the party had come back to me in throbbing, colorful flashes, but there was still a blank when I tried to picture the events surrounding him.

I could always ask Xander or Alec to tell me the details, but they were still gone doing band stuff. Maybe things would be a lot less frustrating if I just asked Oliver straight out what went down and stopped being so embarrassed. I could do that, right? After all, we were just friends.

As if on cue, the hotel door slammed open and Oliver appeared carrying three large grocery bags. Trying to carry was a better description. One of the brown paper bags was ripping, and he was struggling to get the load to the kitchen without losing anything. I shot out of my seat and rushed over to help him.

"Thanks, Stella," he said when I relieved him of one of the bags. We set everything down on the counter next to the sink, and an onion, a jalapeño, and a can of tomato paste came spilling out.

"What's all this for?"

"I'm making dinner," he said. "Wash your hands. You can help."

I stared at Oliver, brows raised. If he noticed my hesitation, he didn't say anything. He was already pulling out the groceries, and I quickly noticed the way he was slamming cans of beans down on the counter as he pulled them from the bag. Something was wrong.

Not knowing what else to do, I slid the ponytail holder from around my wrist and pulled my hair back before turning on the faucet. While the water warmed up, I lathered my hands with soap and chewed on my inside cheek. This would be the perfect time to discuss last night, but I couldn't bring myself to mention it, even after practicing for more than an hour. Especially not if Oliver was upset about something.

"Where is everyone?" I asked instead and grabbed a paper towel to dry my hands.

His nostrils flared. "They're *supposed* to be here."

"Supposed to?"

"Yeah. Once a month, we have what I like to call family dinner. I cook, and everyone else helps out. Tonight was supposed to be family dinner, but on the way back from the store, JJ saw the Cheesecake Factory and they all decided to go there instead," he said, his lips curling in an ugly scowl.

He didn't wait for any response on my part. Instead, he spun around and started opening and slamming drawers in search of something. Eventually he pulled out a can opener and hooked its jagged teeth to the lip of a can. He started to crank the handle, but the blade slipped. He tried twice more with the same results, his face turning redder with each failed attempt.

I placed my hand over his and pulled the can opener away. "Oliver, are you okay?"

"Fine," he said through gritted teeth. A second later he shook his head and glanced up at me. "Sorry, Stella. I'm not mad at you. I'm just frustrated."

He seemed a bit more than frustrated, especially considering it was only one missed dinner, but maybe I wasn't catching something. "You don't need to apologize. It's fine."

He nodded. "Well, looks like it's just the two of us. You like chili, yeah?"

"Chili's great."

This seemed to put him in a better mood, because he turned on some music, and we busied ourselves with preparing our meal. For most of the next hour we worked in silence, our only conversation when he gave me instructions. I was uncomfortable at first, mainly because I couldn't stop thinking about last night, but browning ground beef was so mundane that it was strangely calming. When Oliver started to hum along with the radio, I turned away from the stove and watched him chop vegetables. He was shimmying his shoulders back and forth, and I realized that if something awkward had happened last night, he wouldn't be as relaxed as he was now.

Once the chili was simmering on the stove, I set two places for us at the table, and then we sat down and waited for the food to finish cooking.

"So..." Oliver said. He was playing with the spoon set out in front of him and was avoiding looking at me. *Oh crap*, I thought. *Maybe I spoke too soon.* He was about to bring up last night, and if thinking about it made him uncomfortable, then something bad totally happened. "I wasn't purposely listening or anything, but I overheard you and Xander before the show on Monday."

"Oh." That wasn't what I was expecting. "What about?"

"Your sister," he said, starting to speak in a rush. "I would have said something sooner, but there wasn't a good time and—"

The spoon flew from his hand as his fingers slipped, and it clattered against his bowl. Reaching out, I scooped up both of his fidgeting hands and held them still. Oliver raised his gaze to find mine.

"You don't have to say anything," I said. "Really, it's fine. Cara… she's been sick for a while now."

Oliver grimaced and shook his head like he was disappointed in himself. "I've been trying to come up with something perfect to say all week, but I guess that's stupid, isn't it? There's nothing that would make things better. It's just, the thought of having someone so close, and then there's this potential they might suddenly be gone…" Oliver stopped, and his expression was twisted in a way that made it impossible to interpret. "I can't even imagine how difficult that must feel."

The one thing that I *did* understand was that he was upset, and seeing him so choked up was completely unexpected. "Thank you, Oliver. That means a lot to me." He nodded his head, a grave expression still on his face, so I squeezed his hand and said, "If Cara were here right now, she'd point out that she's still alive and that you need to stop acting all doom and gloom."

"You're right," he said. His smile finally returned and he sat up. "Hey, did your sister like her gift?"

"Like it? She just about pissed herself she was so excited."

Oliver's grin widened. "That's great. I can't imagine how she reacted when Paul offered you a job. What'd she say?"

"Well, she threatened to never speak to me again when I

considered turning it down." As soon as the words came out, I wanted to steal them back because Oliver pulled away from me.

"You weren't going to accept?" he asked. "Why the heck not?"

"I don't know," I said, my voice dropping. I didn't like where this conversation was going, so I let my hair fall in front of my face and started combing my fingers through it.

"Really, that's all I get?" he asked as I isolated the blue chunk from the rest of my hair. I wrapped the colorful streak around my finger and avoided his scrutinizing gaze. "Come on, Stella. There has to be a reason. It—it wasn't because of me, was it?"

I let the strand go and laughed as it unraveled from my finger. "Of course not, Oliver. Why would you think that?"

He shrugged. "It's hard to tell what you're thinking sometimes. I thought maybe you didn't want to say anything because it had to do with me."

I breathed a sigh. "It's not you. I promise."

"Then what?"

"I already told you," I said, speaking warily. "I don't know." I was trying to swallow my frustration, but the more Oliver pushed the subject, the more uncomfortable I felt. I knew it wouldn't be long until I popped like the bottle rocket I could sometimes be, and I hunted for a way to change the subject.

"How can you not know?" he pressed, looking at me like I was an idiot. The doubt on his face was all it took.

"Because, Oliver!" I said, throwing my hands into the air. "I just don't. All I know is that there was this disgusting pit in my stomach whenever I thought about leaving." There was no way I was going to tell him that I *still* felt that way whenever I thought too much about Cara.

"Okay, okay," he said, his voice softening as he held his hands out in defense. "I wasn't trying to upset you. I just thought maybe I could help."

"No offense, but what can you do?" It was nice and all for him to try, but if my brother—one of the two people in this world who knew me best—couldn't help, then how could Oliver?

He shrugged. "No clue, but talking about it isn't going to hurt."

"What are you, my therapist?" I knew I sounded harsh, mean even, but I could feel the pull of the rip current again. Joining the band on tour was supposed to help me figure out what was bothering me, but so far all I felt was more confused.

"Actually, I consider myself more a detective," Oliver said, cracking a small smile. "Right now I'm working a case called The Mysterious Upset Stomach." I looked at him, lips pinched tight, but he just raised a brow and crossed his arms. "Relax, Stella. I'm not going to judge you."

Ask yourself what you're so afraid of...

Finally, I sighed. "When Paul called me, I was super-excited," I admitted. "I mean, jumping-up-and-down excited. The first person I went to tell was Cara, and I think—I think it was seeing her bedroom door that made me panic. She has all these pictures of us taped up, and it reminded me of when we first found out she had cancer."

"What happened?"

I lowered my head onto the table and didn't say anything for a while. That was a day I didn't like thinking about.

Cara had told me she was feeling strange, bogged down and constantly tired, but I'd dismissed it as exhaustion from too many long hours at cheer practice. Eventually Mom brought her to the doctors. They decided to run some tests, and I thought, *Okay, maybe Cara is sick, but it's probably just mono or something.*

Her doctor would give her some meds, tell her to take it easy, and she'd be fine. The truth was, I was too busy with our school's winter production of *Guys and Dolls* to pay much attention. The Art Club was designing the set, and I was in charge of the entire project.

When the test results came back, my parents sat Drew and me down at the kitchen table so Cara could explain what was going on. I'd been annoyed—it was a Saturday and I was supposed to be at school putting the finishing touches on the set before Thursday's opening show—so instead of paying attention, I was texting my friends to tell them I'd be late.

"Stella, are you even listening to me?" Cara had screamed. I remembered looking up, seeing the tears on her face, and still not grasping the severity of the situation.

"Yeah, what?" I'd asked.

"It's cancer." That time she didn't yell. The hard line of her jaw was enough, along with the word "cancer." It packed the kind of punch that could only be compared to a championship-winning knockout. That or getting run over by a dump truck.

Shaking my head, I lifted my eyes back up to look at Oliver. "I didn't notice she'd been crying," I said, my own eyes watering. "Something was wrong with my sister, and I didn't even realize it."

"Hey," he said. His chair scraped against the floor as he scooted over and draped his arm over my shoulder. "You're not all-knowing, Stella. How were you supposed to tell she was sick? X-ray vision?"

"That's not the point." I tucked my elbows into my sides so I could hold myself. "I didn't notice anything was wrong because I was too busy to notice."

Oliver shook his head at me. "No, Stella. You were living your life. There's nothing wrong with that."

My nails bit into my palm as I clenched my fist. "You don't get it. If I'd been there"—thinking about this made me squeeze my eyes shut—"I would have known something was wrong. We could have taken her to the doctor sooner, and then maybe her cancer wouldn't be as bad."

He was quiet for a minute as he chose his words. "You're right," he said finally, which made me suck in a sharp breath. "I don't get it. Not at all. You're blaming yourself for something that's out of your control, like a thunderstorm or an alien invasion. Fact: bad things happen sometimes. You're gonna get the shit kicked out of you sooner or later, and that's just part of life. What matters is how you absorb the blow."

"Okay?" I wasn't quite sure if Oliver was saying I'd actually get beaten up or if this was just some terrible guy analogy. "What's that supposed to mean?"

"Stop feeling so guilty, Stella. You're absorbing all wrong."

CHAPTER 16

The Heartbreak Chronicles was doing pretty well, extra stress on the "well" part. Since uploading my first post a week ago, the blog had been viewed more than three million times. Of course, it helped that Paul had shared news about the blog on all of the band's social media channels, but I was still blown away by the number of hits, and that didn't include the thousands of times my pictures were shared across the Internet or the hundreds of comments they each received.

The overnight attention and support gave me a much needed boost of confidence, but I didn't realize just how well it was doing until the boys had a stint on *Talks with Tracy*. Tracy Hoop was the queen of daytime talk shows, the favorite of forty-year-old moms across the country. During the band's interview, I got to sit in the front row of the audience, a spot my own mother would probably run me over for. About twenty minutes in, Tracy turned the conversation in a new direction.

"Now, boys," she said after taking a sip of coffee, "I've been hearing quite a bit of buzz about—what is it? A blog of some sort?"

I nearly fell out of my seat.

"A photo blog," Oliver told her. "Basically it's a website with a running collection of pictures of us hanging out and stuff. The idea behind it is that our fans can see that we're regular dudes who just happen to have a not-so-regular job."

"How creative," Tracy said. "Are these selfies you take, or how does it work?"

"Actually, our friend Stella is a photographer," JJ said, pointing me out in the crowd. "She hangs out with us on a daily basis, takes pictures, and largely deals with making us look good." The audience laughed, but my stomach turned to rock because two different cameramen swiveled in my direction.

"Oh, she's here with you today? How wonderful!" Tracy exclaimed. To me she said, "Stella, is it? Did JJ cover the basics of what you do, or is there anything else interesting you can share with us?"

Oh man, this isn't happening.

The Tracy Hoop was talking to me. Worse, this was going to be on TV! I wanted to lean over and empty my stomach onto the floor, but instead, I glanced up at the boys. Oliver was watching me, and when our eyes met, he smiled and gave me a thumbs-up. The small gesture was enough to help me shake my fear.

You can do this, I told myself.

Taking a deep breath, I turned back to Tracy. "He did a pretty good job," I said, as my adrenaline rushed. "Although he forgot to mention how hard it is for me to make them look so good, but I do what I can."

Everyone laughed, JJ the loudest.

"So if I understand correctly, you get to travel around with the band? That sounds like every girl's dream come true."

"It's pretty awesome," I said. I could feel my palms starting to sweat, but I wiped them on my shorts and forced myself to continue talking. "The guys are great and I get to do something I love, so it's the perfect situation."

Tracy smiled and nodded. "I assume you're talking about photography. Do you have any other projects besides the blog for the band, maybe one of your own?"

Her question confused me, and I took a moment to respond. *A project of my own?* I considered the Heartbreak Chronicles my project. That's how Paul always referred to it, and it was the first time I'd ever displayed my photography for the world to see.

"I have an entire portfolio of work that isn't related to the band," I said slowly, not sure if that was the answer Tracy was looking for. "But nothing I've really shared."

"Well, I'm sure that will change in the near future considering the success you've gained just by working with the Heartbreakers," she told me. "Congratulations on the blog."

After the interview, JJ apologized for what happened, saying he never intended for Tracy to put me on the spot, but I waved him off. As terrifying as the impromptu conversation had been, I couldn't stop thinking about Tracy's final question, and eventually I was struck with a realization.

Before I uploaded my first post, Alec told me something that didn't quite resonate with me. He'd said that I could take a picture of anything related to the band, and people would love it no matter what. While the positive reaction to the blog *did* help boost my confidence, now I understood it wasn't really my work that everyone liked. The boys' fans didn't appreciate my style and careful technique—they enjoyed the blog because of the Heartbreakers.

Talks with Tracy opened my eyes to the fact that the Heartbreak Chronicles didn't really belong to me. Yes, I took the pictures and ran the blog, but was it really a representation of who I was as a photographer? Not really.

And surprisingly, I wasn't upset.

So the blog wasn't truly mine. That didn't mean it wasn't important. My first upload was the perfect warm-up, a practice round that showed me my potential. If I wanted to know what people *really* thought about my work, then maybe I needed to put a little of myself out there and create my own project.

Over the course of the next few days, I spent my free time combing through all the old work on my computer, trying to decide which pictures really defined me. Someone might argue that they all did since I took them, but it didn't work like that. To me, not all pictures were equal.

I considered each one carefully, and some stood out, bright and clear, screaming, "This is Stella!" It was an intuitive process, one that I compared to driving through a storm. As I drove, the rain came down so hard that the windshield wipers could barely keep up, but suddenly I would see the green of a traffic light. The light would glare through a sea of black telling me to go, go, go! When I came across a particular picture like this, it would snap me back to a moment or person or place. That's what made it important. Even though my world had moved on, the memory I'd captured was still the same, and that's what I wanted to share with people.

"Whatcha up to?" Xander asked.

It was Saturday morning, and we were in the airport waiting for our flight to Houston to board. The band's schedule for the day was packed, so I was trying to use the few spare hours to get some work done.

Glancing away from the screen, I looked down at him. "Working."

"Didn't you blog yesterday?" he asked. "How do you possibly have more work to do?"

"I'm not working on the band's blog," I told him. "I'm thinking about creating my own photography website."

I spun my laptop around so he could see what I was working on. After sorting through all my pictures, I'd purchased a domain name and used one of those free website templates to build my own. Most of my portfolio was already uploaded, but whenever I thought about publishing the site I'd decide to fidget with the layout or rewrite my bio instead.

Xander leaned over so he could get a better look. "That's way cool, Stella!" he said, pushing his glasses into place. "Is it live yet?"

"No, but it's pretty much finished. I'm just messing around with little details trying to work up the courage to post the damn thing. Can I get your opinion on something? I don't know if this font really fits the theme of the blog."

"Nope," he said. His response was so unexpected that I nearly dropped my laptop. He must have noticed my shocked look because he added, "What I mean is that you don't need my opinion. It sounds like you're just coming up with excuses to avoid the hard part. Stop second-guessing yourself."

Xander was right—the website had been ready since yesterday, but there was still that fear in the back of my mind that it wouldn't be good enough, that *I* wasn't good enough, that nobody would like it. I was second-guessing myself, just like I had my first week on the job, and I needed to stop.

So I did.

☆ ♭ ♫

"How about *Napoleon Dynamite*?"

"How about not," I said. Oliver and I were lazing on the couch in the boys' hotel room trying to decide on something to watch. The band had a rare day off, so while JJ, Xander, and Alec went sightseeing, the two of us decided to enjoy a quiet afternoon in.

"You're such a crab today," he said, turning the TV off and tossing the remote aside.

"Am not. I just don't have any interest in watching a stupid guy movie," I said, but I knew he was right.

Three weeks had passed since I joined the Heartbreakers on tour, which meant I'd made it twenty-one days on my own. It also meant that today Cara had a scheduled break in her chemo treatment. Without the boys' busy schedule to distract me, I couldn't stop thinking about how I wasn't there with her, and I regretted not going with JJ, Xander, and Alec to see the city. At least that would have kept my mind off my sister.

"Or any movie," he grumbled. "Here, let me see your phone." Oliver flung his arm onto the cushion between us, hand open and reaching like he expected it without question.

"Demanding much?" I asked but surrendered it anyway. "Where's yours?"

Since the night we'd cooked together, things had changed between us. It was like we formed some kind of silent bond of understanding. That or maybe the bond that was broken when I suggested we just be friends had been mended. There were no more uncomfortable silences or stiff pleasantries, and Oliver was back to acting like he had when we first met—goofy and playful—minus the kissing, of course.

"In my pocket," he said, scrolling.

"Why do you need mine?"

Oliver punched the talk button. "Because I'm calling your sister."

I scrambled up in my seat. "What? Oliver, no!" I tried to take my phone back, but he switched it to his other hand, holding it out of reach.

"Shhh!" he said, pressing a finger to his lips. "I'm putting us on speaker."

After our conversation about Cara's cancer, I was much more open to talking about her in general, which made missing home less difficult. But I didn't know if I could handle having a conversation with Cara today. It would only make me more depressed than I already felt.

"Stella, hey!" she said when she picked up. "I'm so glad you called."

"Is this Cara?" Oliver responded, and my sister went quiet. "Um, hello?"

"Who is this?" she asked. Her voice was small, like she already knew the answer to her question but wouldn't allow herself to believe it was true.

"This is Oliver," he said very matter-of-factly. He didn't need to give his last name for Cara to know who he was, and she sucked in a jagged breath.

"Holy freaking bananas." She let out an audible gasp, which made me want to see the wide-eyed awe that I knew was on her face. "Like, for real? You're not messing with me? Because that would not be funny."

"No, it wouldn't," Oliver said. "Besides, Stella would kill anyone who tried to pull something like that."

"You're right," Cara agreed, her tone relaxing much sooner than I would imagine. "She totally would."

"In fact, I think she's considering killing me right now," he said, glancing in my direction. "She's got this murderous look in her eyes."

"Oh, please," I said and crossed my arms.

"Yup," Cara said. "Definitely sounds mad at you. What did you do?"

"I called you without her permission."

"You should have asked!" I exclaimed.

"She would've said no," Oliver explained, talking to Cara instead of me. "She's been a grump all day even though she won't admit it, so I had to do something. I figured talking to you would cheer her up."

Cara's brilliant laughter burst through the phone. "She's stubborn like that."

"Are you two done talking about me yet?" I grumbled, but the irritation I felt for Oliver was lessening each time I heard Cara's laugh.

I didn't even end up talking with Cara. Instead, Oliver stayed on the phone with her for an entire hour talking about all sorts of things, and I listened. When he finally said good-bye and hung up, I silently slipped my phone back into my pocket.

"You're not angry, are you?" he asked after we sat in silence for a few seconds.

"No," I said.

"You sure? You're awfully quiet."

"I'm sure," I said and smiled. "What you did was really sweet."

Not only did he make Cara's day by talking to her, but he cheered me up. Just knowing that she was happy was the medicine I needed. I'd never really thought about Oliver and I having a "friends only" relationship—it was just a decision I'd made on the spot. But now I was realizing it wasn't so bad, because Oliver was proving to be a really caring friend.

"My pleasure," he said, "but my motivation was purely self-serving. I wanted to see that smile of yours."

Then Oliver leaned over and tucked a strand of loose hair behind my ear, and I froze under his fingertips. The smile he claimed he wanted to see faltered. This close, I could smell Oliver—the cinnamon scent of his cologne and the laundry detergent he cleaned his clothes in—and I breathed him in. I knew this was dangerous, how close we were, but I didn't know how to pull away.

"*Oliver!*" JJ shouted, and his sudden outburst made us jump apart. I hadn't heard him return, but it was impossible to miss his yelling. "*Oliver, where are you?*"

"*Dude!*" Oliver called out in response. "Chill. I'm right here."

He whipped his head around so he could see over the back of the couch, and JJ barreled into the room like a bull chasing red.

"What the hell is this?" he demanded.

There was something clutched in his hand, and when he reached us, he slapped it down on the coffee table. We both leaned in to get a better look. At first glance, I thought it was a picture of Oliver, which it was, but then I noticed the text running alongside the image. It was a magazine that JJ had folded in half, open to an article on the Heartbreakers.

Oliver looked from the magazine to JJ and then back down. He studied it for a moment before saying, "I don't get what the problem is."

"Hmm, I don't know. Maybe this bullshit interview?" JJ snatched the magazine back up and started reading out loud. As he did, Oliver sucked his cheeks in. "When asked about the band's future music, Oliver Perry was very forthcoming. 'Our next album will be pretty similar to what we have out now. Our fans obviously love it, so why mess with something that's working?' What the hell, Oliver?"

"I told you I was doing this interview," he said with a shrug. "I still don't understand why you're being such a dick. That sounds good to me."

"This isn't what we talked about," JJ said, jabbing the article with his finger. He was wearing one of his standard, ribbed cutoff tees, and I could see his muscles and veins straining against his skin as he spoke. I'd never seen JJ lose control like this before, and I held my breath, unsure of what to do.

Oliver sucked his teeth. "Yeah? What exactly did we talk about, JJ?"

"Are you kidding me? We spent a whole day brainstorming different ideas for the new album, none of which included the crap we've already done. You said—"

"Well, maybe I changed my mind," Oliver snapped before JJ could finish what he was going to say.

JJ took a step back, and his head moved with a slow, disbelieving shake. "Are you being serious right now?" His neck and ears were still flushed red, but his face had drained of color.

Something about JJ's tone must have registered with Oliver because his face softened and he unclenched his fists. "Look, JJ. I'm sorry. It was just one stupid article. Nothing's set in stone. You know that, right?"

"Do you?" JJ shot back, and I frowned, not quite following the conversation. "Because it doesn't seem like it."

Oliver scratched the back of his neck. "Come on, dude," he started to say, but JJ spun around and stormed off down the hall. "Just give me a second to—" A door slammed down the hall, cutting Oliver off. "God dammit, JJ!"

After working with the Heartbreakers for weeks, I'd been starting to think the breakup rumors were just that, rumors. Sure, I'd seen some tiffs between them, but that was expected since they were together twenty-four seven. But this was something different.

JJ had made sharp, subtle comments about the band's music before, most of which Oliver shrugged off, but this was the first time the subject had materialized into a full-blown argument. Still, I had no clue what was going on, and I knew I was missing some important piece of the puzzle. I turned to Oliver for an explanation, but he rushed off after JJ, and I was left sitting on the couch wondering what the hell had just happened.

CHAPTER 17

The next morning when I asked Oliver about the fight, he shrugged the whole thing off and claimed it was nothing. I knew he was only dodging my questions, and I would have pushed for a better answer, but JJ was humming and acting like everything was fine. Maybe he wasn't the type of person to stay mad for long, but I had a hunch he was setting the matter aside for a different time.

That was because today was special—the Heartbreakers were performing in Portland, and it turned out to be the best show I'd seen by far. Playing in their hometown fired the boys up like I'd never seen, and by the end of the show, I caught myself singing along with the rest of the crowd. When it was over, we all went over to JJ's house for dinner. And by dinner I mean a block party.

Okay, so maybe it wasn't actually a block party, but there were so many children playing in the street when we arrived at JJ's that we had to get out of the car on the corner and walk down to the large, two-story house with blue shutters.

"Who are all these kids?" I asked as we crossed the driveway. The smell of barbecue was drifting toward us from the backyard, along with the sound of a Mellencamp song.

"The Morrises run an orphanage," Oliver joked.

JJ rolled his eyes. "I have a big family."

To me, a big family meant four siblings at most, which JJ found comical. He was the oldest of eight—three boys and five girls. And then there was everyone else who'd shown up to celebrate the band's homecoming: aunt, uncles, cousins, second cousins, neighbors.

There were so many people at the party that I quickly lost track of the boys. Xander was the first to disappear, rushing off to find his family as soon as we stepped inside. Not long after, JJ's younger brothers dragged him and Oliver off to play football. Alec kept me company the longest—since he was from California he didn't have any family at the party—but he got caught up in a conversation with one of JJ's cousins, and I excused myself after ten minutes of listening to them talk about some band I didn't know.

The kitchen seemed to be the center of the party. A huge spread of food was laid out on the table, and people swarmed around it like bugs, snatching up the easy-to-eat finger food. My camera quickly found its way into my hands, and I stood off to the side of the room, snapping pictures of strangers.

A bulky figure stepped in front of me, blocking my view. "Stella, what are you doing?"

I looked up from my camera and found JJ standing over me. A little girl was clinging to his back, an adorable bundle of dark curls and green saucer eyes who couldn't have been more than two.

"I'm not working, I swear," I said, as I adjust the lens and focused in on her. She was too cute to ignore. "Who's this princess?"

"My youngest sister, Audrella." JJ twisted his neck to look at her.

"Aud, can you say hi to Stella?" She shook her head and buried her face in her brother's shoulder. "No? Okay then."

We both laughed.

An older girl who had the same dark curls as Audrella looked up from ransacking the candy bowl. Chocolate was smeared around the corners of her mouth. "Is Stella your girlfriend?" She said "girlfriend" like it was something funny.

"Jenny!" JJ said, gaping at who I assumed was another one of his little sisters.

"What?" Jenny said, all attitude as she propped a hand on her hip. "It's just a question."

"No," he told her, gritting his teeth. "Stella is not my girlfriend. Stop being so nosy."

She sighed, her face falling slightly. "Figures," she mumbled.

"What's that supposed to mean?"

Ignoring her brother's question, Jenny turned her green gaze on me, a new smile already on her face. "Do you think my brother is cute?" she asked, and JJ's scowl was replaced with a look of horror.

Swallowing my laughter, I grinned down at Jenny. "Oh, I think your brother is super cute," I told her.

"Good," she said. "You should marry him. Then we'd be sisters."

This time, I couldn't hold back my laugh. "I'm a bit too young to get married."

Jenny nodded her head in understanding. "My mom says I'm too young to get married too," she told me as she reached for more candy, "but I already have my wedding planned out. Do you know

Oliver Perry? He's the cutest boy in the whole world. When I'm older, I'm going to marry him."

"Are you now?" I said as a slight blush dusted my cheeks. I secretly agreed with her—Oliver was cute. Annoyingly cute.

"All right," JJ said, grabbing Jenny by the arm and taking the chocolate from her hand. "I think that's enough sugar for one day."

"Hey!" Jenny complained. When JJ let her go, she dodged around him and snagged a brownie off one of the trays. Then she stuck her tongue out at him and ran out of the kitchen before he could stop her.

"Sorry about that," JJ said as he set the chocolate back down on the table. "She doesn't have a filter."

I grinned. "Must run in the family."

JJ opened his mouth to respond, but Audrella, who was still clinging to his back like a monkey, tugged on his shirt and pointed down at the candy. "Colate! Colate!" she demanded.

"Okay, but only one piece," JJ said and picked out a red M&M for his little sister. "Don't tell Mommy."

"Jeremiah James!" a woman yelled from the other side of the kitchen. "I better not have just seen what I think I did. You know not to give Audrella candy!"

"Sorry, Mom," he said as he peeled his sister off his back and set her on the ground.

"Jeremiah?" I snickered.

"Shut it," he said. "It's a family name." I didn't get a chance to tease him further because the doorbell rang, and JJ shot off down the hall calling, "I'll get it!"

He returned a minute later, a woman in her late twenties trailing behind him. She had hair so blond it looked white, and her eyes were such a startling shade of gray that I instantly recognized them.

"Vanessa!" Alec shot across the living room like a blur and barreled into the woman. She stumbled back a step, but laughed and returned his hug. I'd never seen him so excited before, and if I hadn't seen the entire incident myself, I'd never have believed it. "What are you doing here?" he asked when they finally pulled apart. "Are you staying long?"

"Chill, baby bro," Vanessa said, ruffling his head, and Alec didn't even flinch as she ruined his always-perfect hair. "One question at a time."

The largest smile I'd ever seen was plastered across his face. "Why didn't you tell me you were coming?"

"Because it was a surprise, silly. Oliver paid for my flight so you wouldn't be the only one here without family."

"He did that?" I blurted out. Vanessa turned her ashen eyes on me and I blushed. "Sorry. Didn't mean to interrupt."

She raised an eyebrow, glanced at her brother, and asked, "Stella, right? The photographer?" He nodded his head, and then she offered me a smile. "Alec showed me some of the pictures you took. They're quite good."

"Um, thanks." Who hadn't Alec shown my pictures to?

"You're welcome. And to answer your question, yes. Oliver flew me up here so I could spend the weekend with Alec. Speaking of, where is he? I haven't properly thanked him."

"Haven't seen him since we got here," Alec said.

Now that I thought about it, I hadn't either. "I'll go look for him," I offered and backed away from the group before I could embarrass myself further.

But there was one more reason I had a sudden urge to find Oliver. Now that I'd met Vanessa, I realized I'd been introduced to every one of the boys' families. That is, everyone's except for Oliver's.

☆ ♭ ♪♫

I'd been looking for near an hour, weaving my way through the crowd in the Morrises' house, but Oliver was MIA. I checked the entire downstairs before moving outside and searching the yard. The place was so crowded that it was hard to know for sure if I'd missed him, but I was almost positive that Oliver wasn't anywhere at the party.

So I decided to venture upstairs.

The second floor was one long hallway of doors, each one labeled with one or more of the Morris kids' names: Audrella and Joanne, Aiden, Jenny and Amy, Jordan, Annasophia. At the end of the hallway I found the door with JJ's name, which had a yellow-and-black sign that read: DANGER! TOXIC ZONE.

Rolling my eyes, I disregarded the warning and pushed open the door, not knowing where else to look for Oliver. The room was small—a single bed ran the length of the left wall, and a dresser and desk were pushed up against the right. Someone had left the lamp atop the desk on, drawing attention to the bulletin board hanging above it. Tacked to the cork was a collection of photographs.

Although Oliver wasn't physically in JJ's room, he was still here, smiling up at me from most of the pictures. There was one of JJ and him when they couldn't have been more than six, covered in mud and smiling like loons. In another they were dressed up for Halloween as Jedi, JJ wielding a green lightsaber and Oliver a red. As the boys got older, Xander started to appear in more of the pictures: a camping trip, a birthday party, a high-school dance.

The bulletin board was like a chronological snapshot of JJ and Oliver's childhood, so it was appropriate that the final picture pinned to the bottom right-hand side was one with Alec, a group shot of the band. Using my nail, I dug the tack from the cork and pulled the photo down to get a better look. It was only dated from two years ago, but all four boys looked different, much younger—JJ's tattoo was missing, Alec was a foot shorter, Xander had braces, and Oliver's hair was long and floppy.

"Hey."

I yelped and dropped the picture, my heart nearly bursting from my chest. Someone started to chuckle, and I jerked my head up to see Oliver leaning against the window frame, arms crossed over his chest. His entire upper body shook as he laughed at me.

"Where the hell did you come from?" I demanded, my heart still thumping hard.

Oliver responded with a mischievous grin before turning around and climbing out the open window. When I didn't immediately follow, he poked his head back in. "You coming or what?"

Curious what the heck he was doing climbing out people's bedroom windows, I nodded. "Yeah, okay," I said and pinned the picture back to the bulletin board. Once I reached the window, I realized there was a section of roof, six by six at the most, for us to sit on without being in any danger of falling. Oliver offered me his hand and helped me climb outside.

When we'd first arrived at the Morrises', there was still a wash of color left in the sky, oranges and pinks and purples as the sun set, but now it was completely dark. The air had cooled off considerably with the arrival of night, and I wished I was wearing more than a tank top as a rush of goose bumps spread up my arms.

"So," I asked after finding a comfortable position on the shingles, "what are you doing up here?"

"Enjoying the party," Oliver said.

"But you're not even at it."

"Of course I am."

"But—"

"Just be quiet for a sec," he instructed me and pointed down.

I followed his gaze and fell silent. From the roof, I could see the entire backyard. White Christmas lights woven through the deck railing and tiki torches positioned throughout the garden lit the area, and most of the party had spilled out of the house into the refreshing night air.

There was a stone fire pit in the middle of the yard where someone had started a bonfire. More than a dozen kids were gathered around roasting marshmallows or cooking pudgy pies, and their laughter was warm and bright, like the crackling of the flames. Most of the adults were on the deck, drinks in hand, talking and laughing and enjoying the company. Every now and then the wind would snatch away part of a conversation and carry it up on a breeze for us to listen to.

"All right," I admitted. "This is a pretty awesome spot."

"When we were younger, JJ and I would scoot all the way down to the gutter so we could dangle our feet over the edge. Mrs. Morris banned us from coming out on here because she was afraid one of us would fall off and break a leg or something, but I think that's why we liked it so much. It drove her crazy."

"You spent a lot of time together." It was meant to sound like a casual observation, but really I was digging for any information Oliver would give me about his childhood and who he was, aside from being the front man of the Heartbreakers.

It was frustrating that Oliver was still a blank slate to me, while he'd uncovered most of the deep details that filled my own page. I could easily google him and find out everything for myself, but it wasn't really the background knowledge that I wanted. Opening up to Oliver about Cara's cancer had been terrifying, like dodging out into traffic with a blindfold on. But I'd trusted him to guide me safely to the other side of the road instead of running me over, and I wanted him to do the same—to trust me. Because if he did, then maybe I could prove that I could be just as good a friend as he had recently been to me.

"My brother from another mother," he said, cracking a smile. "Our moms were good friends in high school, so I spent a lot of time here growing up."

I kept my eyes down and focused on the bumpy texture of the shingles, not wanting him to see just how interested I was. "Oh?" I asked, hoping he would keep talking. This was the first time he'd ever brought up any of his family. I thought I would meet them at the party tonight, but since he'd been hiding up here alone, I was willing to bet they hadn't come.

Next to me, Oliver lay back and tucked his hands behind his head. "Wanna see something cool?" he asked.

I sighed at the change of subject but said, "Sure." Then I copied him, inching back on my elbows so I could gaze up the sky. "What am I looking at?"

"You said your favorite Disney movie was *Hercules*, right?"

A partial smile tugged at my lips; he'd remembered. "Yeah."

"Okay, do you see the four stars that kind of form a square?" Oliver asked, pointing straight overhead.

"I think so," I said, tilting my head and squinting.

"That's the keystone asterism in the Hercules constellation."

"Ah...you lost me."

"So an asterism is a pattern of stars in the sky, which can be made up of part of a constellation, or more than one," Oliver told me. As he explained, I let my head roll to the side so I could watch him. I wasn't paying nearly as much attention to his words as I was to the way his eyes held a hint of the stars above us. They gleamed with excitement as he spoke. "This particular asterism is shaped sorta like a keystone, hence the name."

"Thanks for the astronomy lesson, Galileo," I said, biting my lip and trying not to laugh. "But I'm still confused."

Oliver grinned and propped himself up on his elbow so he was facing me. "Basically you're looking at Hercules's torso. He's got a head and arms and legs too, but I've never really been good at visualizing them," he said. "Oh, and if you look a little more to the left, you can see Pegasus."

I studied his face. "Where'd you learn all this?"

"My uncle. He's into astronomy and that kind of stuff."

"So you do have a family," I said, half joking.

At this, Oliver looked away from me and rolled onto his back. "Of course I do," he said, his tone suddenly tight. Apparently something I said had sucked the good nature right out of our conversation, something that struck a nerve and made Oliver clamp up. When the roles were reversed, he'd pushed me, so I decided to push back.

"Then why aren't they here?"

"How do you know that they're not?" he asked, and his voice was restrained, like he was trying to hide any emotion that might come across.

"Oliver," I said, shooting him a pointed look. "If they were, wouldn't you be down at the party?"

He pushed himself into a sitting position and yanked his hair back, as if it would help sort out whatever matter was currently wrecking havoc in his heard. "Look," he said, releasing his tight grip. His bangs flopped back into place. "Can we just talk about something else?"

I sat up next to him. "Like what?"

His eyes flickered across my face, examining every inch of it. It was one of those long, intense stares that made my heart start to skip, and finally a tired smile relaxed his face. "Do you know that 'Stella' means 'star' in Latin?" he asked. Then he reached up and cupped my cheek with his hand. "There was this sixteenth-century poet, Sir Philip Sidney, who created the name for a collection of sonnets he wrote called *Astrophil and Stella*."

"I know what you're doing," I said a little breathlessly as his thumb started to move in soothing circles just beside my ear.

"Yeah," he said. "And what's that?"

"Trying to distract me."

He leaned in, slowly running his tongue over his lips. "You're wrong," he said, and I could feel the warmth of his breath as he spoke. "If I were trying to distract you, I'd do this."

I knew what was going to happen, but before I could pull away, Oliver wrapped his arm around my waist and tilted his head. As soon as his mouth was on mine, I knew this wasn't like our first kiss. That one was thrilling, filled with the excitement of exploring someone new. This one was aggressive, as if Oliver had been waiting too long for something he desperately wanted, and now he couldn't hold back.

It didn't take long for me to feel completely out of breath, and I pulled away panting. "Oliver, stop," I said, but I kept my forehead pressed against his and my arms around his neck. I didn't want to stop, but I'd made the decision not to do this with him. "We can't do this."

"Why?" he asked. I closed my eyes as he brushed his hand up my arm and across my collarbone. "I know you're feeling the same thing I am. I can tell by the way you're out of breath and the flush on your cheeks, and how you can't even look me in the eye because you know I'm right. So, tell me again not to kiss you and I won't, but you'd better give me a damn good reason."

I could still feel the way Oliver's lips had felt on mine a moment ago, how they tasted like the lemonade Mrs. Morris made, and I knew he was right. I wanted this even though I had a hard time believing he did too.

Oliver didn't give me long to answer before his lips found mine again, kissing my mouth, my neck, my shoulder. He took control quickly, moving his body over mine and guiding me down onto my back. The rough shingles scraped against my bare shoulders, but I hardly noticed. I ran my hand over his arm and down his torso, enjoying the feeling of the tight muscle beneath his skin.

"You know, people can see you up here."

Oliver and I both shot up at the sound of JJ's voice and smacked our foreheads together. He was hanging out the window, a sly grin on his face.

"God, JJ!" Oliver said, scowling and rubbing the sore spot on his head. "You're such a creep. You know that, right?"

"Creepy would be watching without saying anything," JJ responded, and then he shook his head in disbelief. "Sex on the roof? That's way more dangerous than dangling our feet over the edge. My mom would have a heart attack."

"We were not going to screw on the—"

"Just remember, kids, use protection," he said, cutting Oliver off as he waved a finger at us. He started to duck back into the room but stopped to add, "And don't even think about moving to my bed!"

☆ ♭ ♫

When he was gone, Oliver sighed and rolled off me. "Well," he said. "That wasn't awkward at all."

"Nope," I responded, sitting up and brushing myself off. JJ's surprise appearance had shattered the moment, and now that I could think clearly again, I suddenly wished I was anywhere other than alone with Oliver.

I didn't know if I was more humiliated or angry with myself. Kissing Oliver felt so freeing. Like I'd been stumbling around in the dark, and then everything was suddenly in sharp focus. I wanted so much to believe what he'd said, that he felt the same thing I did, but just as his words started to make sense to me, I remembered the girl from rehearsals and the entire situation got all blurry and out of focus again.

"We should probably head back to the party," I said and started scooting backward toward the window.

Oliver wrapped his fingers around my ankle. "Wait," he said. "Why are you leaving? I thought we would talk."

"What is there to talk about?" I don't know what made me say this. There was so much to talk about, especially considering what just happened, but the words left my mouth like an instant reaction.

"About us," he said, and from the look on his face, he didn't understand why I hadn't come to the same conclusion. Still, I didn't move, so he sighed and added, "Just come back over here and I'll do the talking, okay?"

It wouldn't hurt to hear him out, right?

Answering with a small nod, I slid back to my original spot on the roof. Oliver didn't say anything at first, and we sat silently for a full minute as he rubbed his chin and squinted into the night. Eventually he nodded his head to himself and glanced at me.

"I was trying to think of a good way to say this, but there isn't one, so I'm just going to come right out and say it. I don't want to be friends with you. It's not working for me."

His confession completely caught me off guard. I knew our relationship had started out a bit bumpy when I first joined the boys on tour, but I thought our friendship had improved so much over the past few weeks. There was a painful stitch in my chest, like someone had dug their nails deep into my heart, but I kept my face perfectly still. "What do you mean it's not working for you?"

His eyes searched mine for a moment before he responded. "I tried to keep my distance because that's what you wanted, but that's not enough for me," he said. "Call me selfish, but I don't want to just be friends."

Whoa. I mistook his meaning completely. "You want to be with me?" I said slowly, making sure I understood exactly what he was saying.

"Is that so hard to believe?" he asked, his mouth slacking.

"A little." Actually, a whole lot more than a little, but I refrained from saying this to him. "I thought you didn't date."

"I don't. I mean, I didn't." He shook his head and yanked his dog tag up and down on the chain. "What I'm trying to say is that I want to now."

A sudden shriek cut through the air, followed by a string of laughter, and down in the backyard a group of kids chased each other around the fire. I watched them for a moment, tugging on my lip in thought. "What about that other girl you were kissing?" I asked, turning back to him. "The one in Atlanta."

His brows pinched together as if he had no idea what I was

talking about, but then his face flushed as he remembered. "I never kissed her, I swear!" he said in a rush. Then he sighed and rubbed his hand across his face. "Look, she didn't mean anything. I didn't even know her name."

I laughed, but it was sharp and tight. "No offense, Oliver, but if you're trying to reassure me, you're doing the opposite."

Oliver grabbed a huge clump of his hair as he looked back up at Hercules and Pegasus. "Listen," he said, his jaw clenching. "I know it was stupid, but I thought you were into me and then out of nowhere you weren't. That just pissed me off because I didn't understand why, and I needed something to take my mind off you."

It took me a minute to absorb everything he'd said, so I focused on the fire down below. The group around it had grown by a few camp chairs, and I could see Alec and Vanessa sitting on the far side of the circle. Oliver needed something to take his mind off me?

"I was never not into you," I finally said. "I thought it was the other way around."

"What? What'd I possibly do to make you think that?"

"During that radio interview," I said, my voice a whisper, "you mentioned another girl."

Oliver blinked before laughing, the sound hysterical. "I was talking about you, dork," he said.

Again, he left me speechless. How was I supposed to respond when I finally heard everything I'd been hoping Oliver would say all along? "Then why didn't you just say that?" I asked after letting the truth sink in.

If he'd really felt something for me, why didn't he just go for it instead of shuffling around the edges with half-truths like it was some big secret? Then we could've avoided this whole confusing mess. Oliver had never been shy before, and the first time we met, he was so straightforward and assertive.

I watched him draw in a breath as some emotion I couldn't pin down spread across his face. Regret maybe? "The media has a nasty habit of scrutinizing my entire life, Stella. Did you really want to become their next story?"

"Oh," I said, realizing the implications. While I had been worrying about Oliver hurting me, he'd been trying to protect me. "I feel like an idiot. Like, the biggest of idiots."

Oliver smiled at me like this was the best thing I could say. "Then is that a yes?"

"Wait, what?"

"To not being just friends anymore." Oliver wasn't really giving me any time to think about this, and I was so overwhelmed that all I could do was nod my head. "Are you absolutely sure? I was serious when I said they'll make a story of this. They'll dig through your life and pull out all the unpleasant parts that you'd rather have left alone."

He said this with so much animosity that I wondered what unpleasant part of his life they'd dug up and displayed for the whole world to see. I didn't have any dark secrets to hide, but then I wondered… "What about Cara? I don't want her dragged into this. She doesn't need any more stress in her life."

"That's fine," Oliver said a little too quickly. "I totally get it. We can just keep this between us."

"Well…" I started to say. Of course I didn't want Cara to be affected by anything that happened between Oliver and me, but was he talking about having a secret relationship? "I guess?"

"Good," he said and nodded his head. "It's none of their damn business who I date."

I wanted to talk about it more, because the thought of dating Oliver in secret somehow didn't sit right with me, but his jaw was set and there was a blazing look in his eyes. It wasn't demanding, like he wanted me to accept his decision without question, but one of fierce protectiveness, like he didn't want to let me go and nobody, not even the media, was going to stop him. I suppose some girls might have found that romantic, but it only made me worry. What had happened to Oliver that had made him this way, so possessive and distrustful?

The concern must have been clear on my face, because Oliver unclenched his jaw, smiled, and said in a light voice, "I never finished telling you about the sonnets."

I blinked. "Huh?"

"*Astrophil and Stella*," he said, taking my hand. "The name 'Astrophil' is derived from two Greek words that, when combined, mean 'star-lover.'"

"So what does that mean?"

Oliver tilted his head and looked back up at the sky. "That Stella is the star of his love."

CHAPTER 18

Oliver and I went on our first official date later that week. Of course, he failed to mention we were going on a date until two hours beforehand.

"Special delivery from the Love Doctor," JJ said, and plopped down right on top of the desk where I was working. Okay, so I wasn't actually working. I was reading through the mass of comments I received on my latest blog post, but his intrusion was annoying nonetheless.

"Hey," I complained, craning my neck to see the computer screen. "You're in my way."

"But I have a present for you," JJ said, waving a folded up piece of paper in front of my face.

I wrinkled my nose. "I don't think I want any presents from the *Love Doctor*."

JJ scoffed. "It's not from me. It's from your *lover*."

"He's not my lover, you perv," I said as my face heated up. "And who says lover anymore? That's creepy."

I had yet to officially tell the rest of the band about my relationship with Oliver, not because it was a secret—I doubted that Oliver would care if I told his closest friends—but because it was safe to assume they'd already gathered as much.

"Ah," JJ said, wagging a finger at me, "but you knew exactly who I was talking about, didn't you?"

"Just give it to me." I snatched the paper from him and unfolded it.

Stella,

6 p.m. at 137 North Higgins Street. Dress nice.

—Oliver

"What's this?" I asked after reading the message.

"Instructions from Oliver," he said. "Duh."

"I got that. What are they for?"

Although it registered in the back of my mind that Oliver was probably taking me on a date, I was too caught up in all the little details to freak out. It was already four o'clock, which barely left me any time to get ready, and on top of that, I didn't know what to wear.

He shrugged. "Just the delivery boy, Stella, but if I had to guess, I'd say it has something to do with what I caught you two doing on my roof last weekend."

I ignored his jab and scanned the note again. "But what do you think he means by 'dress nice'? Are we going somewhere fancy?"

JJ raised an eyebrow as he looked me over. "It probably means that you should shower and change out of those sweats."

"*Thanks*," I said, pushing my bangs out of my face. As if I needed him to tell me I looked greasy. "What I meant was how nice?

Semiformal? Formal? He didn't give me any specifics here. What if I show up too fancy?" Worse, what if I was underdressed?

"You're the girl, not me. How am I supposed to know? A sundress, maybe? You're making this a bigger deal than it should be."

JJ clearly didn't understand the crisis I was experiencing, so I decided to use what little time Oliver had given me to tear through my suitcase. I didn't own any dresses, but I'd packed a silver sequin top I stole from Cara. After tucking the shirt into my black skater skirt and pairing it with black heels—also Cara's—I decided the outfit was as date-appropriate as I could get under such short notice.

As it turned out, Oliver wasn't entirely senseless. He arranged for a car to pick me up outside our hotel at a quarter to, and fifteen minutes later the driver pulled up to the curb in a chic part of town where the streets were lined with fancy restaurants and posh boutiques.

"Hello?" I said, pulling open the door at 137 North Higgins.

Oliver was waiting just inside. He was wearing a slim black suit, no tie, over a white dress shirt with the top buttons undone, and his usual messy brown waves had been styled back. "You came." There was an amazed smile on his face, almost as if he'd expected me to be a no-show and I'd surprised him.

"How could I not?" I asked.

His mouth parted like he was going to respond, but then he took another look at me, a head-to-toe look, and said, "Stella, you look perfect."

"You think?" I asked, and had to look away from his stare. "I was worried that—"

"Perfect," he assured me. I felt myself blush, and Oliver took my hand. "Come on. I want to show you something."

He pulled open the inside door, and we stepped into a very long, very empty room with wooden floors and industrial-gray ceiling rafters. The walls were painted stark white, but every few feet a piece of art hung on display, a spotlight shining on each one. When I arrived, I'd been so nervous about what I was wearing that I didn't notice we were meeting at an art gallery. I stepped away from Oliver and walked to the middle of the room, and then I turned in a slow circle, taking everything in.

"Do you like?" Oliver asked. He was standing where I had left him with a satisfied smirk on his face.

I did. I'd never given much thought to what would make a perfect date, but now I was struggling to think of anything better than being here. This wasn't just your regular movie and dinner—it was special, because Oliver had considered what was important to me. We walked from piece to piece, stopping to talk about each one, and he decided an oil painting by some artist called DeBuile was his favorite. A silver fork and knife were glued to a canvas filled with random splotches of bright color. Oliver said he liked it because it reminded him of a food fight.

"Where is everyone?" I asked. We'd made it halfway through the gallery before I even noticed we were completely alone.

"The owner is in the back," he said. "I rented out the place for the night so we could have some privacy."

"Oh, right," I said. He didn't mean that kind of privacy. He meant so we could keep our relationship a secret.

"Look over here," Oliver said before I could give his previous words much thought. He pointed to the end of the row of art, and I instantly recognized a vibrant photograph on the wall. "This is why we came."

I stared up at one of Bianca's pictures. It was the original print, but I was more stunned by the fact that I was looking at my favorite of all her pieces, something that Oliver never could've known. It wasn't the first photo of hers I'd seen when introduced to her work, but it was the one I found most inspiring.

The subject was so simple: a little girl, maybe five or six, who was playing in the street during the middle of a summer shower. Her feet were bare and the look on her face said that nothing in the world was better than being covered up to her waist in mud. In her smile, I'd recognized the sort of carefree spirit that Cara, Drew, and I all had as kids. I hadn't felt that way since Cara's first diagnosis, and I realized I wanted it back, if only for the shortest of moments, so I could capture the feeling with my own camera before it was forever gone.

"I…" I started to say. I wanted to tell Oliver what this meant to me, but I was breathless and I kept thinking there was no possible way to finish my sentence, to use words to explain. They weren't enough.

"You like it?" Oliver asked. "I was trying to decide where to go tonight, and then I read somewhere that this gallery had a Bianca piece. I called just to make sure."

"Yes," I said, finally able to speak. Oliver was oblivious to the fact that this particular picture was one of the special few that had inspired my passion for photography.

"Good," he said like that was the only explanation he needed. "I'm glad."

☆ ♭ ♪♫

Dinner was at a local place called Amber India three doors down from the art gallery. They let us sneak in through the back, and there was a private dining room normally reserved for large parties where we could eat in peace. Before the waitress arrived with our food, I excused myself to wash my hands. When I was leaving the bathroom, I noticed a commotion at the front of the restaurant.

"Ladies, please!" The hostess was attempting to push back a group of twenty or so girls. "If you're not here to eat, then you need to leave!"

I rushed back to our table. "Oliver," I said, waving him over to the door. "You'd better come see this."

"Crap," he said after peeking out into the hall.

"How did they find you?" I asked in disbelief. It was like the girls had materialized out of thin air.

"Anyone in the restaurant who saw us could have tweeted about it," he explained. He pulled out his wallet and dropped a few bills on the table. "It happens more often than you'd think."

"Okay, so what do we do?"

"Hopefully we can still sneak out the back."

We weren't that lucky. Oliver tried to hurry down the hall, but he was easily spotted by his fans. When the hysterical screaming began, he grabbed my hand and we started to run.

"Hold on," he said, pulling up short of the rear door. He poked his head around the corner before quickly pulling back. "Shit."

"What's wrong?" I asked. As adrenaline started to pump through my heart, I wondered if our relationship would always be like this: secrets and chases and drama.

"There's a whole bunch of paparazzi. We need to go a different way."

"What other way?"

"Through the kitchen?" he suggested.

We hurried through the swinging metal doors, and some of the cooking staff looked up at us in surprise. The kitchen had one exit. It led out into a tiny, fenced-in area where the Dumpsters were kept hidden from view, but there was a padlock where the fence was supposed to open, trapping us inside.

"Now what?" I was starting to worry that our first secret date wouldn't be secret for that much longer.

Oliver thought for a moment before pulling me back into the small kitchen. He threw open the janitor's closet and pushed me inside before stepping in after me. When he closed the door behind himself, we were shut in darkness.

"Ouch," I hissed as Oliver trampled over my foot.

"Sorry," he mumbled. I couldn't see much of anything, but I was pretty sure that Oliver had shoved the cleaning cart under the doorknob so no one could get in.

"Hey!" someone in the kitchen shouted. "You girls can't be in here!"

Squealing ensued. We waited, our breathing heavy, until the commotion outside the door died down. My heart was finally slowing and I was able to relax slightly, but that didn't solve our current problem—we were still trapped inside a janitor's closet.

"So how exactly are we going to get out of this one?" I asked. I heard Oliver shuffle around. A second later, there was a sudden bright light as his phone woke up, and he hit a number on speed dial.

"Hey," he whispered when someone answered. "Stella and I are trapped at this Indian place. We need someone to pick us up." The phone conversation lasted a few more seconds as Oliver gave whoever was on the other end the address of the restaurant. When he hung up, he said to me, "It will be about twenty minutes."

"What do we do until then?" I asked. "Hide here?"

With his phone back in his pocket I couldn't see Oliver, but I could hear the grin on his face. "I can think of a couple things." He wrapped his arms around my waist and pulled me up against him. "For example…"

And he kissed me instead of finishing his sentence. At first, it was much softer than our previous two kisses. Oliver took his time, slowly pressing his lips to my forehead, cheeks, and neck. But when he finally found my lips, it was a whole different story. He backed me up against the wall of the closet and pressed his chest against mine as he kissed me feverishly. I accidentally kicked something over as we moved. It was small and metal, probably a can of cleaning spray, and a broom clattered to the floor along with it. My fingers went straight into his wavy curls and locked together as I inhaled his scent—cinnamon and laundry soap.

We made out in the closet until Aaron showed up, and when he snuck us out of the restaurant, I felt like I was part of a James Bond movie. But dating Oliver wasn't all thrilling adventures, dangerous chase scenes, and passionate kisses. The very next night, after the Heartbreakers concert, I let the boys talk me into going to an after-party. It was at a night club a few blocks from the arena, and when we arrived, it didn't take me long to learn that the hardest part about secretly dating one of the world's most eligible bachelors was that nobody—nobody meaning girls—knew that he wasn't so eligible anymore.

A crowd flocked around the band as soon as they stepped inside, mainly gorgeous girls who were dolled up for a night of dancing. I never felt self-conscious about my appearance in front of Oliver, but suddenly I felt underwhelming in my frayed jean shorts and tank top.

Our party was given a VIP room next to the DJ booth, and while it gave us some privacy from the rest of the club, we sat with a small group of fans who were lucky enough to be selected by security to join us. Three girls in particular were hanging on Oliver, all tall, golden, and nothing like me. The frustrating thing was that I couldn't hate these girls for their shameless flirting, because they had no idea he was already taken.

I took a spot on one of the leather couches and tried to look as nonchalant as possible, playing with my phone and watching the mob of people pulse together on the dance floor. At one point, Oliver caught my gaze and looked at me with apologetic eyes, but for most of the night we stayed apart to keep up appearances.

"Hey, you okay?" JJ asked when the club was finally closing. "You've been awfully quiet."

"Me?" I asked, trying to sound surprised. "Never better."

☆ ♭ ♪♫

"Veggie smoothie?" Xander asked me.

I was sitting at the kitchen counter in the boys' hotel suite working on my second cup of coffee. It was early morning and everyone was still in bed with the exception of Xander. Fifteen minutes earlier he'd emerged from his room, still half asleep, and headed straight down to the hotel kitchen. When he returned, he had a huge glass of something green and poisonous looking in his hand.

"No thanks," I said, wrinkling my nose. "I think I'll stick to my usual bagel."

Because of all his food allergies, Xander had the strangest diet of anyone I'd ever met. Normally all he ate were scrambled eggs, chicken, salads, and occasionally he'd mix things up with a blender. He was gluten intolerant, nut intolerant, shellfish intolerant, and there was even a list of fruits he couldn't safely eat—I could live without the seafood, but the carb lover inside of me cried at the thought of missing out on bowls of spaghetti.

"Suit yourself," he said, happily sipping his vegetables as he pulled out the bar stool next to me. "So why are you up so early?"

"Couldn't sleep," I told him. "I added some new pictures to my website yesterday, and I couldn't stop thinking about it."

So far my personal website was doing well. It didn't have nearly as many views as the Heartbreak Chronicles—in fact, it only had a few hundred—but that was to be expected. I was still proud of myself, and every time someone left me a positive message, I found it reassuring.

So last night I worked up the courage to post the pictures I'd taken of Cara—the ones I'd shown Alec—and although the response was positive so far, it was still nerve-racking to bare the most personal part of my life to the world. I felt vulnerable somehow, like I was playing cards and while my hand was exposed for the entire table to look at, I couldn't even see who my opponents were.

"Oh yeah?" he said. "How's that going?"

"Well," I said, "so far so good…at least I think."

Xander scoffed and waved his hand to dismiss my doubts. "I'm sure it's amazing, Stella. Have you thought about what you want to do when your contract is up?"

"Not really," I said, the words faint on my lips. His question brought on a whole new wave of worries and concerns, things I didn't want to think about. "I was supposed to start school in the fall, but I deferred when Cara got sick."

He took another sip of his drink and then used his sleeve to wipe away a green mustache. "You think you'll ever decide to go?"

"I don't know." I raised my hands in the air and let them fall, feeling lost. "So much has changed since then."

He was quiet for a second, choosing his words. "Well, what about photography school? Ever consider that?"

I had to stop myself from laughing. "No, of course not."

"How come?" he asked. I thought he was joking, but my amusement faded quickly when I saw the serious look on his face.

Grasping my coffee mug between my hands, I stared at an unfixed spot on the wall. "It never occurred to me," I admitted after a minute of consideration. "I wouldn't even know what schools have good programs."

Xander perked up. "Let's look," he said and gestured at my

computer. It was resting on the counter in front of us, waiting to be turned on.

He seemed much more excited about the idea than I did, but to humor him, I set my coffee aside, opened up my laptop, and for the next thirty minutes we researched different schools. We discovered a handful of universities that frequented every top list. Yale was the most surprising because I didn't realize they had a photography program, while the School of the Art Institute of Chicago seemed liked the most practical choice for me since I wouldn't be too far away from home. But the place that really caught my eye was the School of the Visual Arts.

"I like this one," I told Xander as we looked over the website. "I always wanted to live in New York."

"Then apply," he said and clicked on the admissions tab.

"Apply?" I said, and this time I wasn't able to hold back my laughter. "I already missed the deadline. Fall semester starts in September."

"So?" he said, pulling up an online application. "Who said you have to go this semester? There's always spring and next year." He wasn't even looking at me now. Instead, he was concentrated on reading over the information displayed on the screen in front of him.

Okay, I hadn't really considered that, but this idea to go to school was so abrupt and hasty. I needed time to consider how a choice like this could possibly fit into my life. "Yeah, but I don't even know if I want to go," I said, shying away from the computer.

"It's not like you have to make a decision now," he said with a chuckle, already typing in information for me. "Full name?"

"Stella Emily Samuel," I responded, the reaction instant. "Won't there be an application fee?"

Xander shot me a look. "Really, Stella? I'll pay the fee if you're so worried about it. Male or female?"

Now it was my turn to give Xander a look. "Funny," I told him, and he grinned at me.

"Come on, Stella," he said and crossed his arms. "Giving yourself options won't hurt."

I glanced from him to my computer in thought. This was silly. If SVA had one of the top photography programs in the country, there wasn't a big chance I'd get in. That part, as disappointing as it sounded, was the easiest to accept. The real issue was Cara. Leaving for school would be long-term and what if she wasn't better by then? When I accepted Paul's job offer, it was with the knowledge that my contract would be up in two months and then I could go home.

I quickly shook my head to clear the negative thoughts. I hated that I always got so worked up and confused whenever I imagined my future. Here Xander was trying to do something nice for me, and all I could worry about was something I had no control over— well, at least in this moment. He was right; SVA would be a nice option to have even if I wasn't accepted or never went.

"Fine," I said, and gave him a curt nod. "What do I need to do?"

Just in case.

CHAPTER 19

A week later the fighting started again.

"God, you're such a pretentious asshole!" JJ shouted, the hotel door slamming open and bouncing against the wall. I knew from the tone of his voice that, for once, he wasn't joking around.

This morning, the band had some type of meeting with their label to discuss the new record that would go into production as soon as their tour was over. While they were gone, I hung out at the hotel and worked on my post that was due later today.

"Me?" Oliver shouted back. "I'm not the one who kept mouthing off the whole damn time. Were you trying to piss him off?"

Alec was the first to appear in the living room. I jumped to my feet when I saw him, but he didn't stop to tell me what was going on. He swept by silently and disappeared down the hall without a word.

"Oh, I'm sorry," JJ said, clearly anything but. "I didn't realize asking for a little creative freedom was considered mouthing off. Next time I'll consult you before thinking or breathing."

"Dude, why are you mad at me?" Oliver demanded.

"Because! I want to do something different for our next album."

I had a strong feeling that neither Oliver or JJ wanted me to hear their fight, so I decided to hide in the suite's office before they saw me. I scooped up my laptop and dashed across the living room, but when I reached the edge of the room, I realized that their voices weren't getting any closer.

"What's wrong with what we have?"

"It's not us, Oliver," JJ said as the two continued to fight in the front hall.

"Of course it is," he shot back. "I wrote it."

"No, it's not. You only wrote what they wanted to hear. I'm sick of the sucking up and the sugary music and the stupid clothes. I want things to be like they used to when we had fun and you wrote killer songs."

I held my breath and tried to ignore the slow burning feeling of guilt in my stomach; I knew I shouldn't have been standing here, eavesdropping on an exchange that was probably private, but I was tired of not knowing and I couldn't make myself move. Whenever there was some kind of tension with the band, I always felt like I was catching the tail end of the conversation. Not because I was literally only hearing half of what was said, but because the Heartbreakers seemed to have all these little secrets that everyone knew, but weren't willing to talk about.

"I'm not sucking up!" Oliver shot back.

"Yeah?" JJ said. "Prove it. Let's play one of our old Infinity and Beyond songs tomorrow night."

Oliver's voice dropped, and I almost didn't hear his response. "You know we can't do that."

"Why not? Because they don't want us to? Don't you get it, Oliver? We made it. We don't have to take their shit anymore."

"The set list is already set and—"

"*Screw the set list! Screw them!*" JJ shouted. "And you know what? Screw you too!"

The door opened and slammed again. It was quiet for a moment and then, before I realized that the fight was over, Oliver stepped into the living room. When he saw me, he scowled.

"Were you listening to that?"

"I'm sorry," I said quickly, my cheeks warm. "I wasn't trying to, but you guys were shouting and it was kinda hard not to hear."

"God dammit!" Oliver swore and kicked the armchair in front of him. Then he dropped down in the seat and buried his face in his hands. After three painfully long seconds he said, "Sorry for yelling, Stella. You didn't do anything wrong."

As I looked at him I was hit with another wave of guilt, but I pushed the feeling away. "Do you want to talk about it?" I asked tentatively, and he was quiet for so long that I thought maybe he hadn't heard my question.

"Thanks for the offer," he finally said without looking at me. "Maybe tomorrow. Right now I kinda want to be alone."

"Oh, okay," I said after swallowing a few times. It hurt that he didn't want my comfort, but he sounded so dejected that I couldn't be mad and I left him in the living room to his thoughts.

At first, I didn't know where I was going—maybe the office where I originally planned to slip off to or one of the many balconies where I could get some fresh air—and I wandered down the hall slowly, trying to process what just happened.

This most recent fight helped clear up some of the mystery

surrounding the band's breakup rumors, filling in details that I'd been oblivious to, but I wanted the full picture. Xander hadn't returned to the hotel with the rest of the band, and with JJ gone and Oliver not willing to talk, there was only one person I could ask.

I hesitated when I reached Alec's door. He was a hard person to gauge, and I didn't know if he'd even be willing to talk to me. I twisted my nose stud around a few times before taking a deep breath and knocking on the door. There was no answer, but the light was on and I could hear someone moving around inside.

"Alec?" I called, knocking again. I bet he had his headphones in and couldn't even hear me. After a moment of silent debate, I twisted the doorknob and poked my head in. Sure enough, Alec was pacing the room, buds in his ears. "Sorry," I said, when he turned to me. "I knocked, but you didn't answer."

"Hi, Stella," he said, and I took that as an invitation to come in.

"What's going on?" I asked, not beating around the bush. As the question left my lips, a million more came forward. "I mean, with the band. Why were JJ and Oliver so mad at each other? Is the label making you do something you don't like?"

Alec turned toward the window and fixed his gaze on the city outside. "It's kind of a long story."

"I don't have anywhere else to be," I said, which wasn't entirely true. My latest blog post was almost due, but I still had some time. I needed to hear what Alec was going to say.

"All right," he said, breathing a long sigh; it wasn't one of exasperation, but of weariness. He gestured toward the bed. "Do you want to sit?"

Nodding, I tucked a leg under my butt as I plopped down. Alec sat next to me, but instead of diving into the story like I thought he would, he pulled his headphones from his neck. Without a word, he handed them to me.

Curious, I stuffed one of the buds into my ear. It was silent as Alec searched for something on his iPod, but then he clicked a button and a song started to play. It was grungier than the music I usually listened to, but the feedback effect with the song's slow tempo and gruff vocalist worked well together. My eyes closed as I enjoyed the rest of the song. There was something strange about it—I knew I'd never heard it before, and yet I had.

When the music faded out, I handed the headphones back to Alec. "It was good. Who is it?"

"Infinity and Beyond," Alec said, watching me closely.

"Bull," I said, but I knew he wasn't lying. It was Oliver's voice that I recognized. Without the backdrop of a sickly sweet melody, his voice opened up, the sound throatier and layered with edge.

"This is one of their old songs," he said. "Before we were the Heartbreakers."

"They were so good," I said. *What happened?* I almost asked, but I didn't want to insult Alec. I carefully worded what I asked next: "Why'd they change?"

Alec ignored my question and chose to respond with another. "Did anyone ever tell you how this all happened?" he asked, waving his hand around.

"You mean the band?" I responded. "Yeah, Oliver did. Isn't your dad the CEO of Mongo Records?"

He nodded. "Yeah, and he didn't want me to be a musician." Oliver had told me that too, but I wasn't going to interrupt Alec's story. "And he definitely didn't want to sign me."

"Why not?"

"Ever heard of Jackson Williams before?" he asked, and I shook my head. "Not surprised. He was a one-hit wonder. My dad took him on a few years after he started the record label. He helped Jackson produce his first single. It did really well, but then Jackson wanted to do his own thing, take his music in a completely different direction."

"So what happened?"

"My dad let him because he's family. Jackson is my cousin, his nephew. When the record flopped, my dad blamed himself."

I frowned. "It was just one record, right? That happens to artists all the time."

"Yeah, but this…" Alec said, shaking his head, "this one was bad. Like destroyed-his-career bad."

I suddenly realized where he was going with this. "And he didn't want that to happen to you."

Alec nodded. "He wouldn't even take a chance." His eyes flashed with a rage so fierce that I leaned away—not because I was scared, but because I'd never seen such raw emotion from him before— but Alec clenched his fists, reining in his anger, and it passed as quickly as it appeared. "I was good, *really* good, and he wouldn't even listen."

I pursed my lips as a growing annoyance for Alec's father built inside of me. "What'd you do?"

"I wasn't willing to let it go," he said. "I told myself there were other labels, different producers, more chances for me, but nothing seemed to work out. Nobody wanted to take on a kid whose own dad didn't believe in him. That's when I found Oliver, JJ, and Xander. It was totally by accident. I was just surfing YouTube, watching music videos and stuff, and then I came across this band. They were sick, and I knew my dad would want them, so I emailed Oliver saying I could get them a meeting, but only if they let me join."

"You were right," I said, and for the first time since Alec started his story, a smile spread across my face. "Your dad liked them."

"He still hated the idea of my involvement, but eventually he agreed to sign them, me included. Of course, there was a catch—we had to agree to a whole list of conditions."

I'd gathered as much from past conversations with Oliver and his fights with JJ, but I wanted to know all the details. "Like what?"

"Everything. He wanted complete control—the music, our image, even the name of the band. He wanted to make sure what happened with Jackson wouldn't happen again, and we went along with it," Alec said. He was speaking quickly now, the words flowing from his mouth. His voice was on the verge of cracking, and I knew the more Alec spoke about this, the harder it was for him to hide his mounting anger. "But now, even though we're more successful than anyone ever thought we'd be, my dad won't loosen the reins. He's strangling us."

"What's that got to do with JJ being pissed at Oliver?" I asked in a gentle voice.

"JJ's sick of doing whatever the label says. He wants us to write our own music again. Actually, we all do, but Oliver..." Alec grunted in frustration. "It's like he's on my dad's side. He refuses to go against him, even though we all know he misses how things used to be. JJ and Oliver started fighting when we left for the tour. It got so bad that rumors started spreading about us breaking up. Things cooled off for a little bit when you joined us, and I thought maybe they'd settled things, but then...well, you heard what happened."

When Alec finally finished, he glanced at me with an old-before-his-time look. My heart sank as I stared back at him, and it was impossible not to sense the pain wafting off him in waves. He thought *he* was responsible for this whole mess—the rules, the arguing, the rumors. I desperately wanted to say something, anything that would ease his guilt, but I had a feeling it wouldn't matter what I said.

I tried anyway. "It's not your fault, you know," I said, reaching out to comfort him.

Alec looked down at our touching hands before making eye contact with me and shaking his head. "But I forced them to let me join their band."

"You didn't force them to do anything," I told him. "They could have said no."

"I guess," Alec said. "It doesn't really matter though, does it? Oliver and JJ are fighting, and my dad is still being an asshole."

"Maybe," I said, a small smile forming on my lips, "but I think I have an idea. Do you mind if I borrow your iPod?"

☆♭♪

"You did *what?*"

It was early morning, and I was sitting at the kitchen counter, legs dangling from the bar stool, in the boys' current hotel suite. They had a show in the evening, so we were all fueling up before the busy day. Courtney's assistant had dropped off breakfast, an assortment of Panera bagels, four different flavors of cream cheese, and orange juice.

Yesterday's fight still lingered in the air, and everyone was relatively quiet. That was, until I told Oliver that I'd added an Infinity and Beyond song to my blog update last night. It was the first time I'd added music to a post, but Paul had shown me how to do it when he first taught me how to use the blog, and it had been simple.

I didn't do it to piss off Oliver or cause more drama. I wanted to know how the Heartbreakers' fans would react to such a different style of music. Alec helped me select which Infinity and Beyond song to use, and I prompted the boys' fans to give me feedback once they'd given it a listen. I didn't once mention that the song was Oliver, JJ, and Xander's from pre-Heartbreakers days, because I wanted an unbiased opinion.

"Why are you so angry?" I asked, calmly spreading veggie cream cheese on my last bite of bagel. "I've been meaning to add music to my posts, and I thought using one of your old tracks was the perfect way to start off."

"Well, you thought wrong," Oliver snapped.

"But it's a great song," I said, defending the music and myself. "Besides, it's not like I told people it's yours."

"You still shouldn't have done that," Oliver was saying, but JJ had a completely different reaction. He leaned forward in his chair and actually set down his bagel.

"You really liked it?" he asked. "No joke?"

"I did," I told him. "Promise."

"It doesn't matter what you think, Stella," Oliver said.

That hurt, but I ignored his comment. "Would you care if your fans liked it?"

"No!" he said, shaking his head, and I knew he wasn't really hearing what I was saying. His knuckles were white from gripping the countertop, and beads of sweat were gathering on his forehead. "You need to take it down. Now."

"Would you just shut up and listen to her for a moment?" JJ said to Oliver.

And that's when Alec took over. He had his laptop ready to go, my latest blog post already pulled up, and all he had to do was turn on the volume. When Oliver's voice started playing from the speakers, Alec spun his computer around and pushed it across the counter. "Just read what people are saying."

JJ's chair squeaked as he scrambled up to get a good look. Oliver, on the other hand, was glaring at Alec and me. There was a harried look about his eyes, but then JJ said, "Oh wow!" and his gaze flickered down to the screen. Slowly, as JJ scrolled through the hundreds of comments that had amassed in one night, his face lightened.

"Oliver," I said, and then the words poured out of my mouth as fast as possible. "Look at all the people who love your song. They don't even know it's yours, but they still want more."

Oliver stayed quiet, but JJ slapped the counter. "I told you," he said, waving his finger in Oliver's face. "Didn't I say people would like it?" I shot JJ a look that said "not helping," and he instantly shut up.

Then Alec took his turn appealing to Oliver. "I know you don't want to piss my dad off, but aren't you tired of playing the same old crap? We need to show him we can be more than the boy band he's written us off to be. We need to shake things up, make some kind of change, but we can't do that without you."

Seconds passed before Oliver said anything. He was so still and quiet that I thought he was trying to contain his anger. The rest of the guys looked nervous: JJ was rocking back and forth on the heels of his feet, Xander kept chewing on his bottom lip, and Alec's mouth was set in a hard line.

Finally he said, "What do you suggest we do?"

I let out a breath of relief, and Alec quickly answered him. "We do what JJ said. We start by playing one of your old songs. Tonight. At the concert."

☆ ♭ ♫

"So we're going to do something a bit different tonight," Oliver said near the end of the concert. "How does that sound?"

Finally, I thought. I had been waiting all night for this moment. The boys refused to tell me when they planned to perform one of their old songs. They wanted it to be a surprise even for me, and no amount of begging had swayed them. As the concert inched closer to the end, one song at a time, I was starting to fear that the boys had chickened out and changed their minds.

Oliver paused as he waited for a response, and he was answered with cheers from the crowd. A light feeling took hold of my chest, and I surprised myself by letting out a quick whoop of excitement and cheering with them.

I felt someone come up beside me. "Do you know what he's doing?" Courtney asked me. "Why are they deviating from the set list?"

"Sorry," I said. "Haven't the slightest idea."

I bit my lip as I tried to contain my smile, and then I crossed my arms and leaned back against the wall as I settled in to listen. Courtney was grumbling to herself and frowning down at her clipboard, but when Oliver started to speak again, she looked back up to watch him.

"This next song might seem new, but it's actually an oldie," he was saying. "We've never performed it before." He paused for a brief second. "Until now."

A ripple of anticipation swept through the arena, and everything got really quiet. It was electric how in sync the audience was with the band. From my spot backstage I could see everything the boys could, and I was starting to understand how playing gave them a rush. I could feel the adrenaline start to flood through my veins, and I rose on my toes and leaned in closer.

My eyes stayed on Oliver. I could see how nervous he was from the rise and fall of his shoulders as he took a deep breath and the way he gripped his guitar tightly. There was a long moment of hesitation, and he looked back at the rest of his bandmates. Xander offered him a thumbs-up, JJ raised his drumsticks in salute, and Alec gave him a quick nod of encouragement.

Oliver bowed his head. I could see his lips moving as he recited something to himself, and then he turned back around to face the crowd. "This song is called 'The Missing Pieces,'" he said as he flipped his bangs out of his eyes, "and I'd like to dedicate this to a special person who gave me the courage to stand up here tonight and share it with you all."

My gasp was inaudible over the sound of Oliver starting to sing, but I could feel the tightening in my chest as I sucked in a sharp breath.

Courtney glanced at me with a pointed look. "Haven't the slightest idea, huh?" she said, but I was too shocked to care if she was mad.

I glanced up at her with wide eyes. "Did he just…"

"Dedicate a song to 'someone special'?" she finished for me. "Yes, he did." Something about her own words must have struck Courtney, because she tilted her head to the side. "You know, he's never done that before."

"Ever?"

"No," Courtney said, her lips forming a smile. "Not for anyone."

When the boys came offstage three minutes later, leaping and bouncing and slapping each other's shoulders, I was still frozen. Everyone loved the song, and by the end of it, most of the audience was swaying back and forth with cell phones and lighters held high in the air. My mind was still reeling from what Courtney had said, so most of the lyrics washed right over me, but I knew I loved the song.

"That was frickin' awesome!" Oliver shouted, punching his fists in the air. When he saw me standing a few feet away, he rushed over, and before I realized it, he scooped me up and spun me around in the air. "Did you hear us, Stella? We killed it!"

"I can't believe we just did that," Xander exclaimed. "That was crazy." He was shaking his head in disbelief, but his eyes were gleaming. Alec stood next to him with a full-blown grin stretching across his face.

"You guys were amazing," I said when Oliver set me down. My voice was high and giddy.

"No, you're amazing," Oliver said, cupping my face in his hands. He quickly pressed his lips to mine before pulling away to continue jumping up and down, still celebrating the moment.

"Guys, listen," JJ said, turning back toward the stage. There was an encore at the end of every concert, but this was different. The chant from the crowd was thundering, and I could feel it pounding against my heart.

Courtney appeared again, hands on her hips. "I have no clue what the hell just happened," she said, her face tight. Everyone stopped. She turned her stern glare on each of the boys, and I was afraid she would lash out, but then she smirked. "But you four need to get your butts back out there."

Nobody spoke for a long second, but then JJ started laughing, and then we were all laughing. The stage crew handed the boys' instruments back to them, and they started moving toward the chanting crowd, wild smiles commanding their faces. Just as they were about to step back onstage, Oliver spun around and reached out to me.

"Thank you," he said, grabbing my hand. He squeezed my fingers and gave me one last dazzling look. Then he was racing out toward the stage, and the crowd was chanting his name.

CHAPTER 20

"I like that one," Paul said, using the pen in his hand to point to my screen. "It's priceless."

We were in the process of finalizing this week's post for the blog. There was only room for one more picture, and we'd narrowed it down to the last two potentials.

"Yeah, that's a good one," I said and clicked on the image.

It was a picture of JJ with his hand propped on his hip. He looked like a total diva, but that wasn't why the picture was priceless.

A couple weeks had passed without any of Oliver's usual pranks, so JJ received quite the surprise yesterday morning when he got dressed. Every one of his shirts had been cut so that there were two circular holes, one over each side of his chest, *Mean Girls* style. I had to give credit to Oliver—it was impressive that he'd found enough time in a single night to cut up all the tops JJ owned. JJ took the joke surprisingly well—I, for one, would have been pissed if someone purposely ruined any of my clothes—but for the entire morning, JJ pranced around the hotel room in one of his new designs, nipples on full display as he quoted Regina George. That's when I'd managed to get the picture.

"Perfect," Paul said, dropping his pen and sitting back in his chair. "You can finish off the rest of this stuff, right?"

"Yup. As soon as all these pictures finish loading, I'll add some captions and we'll be all set to upload."

"Wonderful," he said, "because there's something I've been meaning to discuss with you. It's about your contract."

I stopped what I was doing and turned to face Paul. Because of Cara's cancer, I didn't work a high-school job, which meant I'd never had a boss before Paul. In terms of good bosses, I was fairly positive that he was as cool as they came, regardless of my lack of past employers to compare him to. Most of the time he gave me free range over the blog, and when we did work on things together, I felt like I was hanging out with a friend. But now his tone took on a more serious note, and I was reminded of my position as his employee.

"My contract," I repeated, as I sat up in my seat. Was something wrong?

Paul nodded. "The fans' reaction to the blog has been phenomenal, Stella. You've done such a great job so far."

"Oh," I said, my shoulders relaxing. "Thank you."

"Of course, darling. I wouldn't say that if I didn't mean it. The reason I wanted to talk to you is because I can't imagine what I'm going to do without you."

"I—what?"

"I want to extend your contract. Well—actually, I want to make you my full-time employee."

I don't know what I was expecting Paul to say, but a new job offer wasn't it. It was so left field that I couldn't even figure out if what I was feeling was excitement or joy or pride. Probably all three.

Reaching up, I touched my nose out of habit, running my finger over the diamond stud, and I had a sudden flash of the girl from my English class freshman year—her intimidating bull ring and the wild purple hair that reminded me of octopus tentacles—and I wondered: If she saw me now, would she still remember me as one of the Samuel triplets? My appearance hadn't changed much, but I suddenly felt so different from the girl I was then, even the girl I was two months ago.

By joining the Heartbreakers on tour, I'd finally taken back some of the time—my moments of independence—that I thought I'd lost in high school. Here I was, running my own photography website and applying to SVA. When I'd decided to accept Paul's first offer, I thought I'd be returning home in two months. But so much had happened in such a short time. Did I want to go home or did I want to stay on with the band? What if there was something else out there for me?

"I don't want to pressure you, Stella," Paul said when I didn't answer. "I'll leave you alone to think things over, and you can get back to me when you're ready."

Paul quietly collected his things, and when he was gone, I was left wondering: What do I do next?

☆♭♫

I felt Oliver's eyes on me. "Have you made up your mind yet?" he asked.

I sighed and hit "pause." For this particular leg of the boys' tour, we were traveling via tour bus, and Oliver and I were crammed onto the small lounge couch watching another James Bond movie.

"Oliver," I said. I kept my voice low as I glanced at Alec and Xander. They were busy playing a video game across from us, and JJ was in one of the back bunks sleeping. "It hasn't even been two days yet. Give me a break."

He was the first and only person I'd told about Paul's new job offer. It wasn't that I didn't want the rest of the band to know, but I needed some time to think through my options before all the boys ganged up on me, urging me to stay.

Oliver did a good job of downplaying his excitement when he heard the news, but I still sensed that he was eager for me to accept. He made a point of talking about it as much as possible, and when he started fidgeting thirty minutes into *Casino Royal*, I'd known it wouldn't take long until he brought it back up.

My answer wasn't what he wanted to hear. "Yeah, I know," he said sheepishly. "I'm just excited you'll get to spend more time with us."

He said "us" as in the band, but I knew he really meant him. And that was my main dilemma. Things with Oliver were going so well, but what would happen if I was back home or at school while he was traveling the world? Would a relationship even be possible? I was afraid that turning down Paul's offer would mean giving up Oliver.

In addition, since sending in my application, I'd spent more and more time researching SVA, reading about campus and the different courses I could take. I could gain invaluable experience in New York that I would never get if I continued to work for the band. On the other hand, what if turning down Paul's job meant letting go of the best opportunity I'd ever have in my life? If I chose Paul and the Heartbreakers, did that mean I was playing it safe?

Completely lost in thought, I didn't realize that I'd forgotten to respond to Oliver. Or listen to him for that matter, because apparently he was still talking to me.

"Stella, you in there?" he asked, waving a hand in front of my face.

"Huh?"

"I said I have something for you." He leaned back into the couch, trying to give himself enough room to dig something out of his pocket. Whatever it was, it was big and bulky, so he ended up having to stand to free it. Finally he produced a tiny box with a gold ribbon tied around it. The wrapping paper was the same color as the aqua strand in my hair, and it looked suspiciously like a jewelry box.

"Oliver, you didn't need to get me anything," I said, suddenly forgetting my problems. Smiling, I turned the box over in my hands. "What is it? Give me a clue."

He bumped his shoulder into mine as he grinned back at me. "Just open it."

"You're no fun," I said, but I looked down at the box and slipped off the ribbon. When I tore away the paper and lifted the cover, there was a tiny, silver music note resting between the cushions.

"It's a charm from my mother's bracelet," he explained before I could even ask. "I thought you could put it on your camera. You know, for good luck. Otherwise you can just wear it on a necklace." He shoved his hands in his pockets as if he expected me to think the idea was stupid.

"Wow, Oliver." I pulled it out and held it up in the light. "It's beautiful."

The charm was stunning, but I was blown away by the fact that it was his mother's. Oliver had only mentioned her once before, and now he was giving me something that belonged to her?

"So you like it?" he asked, and I could tell he was holding his breath.

"I think it's perfect," I told him. "I'm just curious—is your mom okay with it? This bracelet of hers sounds like something special."

Oliver paused, his eyes flickering away from me for a moment. "She hasn't worn the bracelet in a long time."

"So…she's okay with you giving me the charm?"

"Yeah, totally," he said and waved me off.

I watched him for a moment. As soon as I'd started asking questions about his mother, he'd tensed up and I just wanted to know why. Did they have a bad relationship? If that was the case, I doubt she'd give him a charm off her bracelet so willingly. "Well, your mom sounds cool," I said after a few seconds of consideration. Oliver took his bottom lip into his mouth and didn't say anything so I added, "I'd like to meet her sometime."

"Yeah," he said, nodding his head absentmindedly. "I bet she'd like that too."

I could already see him folding in on himself, no longer wanting to talk, so I was quick to change the subject. "So is there a specific occasion?" I asked. It occurred to me that Oliver might be trying to bribe me into accepting Paul's new contract. "For the gift, I mean."

His shoulders relaxed, and he looked down at me, a slow half-grin pulling at his lips. "Kind of," he said. "There's this movie premiere in LA the band has to attend. Would you like to go?"

"Movie premiere," I repeated.

"Yeah, with me," he added.

It sounded like Oliver had just asked me on an actual public date, but all my brain could process was movie premiere. "As in, the red carpet?"

"Um, yeah," Oliver said. "Is that a problem?"

"You want me," I said to clarify, "with you, like, on the red carpet?"

This made Oliver smirk. "Like no," he joked, trying not to laugh. "I was actually hoping you'd turn me down so I could go with JJ instead."

"Wow," was all I could say.

Oliver asking me to the movie premiere was huge! Just thinking about it made me feel giddy, and at the same time it was a relief. That he wanted to be seen in public with me was a step forward. I'd been thinking about our relationship a lot lately, especially considering the choices I had to make in the near future, and I realized that keeping the whole thing a secret didn't sit well with me. So I'd confessed to Cara that the only reason I feared going public with Oliver was the media digging into our private lives.

"What kind of dirt could they possibly find on us?" Cara had asked as she laughed into the phone. "We were homeschooled. It's not like we had many opportunities to rob a bank or get arrested."

"But what if they write about your cancer?" I asked.

Cara scoffed. "So what? Like that's something we don't already know."

Our conversation cheered me up. If Cara didn't care, then we didn't need to date in secret for her sake. I'd been meaning to talk to Oliver about it for days, but there hadn't been any good chances and now he'd beaten me to it.

"I take that as a yes?" Oliver asked, his eyes sparkling with amusement. Unable to respond, I nodded my head. "Good," he said with a crisp nod. The corners of his mouth rose in a crooked grin, and then he gently pressed his lips to my forehead, still smiling.

After a minute or two of grinning to myself, I grabbed my camera off the table in front of us and hooked the charm onto its strap. "I still don't know why you needed to get me a gift," I said. "I'm not complaining or anything, but were you trying to butter me up?"

"Well," Oliver said, smirking at me, "I figured it wouldn't hurt."

☆ ♭ ♫

"You got a letter," Drew told me over the phone. "I think it might be some kind of junk mail."

I heard the sound of shuffling paper on his end of the line, and I wondered if he was checking the mail pile as we spoke. Mom always dumped it by the fruit bowl, and there was a clear vision in my head of him leaning against the counter, phone wedged between his shoulder and ear as he went through it all.

"Oh yeah?" I said. I was lying in a bunk on the tour bus, picking at my nail polish. Being away from home was becoming much less painful the more time I spent with the Heartbreakers, but thinking about my brother standing in our kitchen doing something as ordinary as sorting the mail sent a pang through my heart. "Who's it from?"

We'd been talking for the past hour, catching up on what was happening in each other's lives. Besides finishing the last book on his summer reading list, Drew was spending as much time as possible with Cara before he left for school. The final round of her chemo had finished, and soon she'd have the high-dose treatment before her transplant.

"The School of Visual Arts? Looks like some mass recruitment letter. Want me to toss it?"

I shot straight up in bed and nearly slammed my head on the bunk above. "Oh my God," I gasped. "Open it, Drew!"

"What is it?" he asked, and I heard the tearing of paper. "It's a pretty thick letter."

"What does it say?" I was too eager to answer his question.

"Dear Ms. Samuel," he said, reading it off to me. "On behalf of the Admission Committee, it is my pleasure to offer you acceptance to SVA—wait, Stella. Did you apply to another college?"

"Holy crap, are you shitting me?" Squeezing my eyes shut, I tried to keep from squealing as I danced in place. Prior to this moment, I hadn't realized how much I was anticipating my potential acceptance.

"What's going on?"

"Drew," I said, after I calmed down enough to explain. "I just got accepted into a school with one of the top photography programs in the country."

"Really, Rocket? That's awesome! Does Cara know about this?"

"Not yet," I told him. "Honestly, I just applied for kicks. It was all Xander's idea." From there, I brought Drew up to speed on Paul's new job offer and how I didn't know what I was going to do.

"Sounds like you have a tough choice to make," he said. "But aren't you glad you decided to go in the first place?"

"Yeah," I said, nodding and smiling. "Yeah, I am."

CHAPTER 21

On the morning of the movie premiere, I still didn't have an outfit to wear. Oliver was planning on taking me shopping, but then his phone rang.

"Hello?" He started to pace around the room, answering whoever was on the other end with a series of "yeses." Finally he told the caller that he would be there shortly and hung up.

"What's going on?" I asked.

"Have to run downtown and stop by Mongo headquarters," he explained. "You don't mind going shopping without me, do you?"

"No, but is everything okay?"

"Yeah," he said, shoving his phone into his pocket. He leaned over and kissed my forehead. "Have fun, okay? See you tonight."

Five dresses, three pairs of heels, and two necklaces later, I managed to make it back to the hotel without spending all the money I had earned over the past month. JJ was on the couch playing a video game when I stepped in, so I dropped my shopping bags and plopped down next to him.

"I'm wiped," I told him. Maybe I'd have time for a nap before we needed to get ready.

"I can see that," he said. "Looks like you bought an entire mall."

"I couldn't make up my mind," I told him sheepishly.

"On what?"

"Which dress to wear tonight, so I just got them all."

JJ set down the controller and turned to me. "Well, let's see them. I'll help you pick."

So I pulled each dress out of the bag. First was the flowing, purple A-line with a sparkly bodice.

"Nope. Too prommy," JJ said as I held it up against my chest. Next I pulled out a long, red mermaid gown, which had probably been my most expensive purchase of the day. "Hmm," JJ said, stroking his chin as he considered. "That has potential. Next."

Then there was the light-blue high-low dress, which JJ nixed because he thought it was too little-girlish, and a halter that he didn't like because it was overwhelmingly pink. There was only one dress left, and I was worried that my shopping trip had been a complete failure.

"Last one," I said, pulling the dress out. I'd spotted it in the window of a boutique on my way back to the hotel, so I'd stopped to try it on. It was the definition of a little black dress—vintage cocktail, but with edgy lace and tarnished golden studs—one that could only be described as Marilyn Monroe meets modern day.

"That one, definitely," JJ said without hesitation as the tissue paper fell away.

"You really think so?"

"No contest."

"Okay." I smiled to myself, happy that one of my choices would work. "But don't tell Oliver. I want it to be a surprise. Is he back yet?"

JJ shrugged, so I left my bags on the coffee table and went in search of him. After knocking on his door, I poked my head inside. On the bed was his suitcase. It was flung open and a few clothing items had spilled out onto the comforter. A pair of shoes had been kicked off next to the armchair, but there were no other signs of him.

The reading lamp had been left on, so I went over to the table to turn it off. Only then did I notice the book resting on the cushion of the armchair. Scooping it up, I sat down and opened the cover. When I saw the first page, I realized that it wasn't a book. It was a photo album. Smiling up at me was a picture of us together, the first day we'd met in Chicago. God, that felt so long ago.

As I flipped through the plastic pages, I realized that Oliver had been printing out photographs I posted on my blog and adding them to his personal collection. The pictures were mainly the ones just of us, but there were a few with the other guys as well. By the time I reached the last page, a huge grin spread across my face. Knowing that I was important enough to Oliver for him to make a photo album of us made me feel loopy in a happy-go-lucky way.

"Stella?" Xander asked, pushing open the door. "Is Oliver here?"

"No," I said, smiling like a crazy person. "I have no clue where he is."

"Why do you look so happy?"

"Oh nothing," I said, biting back my grin.

"Okay," Xander said, giving me a strange look. "Well, we should probably start getting ready for tonight."

"All right," I said. "I'm going to head back to my room and shower."

"When you're done, Julie and Ken will be here."

Julie and Ken were the boys' makeup artist and hair stylist. I'd met the beauty team a plethora of times when the boys needed to get ready for concerts or interviews or any other kind of public appearance, but they'd never styled me before.

"They're going to help me get ready?" I asked, bouncing from foot to foot.

"Yeah, silly," he said with a grin. "You are making a public appearance with us tonight."

"Oh my God," I gushed, and I knew I sounded exactly like Cara. "This is so awesome."

I hurried through my shower routine, barely able to rein in my excitement for the night. After stepping out onto the mat, I wrapped a robe around myself and rushed back to the boys' suite. The kitchen table had been turned into a salon complete with makeup, styling gel, a hair dryer, a curling iron, and a large range of combs and brushes. Alec was already sitting in one of the chairs while Ken worked on his signature hair style.

"Hi, Stella," Julie said when she spotted me. "I hear you're going to the premiere tonight."

"Yup," I said, grinning at her.

"All right, why don't you sit down and I'll get started on your makeup."

My whole transformation took nearly three hours. Julie went slowly, planning everything from my eye shadow down to my lips. After a year of only doing the boys' makeup, which consisted of a layer of foundation to smooth out any blemishes, working on a girl must have been a treat. In the end, she decided on a golden, smoky eye and bright-red lips.

After my makeup was finished, Ken took his turn. First, he curled my hair into elegant waves. Then he took the bottom layer of my hair, pulled it back into a ponytail, and pinned it up. After almost a full can of hair spray, he managed to mold my hair into a beautiful marcel wave with my blue streak running through the middle like a bolt of blue lightning.

"You like?" he asked when he finally held up a mirror for me to see.

"Can you do my hair every day?" I asked jokingly.

I never thought I'd use the term to describe myself, but I looked sophisticated. After I pulled on my black dress and heels, I twirled in front of my bathroom mirror to see my completed look. Not to brag, but Oliver was going to be blown away.

"Damn," someone whistled. I turned to see JJ resting against the door frame, looking smart in a black tuxedo. "Looking like a hot mama tonight."

"You think?" I asked, glancing at my dress.

JJ looked me up and down in a not-so-subtle way. A slow smirk pulled at his lips, and he stepped up to me. "Oliver's gonna blow his load when he sees you."

At this, I gasped and smacked JJ on the arm, pretending to be offended. In reality, his words were flattering even if I was too embarrassed to admit that out loud. "Do you always have to be so vulgar?"

"What?" he asked, pressing a hand to his heart in mock-offense. "That was a compliment."

I rolled my eyes. "In your own nasty, perverted way, I know you were trying to be nice," I said, "but still."

"What about me?" he asked with a pout. "Aren't you going to tell me how dashing I look?"

"I suppose you clean up nicely," I teased, which was stingy of me—JJ always looked handsome.

"That's it? Not so hot that you're going to dump Oliver for me?"

I shot JJ a pointed look. He cracked a grin in response, and soon we were both laughing. As much as JJ flirted with me, I knew he didn't mean anything by it. JJ was like that around any girl, he was just that type of guy, and it never affected our relationship in a negative way. Truthfully, he was always so easygoing and entertaining that I felt like we'd been friends for years, ones that were so comfortable around each other that we could joke about anything.

It surprised me that he didn't have a girlfriend. He was hilarious and kind, not to mention that most of the female population would bend over backward to date him. I'd asked him about it one afternoon, and he explained that he took relationships very seriously. Since the boys' lives were so hectic and busy, JJ said he'd never be able to devote enough of his time to make a girl happy, and I thought that was adorable.

"Hey, Stella?" Xander called, bursting into the bedroom.

I looked up at him, noting the concern in his voice. "Yeah?"

"Oliver hasn't—whoa," he said, stopping when he saw me.

"She's hot, right?" JJ asked, nodding at his friend.

Xander blushed. "Yeah," he said sheepishly. "You look nice, Stella."

"Thanks. You look good yourself," I told him. "What were you going to say about Oliver?"

"He hasn't called you, has he?" he asked, trying to sound hopeful.

"No, why?" I'd checked my phone several times today, so I knew I had no new messages, but I reached for my cell out of instinct.

"He still hasn't shown up yet," Xander said, his forehead wrinkling with worry. His words made me frown. "It isn't like him to just disappear."

"Have you talked to Courtney?" I asked. If anyone knew where Oliver was it would be her. She always kept tabs on the boys, not because she was a control freak and it was her job, but because if she didn't, they'd probably get in to some kind of mischief.

"That's the strange thing," Xander said, the lines in his brow deepening. "I called her, and she doesn't seem worried at all."

"What?" JJ responded, and joined us in frowning. "That doesn't sound like Courtney. Normally she'd freak out."

Xander nodded quickly in agreement. "I know, right? She told us to meet her in the lobby in ten, so I guess we'll have to ask her then."

Ten minutes passed quickly, and Oliver still hadn't returned. All the excitement I felt for the evening was slowly trickling away, and it was being replaced with a stomach dropping feeling.

Alec looked down at his phone. "Guys, we need to leave."

"I think I'm going to stay here," I told the boys. If something bad had happened to Oliver, I didn't want to show up at the movie premiere without him.

"You sure?" Alec asked me.

I nodded and said, "So I guess I'll see you guys there?"

"You bet," Xander said and gave me a hug.

"Good luck," JJ added, flashing me a wicked grin. "Don't trip on the carpet."

"Thanks," I said sarcastically, my heart suddenly racing.

When the door slammed shut, leaving me alone, I perched on the edge of the couch and waited for Oliver to arrive.

I waited. And then I waited some more. I looked down at my cell phone and saw that it was ten o'clock, and I knew that he wasn't coming. I sat there anyway, hoping that I was wrong. After that, I didn't keep track of the time, and the night passed in a blur. It must have been a little after midnight when the front door opened and a concerned voice called my name.

"Stella, are you here?" I hardly noticed as Xander joined me on the couch. "Hey, are you okay?" I didn't respond. I could barely hear him over the sound of the blood rushing in my ears.

"Stella?" JJ asked, crouching next to me. He waved a hand in front of my face. "Stella, snap out of it."

I blinked and looked up at them. Xander looked horrified, like he had been told someone died, and JJ was red in the face. Alec was standing behind them and he looked…deadly. The gleam in his eyes was almost frightening.

"He didn't come," I said finally and looked up at my friends.

"We know," Xander said. "We saw him there." He bit his lip, and I knew he was holding something back.

"What is it?" I asked. My heart was hammering against my chest in anticipation, but I could feel the dread like poison in my veins.

In that moment, I knew what he was going to say. Xander hesitated, as if he was afraid he was going to break my heart with a few simple words.

Alec said it for him. "Oliver went with someone else."

☆ ♭ ♫

She was a model. The boys hadn't wanted to tell me, but I made them. I had to see the girl Oliver went to the premiere with, the one he ditched me for. Apparently the two arrived shortly after the rest of the band, and when Oliver walked her down the red carpet, the paparazzi and reporters went crazy with speculation. It didn't take me long to google her, and I discovered that Amelia Rose had long, endless legs and stunning red hair.

"She's not Oliver's type at all," JJ said, snapping me back to reality. He was sitting on the opposite couch, and his mouth briefly settled into a white line. "When she stepped out of the limo with him, I was so shocked I almost..." He trailed off and shook his head. "I don't understand."

"Yeah," Xander added. "We've never met her before. She just came out of nowhere."

"Seriously?" Alec hissed, glaring at both of his bandmates. "You guys aren't helping."

"Right, sorry," JJ muttered, looking at me apologetically. Then a fierce look crossed his face and he leaned toward me. "When he gets back, I'm going to beat him senseless."

"Stella, you have to believe us," Xander said then, cutting off JJ before he could make any more threats. "As soon as we realized you weren't with Oliver we wanted to leave, but Courtney wouldn't let us."

"It's fine," I said, brushing the comment off. I wasn't upset with the boys—I was merely trying to sound removed, like Oliver's actions hadn't torn my insides apart and left me feeling gutted. They'd done nothing wrong. There was only one heartbreaker in this band.

Xander and Alec exchanged concerned looks, but I took no notice. As I stared at the picture of Amelia Rose glowing back at me on the computer screen, I realized that it didn't matter who Oliver went with. He could have gone with a gorilla and I would still have felt betrayed. Sure, it hurt that he had taken a beautiful girl instead of me, but what really upset me was how he'd stood me up with no warning. It just didn't make sense. The last time I saw Oliver, he was so excited to go with me. What had changed?

Obviously something had happened between when I saw him this morning and the premiere tonight. I just couldn't figure out what. Before I could think of an explanation, the front door slammed shut and we all froze. I knew it had to be Oliver finally returning, and the panic that rose in my chest made it hard to breathe.

I turned to Alec. "Please hide me," I said, letting out a tiny sob. "I don't want to see him right now."

The moment I realized that Oliver wasn't coming to pick me up for the premiere, I should have gone back to my own hotel room. But I'd been so shocked and completely confused about why he didn't show that I couldn't think straight. I kept telling myself that there was a perfectly logical reason for why Oliver did this. There *had* to be.

Alec held out his hand without a word, and as he helped me up,

I could see the understanding in his eyes. He guided me down the hall and into his room, and only when the door was firmly closed behind us did he speak.

"Stella," he said, his voice soft. "Are you okay?" I could tell from the way he asked his question that he knew I wasn't. But he asked anyway because Alec Williams wasn't as rigid and frosty as most people thought.

And that was all it took. The tears started, and I fell into his arms and wept. He stroked my hair, murmuring comforting words in my ear. At one point I heard angry shouts from somewhere else in the hotel suite, but I couldn't stop crying long enough to hear what was going on. I bawled and bawled, letting all of the heartbreak pour out of me like blood from a fresh wound.

I must have cried myself to sleep. When I opened my eyes, I could feel my hair sticking to my face where my tears had dried. Sitting up, I noticed that someone had tucked me into bed and pulled the covers up around my shoulders. That certain someone was sprawled out in an armchair, head tilted back and mouth wide open.

"Alec?" I whispered to see if he was awake.

He jumped with a snort. "Oh. Morning, Stella." He pulled himself into a sitting position. "Sleep well?" he asked after rubbing away his weariness.

"Oh my gosh, Alec!" I gasped, ignoring his question. "Did I take your bed last night?"

He dismissed me with a wave. "Don't worry about it. I'm fine."

The purple circles under his eyes said otherwise, and I knew he hadn't slept well at all. "But you guys have a concert tonight," I said, feeling horrible. "You need to be rested up."

As the words left my mouth, I realized their true meaning. The boys had a concert tonight, which meant I had to work. I would have to face Oliver.

Alec must have seen the horror on my face. "I'm sure if you talk to Paul, he'd understand if you didn't want to go."

"No," I said suddenly, surprising both of us. I felt like an empty shell, like all my insides really had been ripped out, especially my heart, but I wasn't going to let Oliver see that. More importantly, I wasn't going to let our relationship, or as I should call it now our past relationship, interfere with my job.

Because of Cara, I had years of experience with hiding my pain. I knew how to fake strength when all I really felt was helpless, like a blade of grass in the wind. This would be no different. Besides, I'd taken the job because it was an amazing opportunity, not because of Oliver. I wanted to be good at what I did, and I couldn't let Oliver ruin that.

"No?" Alec repeated, his eyebrows arched in confusion.

"I'm going to the concert," I said with as much resolve as I could muster.

"What? Why?" He sounded aghast, like I'd just told him I was going to jump off the top of a really tall building.

"Because," I responded slowly, making sure my voice didn't crack, "I'm not going to be pathetic and run away."

"Stella, that's not what I meant—"

"I know that," I said, standing up. "But I was a slobbery, snotting wreck last night, and I'm not going to let that happen again." When I finished my speech, Alec looked upset, and I realized that I probably sounded angry with him. Crossing the room, I leaned down and gave him a hug. "Thank you so much for taking care of me last night. I couldn't have asked for a better friend."

"Of course," he said when I pulled away. I could tell that he was still baffled by my sudden mood swing, but I wasn't going to let my problems affect him any longer. According to the clock on the nightstand, it was still early, and there was plenty of time for Alec to get some sleep before the day began.

"Why don't you sleep a little?" I suggested and pointed at the now-empty bed. "You can still get in a few good hours."

Alec was watching me, his face completely blank. After a few seconds, he finally nodded his head. "Yeah, good idea."

"All right then," I said as Alec unwound his headphones from around his iPod. "I'll see you later tonight."

☆ ♭ ♫

The rest of the day sucked majorly. To be more accurate, being around Oliver was nothing short of torture. But I had the boys for support—Alec, Xander, and JJ were giving him the cold shoulder. In turn, Oliver avoided us as best he could, which was why I panicked and froze when I heard him call my name after the boys' concert later that night.

"Stella."

The sound of his voice made me suck in a sharp breath. I held it in my chest as I tried to prepare for our upcoming conversation. What could he possibly have to say to me? Would I even be able to talk to him? After a few seconds, a tight, burning tension built up in my lungs, and I finally released my breath and turned around. When I saw him, my hands started to tremble and I quickly tucked them behind my back so he wouldn't see.

I made sure to hold his gaze as he approached. I still didn't know if I'd be able to say anything, to formulate some kind of speech so he'd know how much he'd hurt me, but if I couldn't, I hoped the look in my eyes would do all the talking.

"Hi," he said when he reached me.

The strain in his voice was so sad sounding, and suddenly I was hit with an urge to step into his arms. My heart screamed at me to move forward, to reach out and comfort him, but I knew better. Curling my toes in my shoes, I held my ground.

"Hi," I said, careful to keep my tone flat.

"I've been looking for you." He looked at me expectantly, like he was hoping I'd respond, but I decided to let him take the lead, so I pressed my lips together. Two very unpleasant seconds passed, and finally he said, "Can we talk for a moment?"

I rubbed my forehead before scraping back my bangs. "I'm tired, Oliver."

"Please?" he said. There was a desperate look in his eyes that made me sigh.

"Talk quickly," I told him.

"Okay." He gestured over his shoulder at an empty room. "But this needs to be private." Whatever he wanted to talk about, it must have been important, because Oliver risked grabbing my hand as he pulled me into the room.

"What do you want?" I snapped, yanking my hand away from him. Nothing good was going to come of this conversation. I could feel it.

He paused as if what he'd say next was more frightening than performing in front of thousands of fans, and the next three words that came out of his mouth were so unexpected that I was left speechless. "Iloveyou."

"I—what?" My brain was trying to comprehend what he'd said, but the words wouldn't register. It was like I was getting the same computer message over and over: *An unexpected error has occurred. Please try again.*

He cleared his throat and repeated himself, this time more slowly. "I said, I love you."

Oh, *hell* no. Crossing my arms, I tucked both my hands away to resist reaching out and slapping him. "You can't just stop caring, treat me like shit, and then turn around and say something like that."

Something flashed in Oliver's eyes. If it was anger, he kept it hidden well, because his words came out calmly. "You think I stopped caring about you?"

"Don't make this about me," I said, taking a step forward as my lips curled. "You were the one who stood me up, remember?"

"But I never stopped caring," he said defensively. "Trust me, hurting you was the last thing I wanted to do, but—"

"Stop!" I said and held up my hand. "You can't apologize and expect rainbows and butterflies. There's nothing you can say that will make up for what you did."

Instead of answering, Oliver turned away from me and yanked

on a handful of his hair. He cursed and swung his fist through the air before forcing himself to draw in a steady breath. "You're right," he finally said, his back still to me. "I can't give you the explanation you're looking for."

That's it? That's all he's going to say? "Fuck you, Oliver! You screwed with my heart, and I'm not even worth the truth?" I didn't want to cry in front of him, but I could feel my eyes stinging.

He turned back around. "Be as pissed at me as you want. I deserve it," he said. "But what I did—it had nothing to do with you."

"What are you talking about?" I said as I tried to swipe away my tears. "You're not making any sense."

"I can't tell you!" he snapped. He flinched at his own tone before shaking his head. "All you need to know is that you're still my star. Even if you hate me."

I stared up at him, pleading with my eyes. I needed something, anything, even if it was the smallest hint as to what had gone wrong between us. But he chose to look down at the ground, his mouth clamped shut.

"Whatever," I said, letting all the air and hope and anger rush out of me. My shoulders slumped. "I'm done."

Without looking back at him, I ran out of the room, trying to put as much distance between Oliver and myself as I could. When I found the closest bathroom I barricaded myself inside, ready to surrender to crying my eyes out, but then my phone buzzed. Glancing down at the caller ID, I laughed through my tears. Cara's number flashed across the screen. Between the concert and Oliver, I'd completely forgot that we'd made plans to talk today, and now, more than anything, hearing her voice was what I needed.

"Thank God it's you, Cara," I said when I picked up.

"Stella?" I froze. It wasn't Cara. It was my dad. And from the way he was trying to keep his voice from cracking, I knew something was wrong.

"Oh no," I whispered as my heart dropped into my stomach. "What's wrong?"

"It's your sister," he said quietly. "You need to come home."

CHAPTER 22

This was what I knew so far: Cara's graft had failed. Last week she'd finished her single round of high-dose chemotherapy, and two days after was the transplant. Apparently, she'd won the lottery of transplant failures, because autologous transplants were almost always a success. It meant Cara's own stem cells hadn't reestablished in her bone marrow.

"Rocket," Drew said, putting a hand my shoulder. "Don't put a hole in the floor. They'll be done soon."

But I couldn't stop fidgeting. For the past half an hour, I'd been pacing the hall of the pediatric floor. We were waiting for Cara's head doctor, Lisa Mitchell, and my parents to finish a meeting about different options moving forward. I hadn't even been able to see Cara since arriving, and the whole situation was driving me crazy.

To add to my frustration, I didn't really understand the graft failure. Before the treatment took place, Dr. Mitchell told us it would work. Now I wanted someone to explain what went wrong and then give me a solution—the "how" to saving my sister.

"Don't touch me," I said and shrugged off his hand.

"Hey, don't get mad at me," Drew said, glaring in my direction. "This isn't my fault."

There were circles under his eyes and his shirt was rumbled, and the realization that he'd probably stayed here overnight made me sigh. I slumped down on the bench outside Cara's room.

"I know," I said in a quiet voice. Drew was right—this wasn't his fault and I shouldn't take it out on him. I looked down at my hands, knowing there was only one person I could blame. This one was all on me…

The flight from Los Angeles to Minnesota had messed me up good. Buckled in at an altitude of thirty-five thousand feet above the ground, I didn't have much to do but sit and think. And think. And think. And it wasn't long until I was pulled down by that rip current, drowning in my own thoughts.

Why did I leave in the first place? Why couldn't I have trusted that horrible gut feeling I got after Paul first called me? The one that terrified me. From the start, I knew that leaving was a bad idea, but I'd convinced myself that there was only one way to face my fear—to go on some stupid quest of self-discovery by touring with the Heartbreakers.

I'd been so consumed by my fears and my problems that all I was thinking about was me, me, me. That was exactly what had happened when Cara got sick the first time. There were signs that something was wrong—her lack of energy and usual enthusiasm—but I was too busy living in my own little world to notice, and then *bam*! I was hit with the world's largest reality check. Yet somehow, impossibly, I'd managed to forget that and here I was. I'd left Cara again even when I should've known better.

There was a sound of a door opening and closing, and I looked up to see a woman wearing a white lab coat. She was probably somewhere in her midfifties, and her long, gray hair was pulled back into a simple ponytail—Dr. Mitchell at last.

"Stella," she said in acknowledgment when she saw me. "You got here quickly."

From there, Dr. Mitchell wasted no time in explaining Cara's situation. There were only a few causes for autologous graft failure. The first was extensive bone marrow fibrosis. I wasn't sure what that meant, but Dr. Mitchell assured us that this wasn't why Cara's transplant was unsuccessful. The second potential cause was viral illness, but Cara wasn't sick, at least not like that. The final possibility was failure due to certain types of chemo drugs, none of which had been used to treat Cara.

"Then why the hell didn't it work?" I demanded after she finished.

"Stella," my dad said, his voice a gentle warning.

I ignored him, not really caring that I was being rude. Both my parents had already heard what Dr. Mitchell was saying, and I just wanted her to get on with it. Instead, she was taking time to explain details she'd normally skip over.

"Sometimes," Dr. Mitchell said, "the reason for failure is unknown."

My vision started to cloud as I stared at Cara's doctor. How was *that* an answer? I wanted to punch her in the face, because really? What total bullshit. How could she not know why the treatment that was supposed to save Cara's life didn't work?

"That's it?" I snapped. "What's that supposed to mean?"

Dr. Mitchell looked down at the clipboard before her eyes flickered back up to me. "It means things don't look good," she said.

I gritted my teeth together for a painful moment, trying to contain my anger. It didn't work. "So she's just going to die because the shitty treatment you suggested didn't work for some unknown reason?"

"You need to lower your voice right now," my mom said, no nonsense. She reached out and grabbed my arm. "Just listen."

I knew this wasn't really Dr. Mitchell's fault, but I wanted to hear solutions, not bad news. I pulled away from my mom as hot tears streamed down my face. "How can you be so calm when she's just giving up on Cara?"

"I'm not giving up on your sister. There is still something we can do for her," Dr. Mitchell told me sternly. She glanced at my parents before continuing. "Since there was no determining factor for the transplant failure, I think Cara's best option is to have another."

She stared me straight in the eye as she made her announcement, almost as if it held some type of hidden meaning.

"How?" I asked.

"Stella," she told me slowly, "you'd be the perfect donor for your sister."

☆ ♭ ♫

I knew what my decision was in an instant. There was no way I *wouldn't* donate for Cara, so making that choice was as easy as flipping on a light switch. Dr. Mitchell called the transplant "syngeneic" or "syngepic" or something that started with an *s* and was along those lines. Basically, it was a procedure in which a cancer patient, Cara, received stem cells donated by an identical twin, me.

Even though my mind was already made up, I told everyone I

wanted some time to think things through, and I disappeared to the patient communication center where I could use a computer. There were some loose ends that needed attention before I could go through with the operation.

From the start, Cara's odds were never anything spectacular, but even if the world is ending, some people refuse to be beaten down. Not every cancer patient had the same optimism as my sister though, because while Cara's survival was unclear, some people were beaten from the start—Stage IV and terminal. I'd seen a few kids like that and, while some chose to chug along like my sister, most decided to get their things in order, to prepare for the irrevocable.

And that's what I was doing now, because the fantasy I had about becoming an actual photographer, someone like Bianca Bridge, was as terminal as it could get. Once I accepted the irrevocable, I could focus my attention on Cara.

There wasn't too much for me to do: I'd throw out my SVA acceptance letter and call Paul to decline his new job offer, but that wasn't the hard part. What I was dreading most was shutting down my website, especially after all the hard work I'd put in, but it had to be done. If I didn't, there would always be something left for me to regret.

I logged in to one of the hospital computers, pulled up the Internet, and typed in the address. My neck was stiff, and I rolled my shoulders as I waited for the page to load. When it did, I noticed a small, red number one next to my inbox, notifying me of a new message. I figured there was no harm in reading whatever it said before I deleted everything, so I clicked on the icon.

As per the hospital's usual crappy Wi-Fi, the page took a few seconds to load, but then I saw this:

Dear Ms. Samuel,

My name is Bethany Colt, and while we don't have much in common (I'm a forty-two-year-old housewife from New Jersey), we do share one connection—the terrible knowledge of how it feels to watch someone you love suffer. Like your sister, my daughter Stephanie has cancer. She was diagnosed with acute lymphocytic leukemia last year at the age of twelve.

Like most thirteen-year-old girls, Stephanie is crazy about the Heartbreakers. The walls of her room are plastered with their posters (much to my horror), and she's particularly fond of the blog you run called the Heartbreak Chronicles, as she enjoys keeping up with what's happening in the boys' lives. It was through the blog that I discovered your photography website.

I'm writing you this letter to express how truly moved I was by your gallery, especially the pictures you posted of your sister. The past few months have been very difficult for me. As Stephanie grows weaker, I feel like her cancer is claiming parts of me as well, and they're all the important pieces I need, like my heart and faith and bravery. But seeing your pictures has helped me take those pieces back. Not only does your work reflect your sister's inner strength, but it shows how loving someone so deeply is a source of courage. Courage to hope and courage to fight.

Thank you for giving me my fight back. By sharing your experience, you helped make someone else's more bearable.

Sincerely,
Beth

I read her message again and again. I kept thinking that if I studied the words long enough, if I read them just one more time, then maybe their meaning would finally click inside my head and I would understand. How could my pictures bring back what she'd lost, especially something as intangible as faith or strength? Was that really possible?

My question wasn't whether art was inspirational or not. I knew it was, because I could never forget when I saw my own inspiration for the first time—a little girl covered in mud, eyes ablaze with glee. That was Bianca's job though, to make people feel things. For me, photography was a personal endeavor. I'd never set out to re-create that spark for someone else, only to satisfy something inside myself. I never imagined helping a stranger, but assuming Beth meant what she said, that made *me* her Bianca Bridge.

Maybe my dream wasn't so terminal after all.

For the past four years I'd seen my camera as a crutch, my own personal way to deal with Cara's cancer. But I was wrong. I wasn't using photography to cope with her disease—photography was just something I was passionate about. I was using Cara to cope with my fear of the future. Suddenly I had all these choices to make, like whether I should continue working with the Heartbreakers or go to school, and that was overwhelming in a terrifying way. Coming home and leaving it all behind was my easy out.

I thought back to the conversation I'd had with Oliver, and how he'd said I blamed myself for her sickness. There was so much certainty in his voice, like it was the most obvious thing in the world. At the time, I'd thought he didn't understand, *couldn't* understand, the position I was in, but now it all made sense. It was Isaac Newton and an apple all over again, a sudden epiphany so strong it felt like I'd been struck on the head with a piece of fruit. All this time, I'd been paralyzed with guilt. Guilt for not noticing when Cara first got sick. As a result, I'd developed some weird, twisted psychological aversion to chasing my own dreams.

Oliver had said something else that night, something about absorbing the blow, and I'd brushed it off as nonsense. Reading Beth's letter made me understand. Life is never going to give you a break. It's a hard, unforgiving son of a bitch, and when it steamrolls you over, there are only two choices: stay down, or get back on your feet and fight. After Cara's diagnosis, I spent my time on the ground, surrendering out of fear, but now I needed to stand up and throw a few punches myself.

I looked at my website and all the pictures that defined my life, and instead of erasing everything, I clicked on the search bar. Then, I typed in three letters: *SVA*.

I was going to save my sister, but first I had some absorbing to do.

☆ ♭ ♫

When I returned to the pediatric floor an hour later, I found the door to Cara's room wide open. My parents were nowhere in sight—they were probably at the cafeteria getting coffee or catching up on sleep in the lounge—but I found my siblings together. Drew had dragged a chair up to Cara's bed, and the two were in the middle of a game of Rummy 500.

Neither noticed me, so I leaned against the door frame and took a moment to watch. It was Drew's turn. He picked up the king of spades, which completed a flush, but he dumped the card in the discard pile like it was useless. I frowned and cocked my head.

"Really?" Cara said, setting down her hand. "Playing is no fun if you're going to let me win."

"Let you win?" Drew leaned away from her as if he was insulted, but there was a hint of a smile on his face. "I'd *never* do that."

"Yeah, uh-huh," she said and rolled her eyes. "If you didn't take the jack at the start of the game, maybe I'd believe you."

"He's got the queen too," I said, pushing away from the door and making myself known.

At the sound of my voice, Drew's head swiveled in my direction. "Stella, hey," he said. "What's up?"

"Not much." I stepped into the room. "I was just wondering if I could have a moment with Cara."

"Sure, no problem." He collected the cards, and as he crammed them back inside their flimsy cardboard box, he said to her, "Rematch later?"

She nodded, and then we both watched Drew stand up and cross the room. When he reached me, he gave my shoulder a quick squeeze before continuing out into the hall. Once he was gone, I looked back at Cara and inhaled a long breath through my nose, telling myself to relax. It wasn't that I was nervous, but what I was about to say to her was important and I wanted my head straight.

"You came," Cara said. There was something off about her voice.

"Well, yeah, dork," I responded, making a face at her. "There's nothing in the world that would keep me from you."

That must have been the wrong thing to say, because Cara sighed and folded her hands in her lap. "Thanks, Stel," she said. Her tone was dull, and I felt like she was speaking to an empty room because she wouldn't look in my direction.

"You mind if I join?" I asked, gesturing at the bed. She nodded, still avoiding my gaze.

Okay, strange, I thought as I took a spot on the edge. Something was definitely bothering her, and I figured it most likely involved me, considering that she'd been fine a minute ago with Drew. I waited for a second, giving her a chance to speak up, but then five seconds turned into ten, and ten to twenty.

"Cara, what's wrong?"

"Besides the obvious? I'm fine." She smiled, but it was halfhearted and faded in an instant.

"Doesn't seem liked it," I said, crossing my arms. "Are you mad at me or something?"

"No." Cara twisted her hands together before finally glancing up at me. "Dr. Mitchell told me I need another transplant"—she hesitated, the expression on her face grave—"if you're willing to be my donor."

I almost laughed. She was worried because she thought I wouldn't donate for her? "Cara." I grabbed her hand and gave it a gentle squeeze. "Of course I will be your donor. How could I not?"

She pulled away from me. "It's not that. I'm afraid…" She trailed off, leaving her fear unfinished.

"Hey," I said, reaching out for her again. "Don't worry. This will work."

I was nervous too, but Dr. Mitchell seemed confident about the procedure's success. First, I would undergo a physical exam to make sure I was healthy enough to donate. Once that was out of the way, the actual surgery could take place. Under normal circumstances, she would have to do human leukocyte antigen (HLA) typing—a test to make sure donor stem cells matched the recipient's—but since we were identical twins, a confirmation was unnecessary.

My bone marrow would be harvested from both sides of my pelvic bone, which kind of freaked me out, but Dr. Mitchell assured me that I would be under anesthesia and that the surgery would be painless. It was a relatively simple operation, and I could be released from the hospital the very next day.

Since the transplant was syngeneic, my healthy cells could be given to Cara shortly after being harvested. They would be infused into her bloodstream, much like a blood transfusion, and the process itself would only take a few hours. After the transplant was complete, Dr. Mitchell would monitor Cara for signs of new, blood-forming cells that produced healthy blood cells. The growth was called "engraftment" and was the first sign of a successful treatment.

"That's not what I meant," she said, shaking her head.

"Then what?"

"I don't…" She trailed off for a second time. I waited for her to collect her thoughts, and finally she took a deep breath and said, "I don't know if I want you to go through with the donation."

"What?" I exclaimed, the word hissing out of my mouth in a breathless manner. "Cara, I have to. If I don't, then you won't get better."

She shrugged and looked away from me. "You don't know that for sure."

"Your doctors do." My stomach was clenching with a sudden pain, and I felt like I'd been shot with a bullet of ice. A cold, tingling sensation was spreading through my body. "Besides, why would you be willing to take that kind of chance?"

Who is this person sitting next to me? It couldn't be my sister. She'd been a fighter since day one. She would never roll over and let cancer beat her. She was a pro at absorbing punches. I didn't understand where this white flag was coming from.

Cara's eyes were dark, and she sat unmoving for a long stretch of silence. "Stella, I'm scared," she finally said, and her voice was so quiet that I had to lean in to hear her. "I don't want to die, but—but I can't stop thinking that I'm ruining your life, and that scares me so much more."

"Look at me, Cara," I said, shaking her shoulder. "You are not ruining my life. How could you ever think that?"

When she glanced up, there was a pinched expression on her face. "Oh, come on. Don't pretend like our world doesn't revolve around this place and the treatments and the cancer, because it does, Stella. It's a big, shitty black hole that sucks everyone in." She was sneering at me now, but her voice trembled and I knew she was more distraught than angry. "Then you got your job, and I was so happy. For a moment I thought you'd done it, you'd escaped, but all it took was a phone call and some bad news, and now you're stuck here again."

My throat lumped up as the tears that had been hanging in her eyes finally fell and streamed down her face. "How can I be stuck in a place if it's exactly where I want to be?" I asked her. "Black hole or not, you're still my sister."

Cara laughed through her tears, but the sound was bitter. "Because, Stella. There's this thought that keeps running through my head, and it's tormenting me because I know it's true. If I'm not here anymore, then you don't have to be either."

Hearing this, I turned away from Cara. My heart was twisting, and I felt the pain of the past four years like I never had before. I didn't want her to see any guilt on my face, so I closed my eyes and counted out three deep breaths before clearing my throat. "Fine," I said, turning back to her. "Let's make a deal."

"I—okay?" she said, her eyes huge and glistening.

"I'm going through with the donation whether you like it or not, and you're going to have another transplant," I told her firmly. "Then, when you get better, we're both going to walk out of here and I can go to SVA."

"SVA?" she repeated, her eyebrows bunching up like a piece of fuzzy pipe cleaner pushed together. "What's that?"

"The School of Visual Arts. It's in New York," I explained. "I was accepted into the photography program for spring semester."

"Oh my God," Cara said, and a smile broke through her tears.

"You're gonna go to school for photography? I'm so proud of you, Stella."

"Thanks, Cara. That means the world to me," I said and smiled back, "but I'm only going if you help me. We do this together. Otherwise, neither of us is leaving."

"Yes, okay," she said, nodding her head.

There were still tears running down her cheeks, but these were different. Maybe not tears of joy, but they were happy nonetheless.

☆ ♭ ♫

Everything was black. It surrounded me like a blanket of cement, and the weight was too heavy for me to move. Before panic could sink in, a dot of red appeared in front of my eyes. As it grew, the weight lifted from my chest and my arms and legs began to tingle. Moving was like trying to swim through syrup, but I kept my gaze focused on the dot and pushed myself forward.

Then I opened my eyes.

I was in a hospital room. It was a replica of the one Cara always stayed in, only this time I was the patient. My surgery had taken place early in the afternoon, and judging by the dimness outside my window, it was almost nighttime. The room's only source of light was a small lamp on my bedside table. Its glow struggled to reach the entire room, casting long shadows that disappeared into the gloomy corners.

At first, I thought I was alone, but then I spotted *him* in the armchair next to my bed. His long legs were sprawled out in front of him, and his head lolled to the side as he slept. He looked uncomfortable, and the circles under his eyes suggested that this was the only sleep he'd received in quite some time.

What the heck is he doing here?

"Oliver?" I called out softly. He stirred in the chair momentarily, but then continued to snore. "Oliver!" I said again, this time louder.

He woke with a start. "Huh—wha?" he mumbled, his voice still filled with sleep. When he saw me awake in bed, the effect was immediate. He scrambled out of the chair. "Stella! You're awake!"

I nodded as I pushed myself up. "What are you doing here?" I said and winced. My hips and entire backside ached like I'd fallen down a flight of stairs and landed on my tailbone. "Where's my family?"

"They're down in the cafeteria eating dinner."

"Okay?" I crossed my arms over my chest and waited for him to answer my first question.

Oliver moved into the light, and that's when I noticed his wrinkled clothes and limp hair. "I know I'm probably the last person you want to see right now," he said and shuffled a bit closer, "but I had to make sure you were okay."

"I'm fine," I said, holding up a hand to ward him off. I didn't want him to get any closer, because even in his unkempt state, Oliver was achingly handsome. Just looking at him made me want to reach out and touch him, to feel him and have him hold me. But seeing him also reminded me of what he'd done, and my heart and stomach both became painfully tight.

Oliver pressed a fist to his lips and took a step back. He stood there momentarily, his chest heaving, but then he dropped his hand and sighed. "I came to explain, you know, why I did what I did." I opened my mouth to argue—he already wasted his chance

293

to explain—but he cut me off. "You don't have to say anything. Please, I just need you to listen."

I pinched my bottom lip, not sure what to say. Stuck in my hospital bed, I felt unable to escape what Oliver was going to say, whether I wanted to hear him out or not. At the same time, if he'd flown all this way to see me, would it really hurt to listen? Maybe it was best if he said his piece and left, because then we could both get on with our lives. After a few more moments of silent debate, I gave him a hesitant nod.

"Okay," he said, swallowing and nodding. "I don't really know where to begin, so I guess I'll start with my family."

My head snapped up as I sucked in a sharp breath. I *knew* there was something going on with his family. I watched him intently, waiting to hear what he would say, and it took Oliver a few minutes to work up the courage to continue.

"I never knew my parents," he said eventually, and I bit down hard on my lip to keep from gasping. "My mom died giving birth to me, and she never told my grandparents who my father was. They were the ones who raised me, so it never occurred to me that they weren't my parents until my grandpa died when I was six. I mean, I called them Gramps and Nanny, but I never paid attention to the fact that they were older than all the other kids' parents. It was just the way things had always been.

"After his funeral, Nanny sat me down and explained what had happened to my real mom. To be completely honest, I was more upset about losing my grandpa than someone I never knew, so my grandma gave me this to remember him by." Oliver fingered the chain around his neck and lifted the dog tag out from underneath his shirt. "He was a veteran from the Vietnam War."

"Oh, Oliver." I was going to tell him how sorry I was, but then I remembered the silver music note he'd given me, and something occurred to me. "Your mom's charm bracelet?"

"Besides a few pictures," he said, barely meeting my gaze, "that's all I have of her."

I was quiet as I processed this, but then another horrible thought came to mind. "What about your grandma?"

My question made Oliver go quiet, and he stood unmoving for an unbearably long time. "She passed away when I was twelve," he said eventually, his tone bleak. "Some kind of heart complication."

From his initial reaction, I'd had a bad feeling about what he would say, but I was still unable to contain my gasp. "Oliver, I'm so sorry."

He shrugged. "That's life. She lived a good one," he said. "After she died, I was sent to live with her brother, my great-uncle Steven."

I could tell by the way he said the name that Oliver didn't have the same fondness for his uncle as he did for his grandparents. "The one who taught you about constellations?"

"Yeah, that was about the only cool thing we ever did together. My uncle's a historian, so he spends more time reading books than anything else. Didn't really have time for a kid."

"That's horrible." I never imagined Oliver's story would be so…tragic.

"It was pretty lonely," he admitted, "but my uncle only lived a town over from my grandparents, so I was allowed to stay in the same school and be with my friends. That's why JJ, Xander, and I got so close. They became my family."

"So then what happened?" I asked. I was glad that Oliver was telling me all of this, but I didn't understand what it had to do with us.

"Then we signed our record deal, and everything changed," he said. "You already know most of the story: Mongo made us change our name and our music so we would be more marketable, and we went with it because it was such a great opportunity and probably our only shot. When we made it big, we thought we could transition back into our old music, but Alec's dad wouldn't let us. JJ tried fighting him on it, but I—I didn't have his back."

"Why not?"

Oliver sighed and his shoulders slouched. "I suppose I was afraid of what would happen if we pissed off Alec's dad. There was this image in my head of my life falling apart: Xander going off to college, Alec starting a solo career, JJ becoming an actor, and there I'd be, all alone." He looked back up at me, and I could see the fear still reflected in his eyes. "The band—that's all I have, Stella. They're my family. I wasn't going to chance losing them."

His fear was understandable, but the reasoning? Not so much. "But isn't that kind of what you did?" I asked. "You and JJ were fighting all the time, and then there were the rumors."

"God, I know," he said, hanging his head. "It's not like I knew that was going to happen. It wasn't my goal. I was just too scared to see that JJ was right, and then *you* happened. I never would have played that song if it weren't for you."

"And?" I said, my tone sharp. I just wanted to hear the punch line. "That doesn't explain why you did what you did, Oliver."

He grimaced, and then his whole upper body—head, shoulders, arms, hands—went limp. "I'm not allowed to date," he told me. I opened my mouth to say something, anything, but nothing came out. "It was one of the rules that Alec's dad made me agree too. He thought it would make me more appealing to fans or some bullshit like that."

My heart began to race as all the little details, the hints and glimpses I'd seen over the past weeks, finally fell into place. "That's why you asked to keep us a secret," I said.

He nodded. "Yeah, but our fans loved our old Infinity and Beyond song, and I thought we could finally show Alec's dad that we didn't need all his rules. I was wrong. When he found out you and I were together, he called me in for a meeting and told me I had to stop seeing you."

I remembered Oliver going to Mongo's headquarters the day of the movie premiere—he'd kissed me before he left, and the next time I saw him, everything was different. All my questions had finally been answered, but that only left me with new ones.

"Why the hell didn't you say anything?" I exclaimed even though I knew my question was unfair. Oliver had let his fear control him, and that was something I had experience with myself. Fear made you do stupid, irrational things.

"I don't know, Stella," he said, tugging on the chain around his neck. "I wasn't thinking straight."

"I'm sorry," I responded, surprising both of us. "I understand that you couldn't risk your family." If I were put in the same position, I'd make the same decision as him. Of course, I never would've gone about it the way he did, but that wasn't the point.

Oliver took a hesitant step forward. "You do?" He stared at me, his face shining as he held his breath.

"Yes," I said, nodding my head. "But just because I understand *why* you did it doesn't mean I forgive the *how*. What you did sucked, Oliver."

"Okay, I deserve that," he said, a flush creeping across his cheeks. "I was terrible, but I figured if you hated me, then it would be easier for you to move on and be happy."

I lifted an eyebrow. "You thought standing me up would make me happy?"

"When you say it like that, I sound like the world's biggest idiot."

"You are the world's biggest idiot," I said with a small smile. "Although JJ and Drew are close runners-up." The more time I spent talking with Oliver, the more I realized that I was past being mad at him.

A tiny smile appeared on his face too. It was there for a moment, but then it slipped away. "You're still not going to forgive me, are you?"

"I appreciate you taking the time to tell me the truth, so yes, I do forgive you," I said carefully, and the uncertain look on his face turned into a grin. "But that doesn't mean anything has changed between us."

His smile wavered. "Meaning what?"

"I called Paul yesterday," I said slowly. I didn't know why I suddenly felt nervous about telling him this, but I could feel my pulse in the back of my throat. "I'm not coming back to work. I have enough material to keep the blog running until the end of the tour. After Cara gets better, I'm going to college and—I don't think I can handle seeing you again."

Neither of us spoke. Out in the hall I heard a woman's voice, probably one of the nurses, followed by a response from what sounded liked my brother.

Oliver cleared his throat. "So this is it then." It wasn't a question; he understood that we were really, truly over.

"Yeah," I said, my chin trembling. "This is it."

He was silent for a long time before finally nodding his head. Then he leaned over the side of the bed and placed a soft kiss on my forehead. "Good-bye, Stella," he said in a thick voice. "Thank you so much for allowing me to be a part of your life."

CHAPTER 23

I was right about hearing my brother out in the hall. A few minutes after Oliver left, Drew pushed open my door. "Knock, knock," he said, rapping his knuckles against the frame. "How you feeling, Rocket?"

"Not as bad as I thought I would," I said. "Come in."

Drew hesitated for a second, lingering in the space between the hall and my room, but then stepped inside. He was quiet as he moved toward the chair where Oliver had been minutes before, and when he reached it, he smoothed out his shirt before sitting down.

"What's up?" I asked. Something about the way he was holding himself was strange.

Drew shook his head. "It's nothing."

"Oh yeah," I said, crossing my arms. "Clearly."

"Well"—he paused and fidgeted in his seat—"I guess I was wondering about Oliver."

"What about him?" I asked, trying my best not to sigh. If Drew was outside my room when Oliver left, the two had obviously seen each other, and although I'd known he'd ask sooner or later, I'd hoped my brother would forget to interrogate me.

"He flew all the way out here?"

I shrugged, trying to look casual. "Yeah. He wanted to make sure I was okay."

My response made him frown. "And he's already left? That wasn't a very long visit."

"He's a busy guy, Drew," I said. "He probably didn't have time to hang out and play cards." I knew I was being short with Drew, but I didn't want to explain my relationship problems to my brother. Not that there was a relationship to have a problem with since Oliver and I were over.

The thing was, even though I found comfort in knowing the truth about what had happened between us, and despite the fact that I'd forgiven Oliver, I still felt heavy on the inside whenever I thought about him. Before he ruined us, I'm fairly positive that I was on my way to loving him, and that wasn't a feeling that would disappear overnight. It would linger in my heart for a while, and that was something that I would have to deal with. But not right now. Not here in this moment with Drew, and most definitely not when I had more important issues to wrestle with, such as my sister's health.

"I guess you're right," he said.

"But?" I asked.

He rubbed his chin. "Dunno. I thought maybe there was something going on between you two."

"Are you asking if we're dating?" I narrowed my eyes. "'Cause we're not."

"Okay," he said and held up his hands. "I was just wondering."

After that, Drew slumped back into his seat. He looked worn out, which, after everything, was not surprising, but what bothered me was the look in his eyes. Or maybe it was a lack of a look, his eyes dull and distant.

"Drew," I said, my mouth suddenly parched. "Are you okay?"

He took a moment to respond. "Yeah," he said at last, but his expression was still slack.

"You don't seem like it," I told him.

"You know," Drew said, rubbing his face, "you can be a real pain in the butt sometimes."

"It's my specialty," I said and pressed my lips together into a tight line. He wasn't going to joke his way out of this one. "Just tell me."

"Fine." He tipped his head back on his neck and stared up at the ceiling instead of looking at me. "I guess it's just—I can't help but think that this is her last chance."

"What?" I asked with a frown.

"Cara's," he clarified, a slightly faraway look clouding his eyes. "I'm afraid this is her last chance to get better."

Oh. Drew had never been as positive about Cara's recovery as she had been over the course of her illness—nobody was. But at the same time, he'd never openly expressed his fears, especially one as bleak as this. A few months ago, I'd been anxious about the same thing, and I braced myself for the cold, creeping feeling of dread that would most certainly infect my mind.

But it didn't.

"Cara doesn't need any more chances," I said when I realized I wasn't scared. "She's going to be fine."

Drew's eyebrows scrunched together. "How can you be sure?"

"Because," I said, "I just am."

When I found out Cara's first transplant had failed, I'd been terrified. I knew I should be now too, because there was no guarantee that this treatment would work, but my pulse and heart were steady. Drew was right—this was Cara's last chance. But it didn't matter. This time things were different. I couldn't know for sure, but I could feel it.

☆♭♫

Three weeks later we brought Cara home from the hospital. Her platelet, red, and white blood cell counts were still low, but the second transplant had been a success.

Although she was being discharged, Dr. Mitchell explained that Cara's recovery would take a long time. It could be months before she started to get some of her strength back and, if her cancer didn't relapse, it could take an entire year for her full health to return. During this time, there would be a huge risk of infection and Cara would have to visit the outpatient clinic on a regular basis so her progress could be tracked.

But there wasn't anything Dr. Mitchell could say that would ruin my high of emotions—I was hyper and ecstatic and overwhelmed all at the same time, but more than anything I was relieved. Cara's last chance had actually worked.

A few days after her official release from the hospital, the two of us were curled up in her bed watching a movie. Since she was still exhausted from her treatment, we spent a lot of time in her room. I didn't mind; I'd always loved the scarlet walls, lacy gold pillows, and vanity covered in mounds of jewelry, makeup, and perfume. Every inch of space reminded me of my sister.

When the credits came on, Cara switched off the TV and turned to me. "So," she started. "There's something I've been wanting to talk to you about."

"Hmm?"

I had yet to take off my hospital bracelet, and I slipped a finger under the plastic and spun it around my wrist. I liked fiddling with it. In black type was all my patient information: my full name, doctor, date of birth, and other important information the nursing staff needed to know. There was no reason for me to still be wearing it, but I'd grown attached—maybe because it was a reminder of what Cara and I had overcome together.

"It's about Oliver," she said. "I know what happened between you two."

My entire body stiffened and I let go of the wristband. "What?" I asked. "How did you find out?" It wasn't that I was purposely keeping the breakup a secret from Cara, but I figured the less I talked about it, the easier it would be to forget.

"He told me," she said, her tone slightly tart. "After visiting you that day in the hospital he came to talk to me. I don't know what was more shocking: actually meeting Oliver Perry or him breaking down and telling me *everything*. It was like he was still trying to apologize by admitting it all to me."

"He did *what*?" I gasped. "Why didn't you say something?"

Cara's glare was glassy. "Oh, like how you gave me all the details about your breakup?"

Her comment stirred the guilt inside me with a jolt, and unable to face my sister, I tossed off the blanket and climbed out of bed. Cara was right. I should have told her about everything, from Oliver standing me up to his explanation and apology, because she shouldn't have had to find out from *him*.

"Well, Stella?" Cara said when I didn't respond. "No comment?"

"Okay," I said as my cheeks started burning. "I should have filled you in on the whole thing, but between my donation and your second transplant, I figured we had enough to worry about."

The sour look on her face dissolved as she sighed. "I get that, Stella," she said. "I really do. You're always looking out for me and I'm so grateful for that, but sometimes you have to let me look out for you too. That's what sisters are supposed to do. Even if all I can be is an ear to listen, I'm here."

"I know that," I said, glancing down at the carpet. "Thank you, Cara."

"Do you though?"

My head snapped back up. "Yes," I said, looking directly at her. I could *never* forget what she'd been willing to sacrifice to give me my life back.

"Good," she said with a crisp nod, "because this isn't what I wanted to talk to you about."

Oh great. There was a strange look on Cara's face, like she was suddenly apprehensive about our upcoming conversation, and that made my stomach fluttery and uncomfortable. Unwittingly, I started to twist my nose stud between my fingers.

"All right," I said. "What's up?"

She bit her bottom lip before taking a quick breath and clearing her throat. "Do you miss him?"

Rather than answering, I focused my gaze out her bedroom window, because I didn't want her to see how much that one question affected me. Across the street, the neighbor kids were playing on their front lawn. They were taking turns raking up the fallen autumn leaves and then jumping into a blazing pile of red, orange, and yellow.

Halloween was at the end of the month and their porch was already decorated for the holiday, a collection of pumpkins waiting to be carved, all lined up on the wooden steps. For a moment I wished I was out there with them, enjoying the last bit of nice weather before winter came.

"Stella?" Cara prompted me.

I sighed. Of course I missed Oliver. It was impossible not to. As hard as I tried to block him from my mind, he kept slipping in through windows and cracks. The cycle was vicious. I'd go a few days without thinking about him, but then I'd see the Heartbreakers posters in Cara's room or hear one of their songs on the radio, and then all the memories and feelings I was keeping at bay would surge into me like I'd been plugged into an outlet.

There were so many things I missed about him, like his easy smile and how he ran his fingers through my hair. Most of all, I missed how being around him turned me into someone new, someone who was strong and confident and ready to take on the world. I was still that person now, but there was no doubt in my mind that if it weren't for Oliver Perry and the Heartbreakers, my new self would still be trapped inside the older, scared version of me.

Minutes of silence lapsed before I could turn back around and face Cara. "Yes," I finally said when our eyes met. "I miss him more than I should."

"More than you should? What do you mean?"

"That moving on is hard."

Cara was slow to answer, and she sat for a long while considering my response. "Did you ever consider," she said hesitantly, "that you can't move on because it's the wrong thing to do?"

I sighed. "It would be nice to think so, but trust me, I'm doing the right thing."

"How can you know that?"

For the past four years, I'd been preparing for my heart to be broken. I knew that Cara's chance of survival was just as great as her chance of dying, and that was something I'd privately acknowledged but never spoken of. There was nothing I could have done to prepare for Oliver though—I never saw him coming.

When I'd been left heartbroken by him instead of my sister, the surprise was so crippling that I was *still* trying to pick up my shattered pieces. Yes, I'd forgiven Oliver. But was I willing to hand back over my heart when there were still a few cracks left to be sealed? Not a chance in the world.

"Because he hurt me, Cara," I said. "Even if he's sorry, there's no guarantee he won't do it again."

Cara shook her head. "But there's no guarantee about anything in life. Sometimes you just have to take a chance."

I knew she was trying to help me, but there was no way she could understand how it felt to have your heart fractured by someone you possibly loved. And beside, after all the pain and hardship of the past few months, I wanted to feel safe and whole again. Talking about this brought the hurt back up in stinging waves, and I took three deep breaths to curb my ache.

"You're wrong," I said, hugging my arms to my chest. "By letting him go, I'm guaranteeing that he can't hurt me again."

She tried to keep the disappointment off her face, but it didn't matter because I could hear it in her words. "If you think it's for the best, then fine," Cara said. "But just so you know, it seems like you're still in pain."

CHAPTER 24

I woke up on Thanksgiving Day to a layer of snow outside my bedroom window. Only a few inches were on the ground, but they were enough to transform our lawn from a sea of brown grass to a pristine white blanket.

"Good morning," my mom said when I wandered into the kitchen in search of a cup of coffee. "Happy Turkey Day!" She was standing at the counter with an apron on, already working on tonight's feast. I frowned and looked up at the clock above the stove.

"Morning, Mom. Why are you cooking already? It's only nine." As soon as the question left my mouth, I realized what I'd just said. "Wait. Why are *you* cooking?" My mom's lack of culinary skills had ruined many meals in the past, and suddenly I had an image in my head of the entire turkey on fire.

"Don't worry," said my dad. He was sitting at the kitchen table with his usual breakfast: half a grapefruit, a cup of green tea, and the sports section. "I'm cooking the bird. Your mother's help is restricted to the mashed potatoes."

"Drew won't be happy," I said. Potatoes were his favorite food at Thanksgiving. Luckily, mine was pumpkin pie.

"Hey!" my mom said, brandishing the kitchen beater in my

direction. Chunks of potato fell from the silver blades and splattered on the floor. "Just you wait. These will be the best taters you've ever tasted."

"Can't wait," I said. "Food poison is my favorite flavor of potato."

I tried not to laugh at my own joke, but then I heard my dad's deep, wheezing chuckle and I couldn't contain myself. My mom pretended to look angry for a few seconds, but it wasn't long before she cracked a smile too.

"So," I said, once we all calmed down, "you never told me why you're cooking so early."

"Your sister requested we celebrate at lunchtime," my mom said. "She has something going on later tonight."

As Dr. Mitchell had warned, Cara's recovery was a slow process. She was still fatigued most of the time, but she'd gained back enough strength to start taking daily walks on the treadmill, and last week we took a trip to the mall. But even though she was steadily getting better, I didn't understand how or why Cara would leave on Thanksgiving, especially when we had so much to be thankful for this year.

"What? Where's she going?"

My mom smiled, and it was one of those I-know-something-you-don't grins. "Can't tell you."

Right when I opened my mouth to grill her further, Cara stepped into the kitchen still wearing her bathrobe and slippers. "Have you guys seen outside? It snowed!"

"Yeah," Drew said, yawning as he appeared beside her. He'd come home from school late last night for the holiday. "I have a feeling I'm going to be the one shoveling the driveway."

"Just look at it this way," my dad told him, turning the page of his paper, "you'll burn off all the fattening food we're about to eat."

Drew grumbled under his breath as he headed toward the coffeepot, and I turned back to Cara. "What's going on tonight?" I asked her.

"That would ruin the surprise," she said, her eyes lighting up with a glow of mischief. "You know how those work, right?"

It turned out my mom wasn't the only one in on the surprise. Four hours, two plates of stuffing, and one piece of pie later, my siblings and I piled into Drew's beat-up Honda Civic. I still had no clue what was happening or where we were going, but apparently Drew did.

"Here, put this on," Cara said, handing me a blindfold as Drew turned on the car.

"Wait," I said, glaring at him. "You get to know, but I don't?"

"Don't complain to me," Drew said, backing out of the garage. "Cara's the mastermind behind the plan. I'm just following orders."

"Relax, Stella," Cara told me. "This is supposed to be fun. You've done so much for me over the past few years. I'm only trying to repay the favor."

"I don't need you to repay me for anything," I said, but I slipped the blindfold on anyway. She was clearly excited about whatever she was planning, and I wasn't going to ruin that for her.

I did my best to pay attention to the route that Drew took. He turned onto the highway after leaving our neighborhood, and when the trip started to stretch into an hour-long drive, I knew we were heading to Minneapolis. After that, it wasn't long before I felt the quick stops and sharp turns of Drew's horrible city driving.

"Are we almost there?" I asked, fidgeting with the bandana over my eyes. I wasn't normally the type of person who got carsick, but sitting in the backseat and not being able to see anything was making me nauseous.

"Don't take that off," Cara said and swatted my hand away. "We'll be there in five."

"I was only readjusting," I said. "This thing is itchy."

Five minutes turned into fifteen, so when Cara told me we'd arrived, I ripped off the blindfold and looked around. The last thing I'd seen was my house, so the stark change of scenery was disorientating, not to mention that it was dark outside. I blinked a few times as I looked around, but finally I realized we were at the Target Center. Drew pulled up to the valet parking, and one of the attendants approached the car.

"Are the Timberwolves playing tonight?" I asked as we stepped outside into the crisp winter air. I wasn't a big basketball fan, so I didn't understand why Cara would take me to a game.

"Nope," Drew said as he handed his keys to the valet.

"Okay, so what's the event?"

"A concert," Cara said. Her face was already rosy from the cold, but she had a wide grin on her face.

"What con—" I didn't finish my question, because that's when I noticed the suspicious number of teenage girls streaming into the arena.

My head dropped back, and I stared up at the digital billboard above the Target Center's front entrance. Smiling down at me were four familiar faces, and one in particular made my stomach roll.

It didn't make any sense. The Heartbreakers' tour ended back in September. What were they doing in Minnesota? Better yet—why did Cara think taking me to a show where I'd have to watch my ex perform was a good idea? Was this some last-ditch attempt to get us back together?

Ever since our talk about my decision to end things with Oliver, Cara had let me be. I knew she wasn't happy with my choice, but she didn't press the matter. Occasionally she'd ask me how I was feeling, but other than that, we didn't talk about Oliver. Had she been planning this all along, letting me think she'd dropped the subject only so she could ambush me later?

Crossing my arms, I cemented my feet on the sidewalk and refused to move. "I'm not going."

"You have to," Cara said. "This concert? The guys are putting it on for *us*."

I narrowed my eyes. "Explain. Now."

"Okay," Cara said, taking a deep breath. "A few weeks ago, I got a call from Oliver. He wanted to see how I was doing, make sure the transplant had gone well, that sort of thing. We talked for a long time. Eventually he mentioned that one of the reasons he was calling was because the band was interested in putting on a special concert—one where all the proceeds would be donated to cancer research. Oliver asked if I wanted to come as a special guest, kinda like a face of the cause, and I said yes, so they arranged to do the show here in Minneapolis so I could attend.

"I know you're still trying to get over Oliver, but this concert isn't about you and him. It's about us and any other person who's had to go through what we did. The guys are doing this because they met you and were inspired by our story. Being here to celebrate that I kicked cancer's ass means the world to me"—Cara paused and there were tears in her eyes—"but I don't want to do it without you."

My mouth had fallen open halfway through Cara's explanation, and now I could barely speak. "They really did all this—because of us?"

Cara nodded her head. Tears were still rushing down her cheeks like a shining trail of diamonds. "Please say you'll come," she said, and the look on her face rattled something loose inside my chest. All I could do was nod back and try not to cry. How could I possibly say no?

☆ ♭ ♩♫

Since she was a special guest, Cara didn't just have regular tickets; she had three VIP passes. While I knew that watching the concert would bring back memories, I wasn't ready for the surge of emotions that slammed into me as soon as we stepped backstage. Maybe it was just JJ.

"*Bear!*" he yelled and barreled into me so hard that I almost fell to the floor.

"JJ, you're crushing me," I said, barely able to breathe.

"Sorry," he said and quickly let go. "I couldn't help it. It's not the same without you around."

"You better watch out," warned a familiar voice, and I turned to see Xander smiling at me. "I'm fairly positive that JJ's planning to kidnap you."

"Oh my God, Xander," I exclaimed when I noticed the change in his appearance. His usual thick-framed glasses were gone. "You look great!"

"You think?" he asked. "I'm trying out contacts because I figured they'd be harder for JJ to break."

"Hey, this time was purely accidental," JJ said. "It's not like I meant to sit on them."

"What about the time you tried using them as a slingshot and flung them off our balcony?" Xander asked. JJ attempted to hold a straight face, but he quickly gave in to his snicker and Xander shook his head. "Yeah, that's what I thought."

"Where's Alec?" I said as I looked around. "I'd like you all to meet my sister."

"Right here," he said, appearing out of the shadows like a silent night creature. Like always, his face was expressionless, but from the force of his hug I knew he was glad to see me.

Oliver had yet to show his face, but since he'd already met Cara, I spent the next minute doing introductions without him. Afterward, Drew took his turn shaking the guys' hands and getting reacquainted, and I stood back and took everything in. Being at one of the Heartbreakers' concerts again gave me a strange feeling, like I'd suddenly been yanked back into summer. Seeing Courtney, Paul, and the usual crew going about their usual business made me feel like nothing had changed, even though that was far from the truth.

"I've always had a bit of a crush on your sister," I heard JJ joke, so I turned back toward the group to listen. He was smiling down at

Cara, and the look on his face—rosy cheeks and wide eyes—made me pause. "But I really have a thing for blonds."

For someone who was normally sensitive about her hair loss, Cara blushed and laughed. Since the end of her chemo, about an inch had grown back, so tonight she'd worn what she liked to call her Scarlett Johansson wig.

"Remember what happened the last time you tried hitting on one of my sisters?" Drew said in a warning tone, but I could tell from the glint in his eyes that he was only teasing. I never heard JJ's response because someone tapped me on the shoulder.

I knew who it was without looking, and even though I'd known I'd have to face Oliver at some point during the night, my heart lurched when I finally turned to him. His hands were shoved in the front pockets of his jeans. On his head was a beanie that reminded me of the first time we met, and a few of his brown locks curled out around his ears. Normally he stuck to plain black or white shirts, but tonight he wore a navy one that made his eyes pop like an explosion of aqua.

"Hey, Stella," he said, looking almost shy.

"Hey, Oliver."

Then we both just stood there and stared at each other. As the silence mounted between us, I tried to think of what I could possibly say. Thankfully, Oliver reached up, rubbed the back of his neck, and spoke first.

"How are you?" he asked, and the tension in my stomach eased a bit.

"Good, good," I said, nodding my head quickly. "What about you? How are things going with the band?"

"Better," he said. "We told Alec's dad that if he didn't give us some freedom to do our own thing, then we were done."

"And he agreed to that?"

"Yeah, I guess he didn't want to chance losing his biggest dollar sign. I've already started writing some different songs for our new album."

"That's great news, Oliver. I can't wait to hear them when it's released."

"You won't have to wait that long," he said, flashing me a small smile. It wasn't like the one I'd come to love, full faced and crooked. This was only a shadow, a cast-off of the real thing. "We'll be playing one tonight."

Smiley, the Heartbreakers' stage manager, came up behind Oliver and clamped him on the shoulder before I could answer. "Come on, O-man," he said, and pulled him toward JJ, Xander, and Alec who'd already assembled in their preshow places. "All right, gentlemen," Smiley said once they were all in position. "It's time to make some girls' panties drop."

Courtney shot Smiley a cross look. "That's so inappropriate, Fred," she scolded him. "And nobody says 'panties' anymore."

Everybody laughed, and the back-line crew rushed up to the Heartbreakers. Someone helped Oliver with his earpiece, another passed Xander and Alec their instruments, and a third handed JJ a pair of drumsticks that he instantly tucked into the back pocket of his jeans. Then the lights dimmed, and the hair on the back of my neck rose in anticipation. It was time for the concert.

I had to squint to find my siblings in the dark. They were standing close to the side of the stage where they could actually watch the show, and when I joined them, Cara greeted me with a thumbs-up. Drew had his hands pressed over his ears as the audience started to scream, and I smiled and shook my head. From experience, I knew that the Heartbreakers' fans were loud enough to command an entire arena. Not even a pair of soundproof headphones would help my brother now.

But today, I hardly noticed the noise. During those few quick seconds before the show began, all I could hear was a dull roar as the crowd suddenly became background music in my mind. It was like I'd been listening to my iPod and then my headphones were ripped from my ears. What was once loud and focused became a whisper of a song, one I could only make out because I'd heard it hundreds of times before.

Maybe it was because at that exact moment, my vision tunneled as I focused on one thing—Oliver. I watched as he shook out his arms to get rid of his jitters, and he must have felt my gaze because he glanced over his shoulder. When he saw me watching him, he nodded as if that was some sort of signal I was supposed to understand. I didn't, but I also didn't have any time to figure out what he meant.

Fred-Smiley shouted something I couldn't hear, and Oliver swung back around to listen. Just like that, our moment ended, and all my senses flooded back to me. First was the sound of the crowd—so deafening that I could feel it thumping against my chest, like bass tones blasting from a speaker. Next came my smell as I caught a whiff of Drew's cologne. Last, I felt Cara laughing next to me.

"What?"

"Remember that time in the hospital when I said you'd never go to a Heartbreakers concert?"

Her statement made me pause. Neither of us had ever imagined this moment, the two of us standing here together, but here we were. Cara had beaten her definites. My sister was right about so many things in our life, but she'd been wrong about never seeing the boys perform. If there was such a thing as fate, she'd changed it.

"Remember when you thought you'd never go to one either?" I asked, eyebrows raised.

Somehow my question was timed perfectly with the beginning of the show. A slow-growing smile stretched across Cara's face, and I couldn't tell if it was the result of my comment or because Oliver's voice was suddenly echoing through the entire arena.

Cara answered by squeezing my hand, and then she turned back toward the stage and, for the first time, watched her favorite band perform.

☆ ♭ ♫

The concert set list was the same as the one used during the boys' tour, so by the time they reached the last song of the night, I'd completely forgotten about Oliver's promise of something new.

"I hope everyone enjoyed themselves tonight! I want to thank you all for supporting a cause that's very near to our hearts," Oliver said, gesturing back at Xander, Alec, and JJ. "By purchasing a ticket tonight, you've helped in the fight against cancer. To show our gratitude, we'd like to share a track that will be on our new album. How does that sound?"

"Oooh, exciting," Cara said, tugging on my arm.

Oliver waited for the cheers to die down before continuing. "This song is called 'Astrophil,'" he said, and then he started to sing:

Sometimes the things left unsaid
Are deadly like bullets and knives.
Mine cut you deep, girl.
We had no chance to survive.

And there's an unspoken truth in my eyes,
But the heart whispers words
That can't be denied.
Mine's telling you that I'm falling,
Falling apart 'cause I fell in love.

You settled into my lungs
And crawled into my heart.
You're in every word I sing
And my star in the dark.

Early-morning coffee
The first time that we met:
Remember the picture you took of me?
That close-up-style vignette.

My world was blurry before you;
I was too scared to see.

But slowly the picture's developing,
And I know what's happening to me.

You settled into my lungs
And crawled into my heart.
You're in every word I sing
And my star in the dark.

Girl, you might think that we fell,
Fell hard from the stars,
But my love's untouched, unmarred.
And I'm telling you that I'm coming apart,
Coming apart 'cause I'm still in love.

You settled into my lungs.
You're in every word I sing,
Every word I sing.

When the song finished, I wished I could hit a replay button like I was listening to my iPod. That way I could hear Oliver say that he loved me over and over again. I knew the instant he started singing that it wasn't just a song but a message for me. It wasn't the title or the lyrics that gave it away, but because I knew that the sound of Oliver's voice—so gruff and broken and otherworldly—could only be the product of raw emotion, and that was something my heart recognized.

"That was beautiful," Cara said, "but I don't get it. Why's the song called 'Astrophil'? What does 'astrophil' even mean?"

I smiled to myself. "Star-lover," I said.

And I was his star.

I remembered back to the conversation I'd had with Cara a month ago, when she'd said there are no guarantees in life. At the time, I didn't hear what she was saying, but now I did. By not giving Oliver a second chance, I was playing it safe like when I deferred from NYU or almost gave up on photography. I'd made a decision to stop living in fear the day I read Beth's letter, and now I needed to follow through.

As Oliver came offstage, his face was closed off and guarded. I completely understood why—if he'd come up to me tonight and told me he loved me, I never would have listened. So through his song, he told me the only way he could. It was a risk, and he'd just displayed his heart for the world to see without knowing if he'd get a response.

But I would give him one.

I smiled and placed my hand over my chest, right above where my own heart rested, so he'd know that this time I'd heard his message. Oliver stopped midstride. He stared at me as if I were a unicorn riding a rainbow, but then the realization snapped across his face and he strode toward me. He was a few yards away when an idea came to mind, so I held up a hand, signaling for him to stop. I pulled out my cell and started scrolling through my contacts. Oliver frowned as I listened to the ringer, but then he jerked and started digging at his pocket when he felt his own phone go off.

"Hello?" His tone was uncertain when he picked up.

"Remember when you gave me your number and made me promise to call?" I asked.

"Yeah," he said, his lips almost tweaking up into a grin. "You never did."

"Well, I hope it's not too late," I said. "I know there's usually a three-day rule, but I figured it was worth a shot."

Only then did I see that real Oliver Perry smile. "Is this your way of asking me out on a date? 'Cause I'll have to talk with my manager and see if I can fit you in."

"Date? I never mentioned a date," I said, but we were both grinning.

We didn't get to talk long after that, because the boys were beckoned back onstage by chants for an encore. As I stood next to my siblings and watched, I was overwhelmed by such a foreign feeling that I didn't know what to do with myself.

Cara bumped her hip against mine to grab my attention. "You okay?" she asked.

"Yeah," I said, nodding once. "I think so."

"What's wrong?"

"Never mind," I said and shrugged her off. "It's going to sound stupid."

Our conversation caught Drew's attention. "Come on, Stella. What's bothering you?"

"Nothing's bothering me," I said immediately. It was the truth, and to prove it, I offered them both a smile. Drew seemed to believe me, and he turned his attention back to the stage. Cara, on the other hand, wasn't willing to let it go. I could tell from the look on her face that she thought I was lying, so I gave in. "Honestly, I don't think I've ever been so happy in my life."

Cara's forehead scrunched up at my response. "Then what's your deal? Why are you acting so mopey?"

"Sorry," I apologized. "I'm not trying to, but it just feels weird, you know? I can't remember the last time that everything's felt this…perfect."

Finally, Cara seemed to understand what I was trying to explain. That empty void I'd been trying to fill since seeing Bianca's picture of the little girl was finally overflowing again. "It does feel strange, doesn't it?" she said. "But you have to stop thinking about it. Just enjoy the moment."

I opened my mouth to respond—because I was totally enjoying the moment—but my words were drowned out by the cheers of the crowd as the boys stepped back onstage. Cara joined in with an ear-piercing screech.

I raised an eyebrow at her.

"What?" she said with a shrug. "I can't help it. I just love the Heartbreakers!"

Her words made something inside me shift, and I surprised us both by letting out my own fan-girl scream. The truth was, I loved the Heartbreakers too. Maybe at one time I'd hated their music, but that was when I was a different girl. The Heartbreakers hadn't just grown on me—they'd grown to be a *part* of me, one that I'd never be able to sever. These boys were like my second family, and I wouldn't have it any other way.

Cara snorted. "Okay, what the hell was that?" she asked and put a hand on her hip.

"What?" I said. "I can't show a little appreciation too?"

She narrowed her eyes for a moment as if considering my answer, and then she burst out laughing. It only took seconds before I was laughing along with her. For the next five minutes we stood backstage as the Heartbreakers sang their final song and laughed until our sides ached. Maybe it was the adrenaline from hearing Oliver's song for me, or the electricity that always seemed to be in the air at concerts, the ebb and flow of energy that moved between the performers and the audience. Or maybe it was just the love from one sister to another. Whatever it was, it was making us giddy. We both felt the change. It was in the air and our hearts, and this time it was real. It made me feel like I was flying.

"I love you, loser," Cara wheezed as we tried to catch our breath.

"Yeah," I said back. "I love you too."

There wasn't a better moment than now. We were together. We were happy. We were free.

EPILOGUE

"Dang, Stella. Did you let Cara pack for you?" Drew asked, grunting as he set down another heavy box. Even though it was freezing outside, and I spotted a small ring of sweat around the collar of his T-shirt.

"What's that supposed to mean?" I asked from my spot on the floor. I'd opened one of my duffels in the middle of the room and was sorting through clothes.

"That you packed way too much," he said before pressing a water bottle to his lips and chugging. The thin plastic crinkled up as he sucked down all its content, and when he finished, he gasped, "How does one person even have this much junk?"

"It's not junk," I responded. "And I'm going to be living here."

"I get that," Drew said, "but where are you going to put everything?"

"Let me worry about that," I told him and pulled one of my favorite tops out of the bag. Quickly deciding that only my nicest clothes would get a hanger in the closet, I folded the shirt and put it in a pile destined for the dresser. "You finish unloading the car."

We were in the process of moving me into my dorm at school in New York. Drew and I had arrived early this morning, pulling up in the family van just in time to see the sun's first rays glimmer off the frozen snow as we carried a load of boxes across the lawn. For the past two hours, Drew had been running back and forth between my room and the van as he emptied the car of my luggage.

It was expensive to ship my belongings, so Drew had suggested we drive everything out. Even though it was almost an eighteen-hour drive, I'd eagerly agreed and packed the van with everything I owned. Our last road trip had been the start of an adventure for me, one that had shaped me into a new person. On the contrary, maybe my time with the Heartbreakers only opened my eyes to the person I already was. All I'd had to do was find the courage to peel off the layers I was hiding under and embrace myself. Either way, I was a different person, and I hoped this most recent trip would bring as many exciting experiences as the last one.

"Maybe if your lazy lump of a boyfriend helped me, I'd already be done." Drew gave the stink eye to Oliver, who was lying on the futon, arms crossed over his chest and beanie pulled down over his eyes as he tried to nap.

"I'm way too pretty for manual labor," he told Drew. "Besides, I've been working all week. I'm spent."

And Oliver wasn't joking, at least in regard to the working part. For the past two weeks the Heartbreakers had been in the studio recording their third studio album, *Light Years Away*.

Drew scoffed, and I was fairly positive I heard him grumble, "Pretty, my ass," as he stalked out of the room.

"You know, helping him wouldn't kill you," I told Oliver. "The sooner I finish unpacking, the sooner we get to hang out."

Oliver only had the weekend off, but he'd flown out from LA to see me. When Monday came, he'd be back on a plane to California to finish the album's production process.

"I did help," Oliver said. There was a crooked smile on his face. "I gave him a hand with the futon."

"Yeah," I said and rolled my eyes. "So you could sleep on it."

Before Oliver could come up with another smart-ass comment, there was a knock on the door. Standing outside was a pretty girl with long legs and dark skin who was wearing an SVA sweatshirt.

"Hey," she said when I looked up at her. "My name's Lena. I'm your neighbor across the hall, so I thought I'd introduce myself."

Standing up, I brushed myself off before holding out my hand. "Nice to meet you. I'm Stella."

"Let me guess," Lena said, gesturing her head in the direction of my dresser. The drawers were still empty, but resting on top was my camera. "Photography student?"

"Yup," I said and offered her a smile. "You?"

"I've got my own camera," she said, grinning at me, "but it's for something a little different. I'm film and video."

"Cool," I said, genuinely excited to already be making new friends.

"So…the boy I saw in the hall who's carrying all your stuff in— Mr. Hot and Sweaty," Lena said. "He your boyfriend or something?"

I blinked at Lena, not sure who she was talking about, but then I remembered Drew. "Oh, God no!" I said, making a face. "He's my brother."

"Sorry." Lena flinched, but the way she was biting her lip revealed that she was pleased with my answer. "That's totally embarrassing."

There was a groan of metal from the futon. "Don't worry," Oliver said as he stood up. "You're not the only one who's made *that* mistake before."

Lena's gaze flickered over to Oliver as she noticed him for the first time. He'd pushed his hat back so you could see his face, and Lena's eyes grew huge. She glanced at me and then back at Oliver, and I pressed my lips together, trying to stifle my grin as she realized who he was.

"I don't get it," I joked, shrugging my shoulders. "We don't act like a couple, and we look freaky similar."

Oliver smirked and said, "Yeah, almost like twins." Then he crossed the room and offered his hand to Lena. "I'm Oliver," he told her. "Stella's boyfriend."

Well, I thought to myself as Lena squeaked. *This is definitely the start of another crazy adventure.*

ACKNOWLEDGMENTS

The creation of *The Heartbreakers* was in no way a one-woman operation, and there were countless people involved in making this possible. Although their names are not printed on the cover like mine, their efforts can be found on each page and in every word.

Firstly, I have to thank my amazing army of fans on Wattpad who are just as much the author of this book as I am. They supported and shaped this story before I ever dreamed of having it published. As I've said in the past, without them I would be nowhere.

Second, the Sourcebooks team, specifically my editor, Aubrey Poole, who saw my vision before I had a clear picture of it. This manuscript came to her as a serialized mess, and she was the guiding hand that helped me turn it into a novel.

To the extraordinary people at Wattpad, especially Caitlin and Ashleigh, who acted as my makeshift agents before I had one. I'd also like to thank Chloe Larby, Asha Clarke, and Laura Stracey for helping me write Oliver's song to Stella. I'm no Taylor Swift, but I think we did pretty dang good.

Thank you to Grandma Fletcher, who acted as my own personal copy editor; to my mother, for listening to my endless rants and soothing my frustrations with a good bottle of wine; and finally to

Jared, my husband, for being my own special star—not only did you give me the opportunity to chase my dreams, but you put up with my writing storms, late nights, and panicking.

ABOUT THE AUTHOR

Ali Novak is a twenty-three-year-old Wisconsin native and recent graduate of the University of Wisconsin-Madison's creative writing program. She started writing her debut novel *My Life with the Walter Boys* when she was only fifteen, and since then, her work has received more than one hundred million hits online. When she isn't writing, Ali enjoys Netflix marathons and traveling with her husband, Jared. You can follow Ali on Wattpad and Twitter @Fallzswimmer.